PRAISE FOR *THE GREAT GAME*

"Breathtaking! *The Great Game* is nothing short of transcendent. Yes, it is a brilliant, relentlessly paced classic crime thriller of good versus evil, populated with living, breathing characters (some familiar to us, some not, but all so fully fleshed out that they might be our neighbors). Yet it soars beyond that, offering psychological, cultural, and political insights that touch our souls—often on issues that have been tragically neglected. Told in a unique and captivating literary voice, this is a roller coaster of a tale that, I promise, you'll read in one sitting. Bravo!"
—Jeffery Deaver, author of the Colter Shaw novels (the basis for the television series *Tracker*)

"*The Great Game* is a thrilling tale about a fascinating new hero (or two), along with a familiar cast of characters—Holmes! Watson! Raffles! Churchill!—(and a surprise or two!) struggling for the fate of the British Empire. Please, Mr. David, tell us that there will be more!"
—Leslie S. Klinger, editor, *New Annotated Sherlock Holmes*

"David breathes new life into familiar characters with this wry, wickedly arch tale about decolonization, integration, and imperial arrogance, not just interrogating the classic caper but elevating it—stealing it out from under the Empire's nose."
—Dave Rudden, *Sunday Times* bestselling author of *Sister Wake*

"An audacious book . . . [*The Great Game*] has the pace of a thriller, the voice of history, and the charm of a writer who knows his way around a story . . . Full of intrigue and mystery and a completely unique story. One for fans of Vaseem Khan and Abir Mukherjee."
—Imran Mahmood, award-winning author of *You Don't Know Me*

"Arvind Ethan David's *The Great Game* has the heart of Sir Arthur Conan Doyle and the social conscience of Charles Dickens. A wonderful trip to the origin of crime fiction . . . infused with real people from early twentieth-century London and also fictional characters of the day. A tantalizing whodunit."

—Matt Goldman, *New York Times* bestselling author of the Nils Shapiro series

THE
GREAT
GAME

ALSO BY
ARVIND ETHAN DAVID

Graphic Novels

Raymond Chandler's Trouble is My Business
Gray (Volumes 1 & 2)
Darkness Visible (with Mike Carey)
Dirk Gently's Holistic Detective Agency: A Spoon Too Short
Dirk Gently's Holistic Detective Agency: The Salmon of Doubt

Audio Originals

Douglas Adams: The Ends of the Earth
The Crimes of Dorian Gray
The Girl Who Wasn't There
Dr. Vikram Loses His Mind
Would You Like to Choose the Race?
The Neil Gaiman at the End of the Universe
Darkness Visible
In the Lap of the Goddess (with Whitney Mosely)

Plays

Dirk Gently's Holistic Detective Agency (with James Goss)

THE GREAT GAME

A THRILLER

ARVIND ETHAN DAVID

THOMAS & MERCER

Published by Thomas & Mercer, Seattle

www.apub.com

Amazon, the Amazon logo, and Thomas & Mercer are trademarks of Amazon.com, Inc., or its affiliates.

EU product safety contact:
Amazon Media EU S. à r.l.
38, avenue John F. Kennedy, L-1855 Luxembourg
amazonpublishing-gpsr@amazon.com

ISBN-13: 9781662540356 (paperback)
ISBN-13: 9781662534409 (digital)

Cover design by Jarrod Taylor
Cover image: © CSA Images / Getty; © pashabo / Shutterstock

Printed in the United States of America

To ACD, EWH, ERB, OW, JMB, HGW, RJZ, MC,
and SR.
This form of flattery.

You must not make the criminal a hero.
—Arthur Conan Doyle

He is one to be obeyed to the last wink of his
eyelashes. Men say he does magic, but that should
not touch thee . . . Here begins the Great Game.
—Rudyard Kipling, *Kim*

CHAPTER 1

My Friend Raffles

Say what you will about my friend Raffles (and in my time, I've said plenty), he is not a man given to exaggeration, unsubstantiated claims, or hullabaloo of any kind.

Therefore, when, late in the evening on a cold September night in 1905, I responded to a frantic ringing of my doorbell and found Raffles standing outside, his head bare to the elements, his face pale in the flickering light of the street lamp, I was both shocked and intrigued.

"AJ!" I exclaimed. "What on earth's the matter?! You look like you've seen a ghost."

He pushed past me into the warmth of my little hall, muttering as he walked:

"A ghost I could have borne without complaint, Bunny. What I've witnessed tonight was more horrific by far than a mere apparition. It was the worst thing I have ever seen. For God's sake, man, stop gawking and fix us some drinks."

I looked out of my door to a largely empty street as a carriage rolled past, drawn by a handsome black horse, but otherwise the night was desolate, as it typically was at this late hour.

Raffles ascended my staircase, removing his coat and gloves as he walked, discarding them on the floor of my corridors like a great snake shedding its skin. He made his way to my nook of a study and reached for the shelf where he knew I kept the good whiskey just behind a copy of Gibbon's *Decline and Fall,* which I regret to say I have never read.

I got some tumblers out, boggling and baffled. The worst thing he had ever seen? This from a man who had served alongside me in the bloodiest excesses of the Boer War, who had faced down the great batsman Ranji at Lord's, and who only last October had arranged for us to be locked inside a bank vault for the purposes of strategically emptying it.

This level of agitation in him was very far from normal. For the most part, Raffles' cool, calculating mind and his steely, sportsmanlike nerve mean that he is one who favours *under-*, not *over*statement.

In this, as in all else, Raffles goes his own way, priding himself on his ability to keep calm under pressure. It is not natural for one's constitution to respond to situations of danger or threat by becoming even more calm, yet that is what Raffles invariably does.

The hotter the crisis, the colder runs the blood of AJ Raffles.

I suppose this is part of what makes him such an extraordinary cricketer, the finest slow bowler in recent memory, a dangerous bat, and a brilliant field. When confronted by the fastest of fastballs, he neither doubts nor panics, but simply greets it with grace.

This characteristic is also what allows him to excel in his other profession. The profession in which I, to my enduring shame, assist him: that of gentleman thief. You see, Raffles is the greatest amateur cracksman there ever was, the most daring, most notorious, most successful society burglar of our, or any other, age. For more than a decade now, he has helped himself to the bounty of the idle rich: rare jewels, priceless works of art, the family silver—and whatever else catches his fancy.

At the point of these events, I had spent nearly three years as an ally of Raffles, an accomplice thief, and a cat burglar in training. The details of how this had come about are a matter to which I shall return, but know that it began out of necessity when I had fallen on hard and desperate times. Unlike Raffles, who stole, I think, for the sheer fun of it, and only secondarily because he enjoyed the proceeds, I had come to the disreputable business of burglary, to my current life of crime, not out of desire but out of need. I broke the law not because I enjoyed it but because I had no other choice.

At least that is what I told myself.

Finding the bottle, Raffles poured himself a heavy slug and downed it without comment, then refreshed his glass and filled a second, which he extended to me. As I took the drink, I saw, to my deepening surprise, that his hand was shaking.

"Raffles! Dear fellow, you're scaring me. What is it? What have you done?"

He regarded me coldly; the drinks seemed to have done their work, and his usual hard façade was back upon him, his hands once again rock solid. "Done? Bunny, this ill becomes you. I told you I *saw* something. Why should you think I have *done* something?"

I bluffed and bustled, and my guilt at our shared criminal enterprise had me stammering like a schoolgirl: "Why, why, why, that is to say, I mean, dear fellow—you do have rather a habit of getting yourself—of getting me, come to that, of getting us, into all sorts of scrapes. So naturally, when . . ."

He laughed then. Starting with the little cynical chuckle I knew so well, but then something in him shifted, and he laughed more freely till his body was shaking and he was gasping for air. Not knowing what was so funny, and struck by how unusual this behaviour was in him, I nevertheless found myself laughing too, and we held each other for a moment, just laughing together.

When we were spent, he lit a cigarette, sucked it deep, and his grey eyes holding me lightly, exhaled and then spoke through the smoke:

"I was up at General Fitzwilliam's place tonight. For his regular poker game."

"I thought you despised Fitzwilliam!" I responded, surprised.

"I do, the man's a brute, but I'm rather fond of his Golconda diamond."

"You were on reconnaissance?"

"Something like that. In fact, I decided, somewhat on the spur of the moment, that it was the night to do the job." There was a wink in his eye as he said this, knowing how galling I would find this information. As always, I took the bait.

"Raffles! How could you! These things take planning. Going in alone? Without me there to provide backup? What were you thinking?"

"Ah, my dear Bunny. How sweet of you to be upset at being left out. I'm not quite sure the general, good imperialist that he is, would have been comfortable with you at the poker table. But don't worry, the jewels were left untouched, at least by me."

"If not you, then by who?"

"'Whom,' dear boy, 'whom.'"

"I do not require grammar lessons from you, AJ!"

"I apologize, dear fellow. My wits are somewhat scrambled by events. I seek order when I can find it, because there was precious little available to me tonight. Let's fix another drink and I'll tell you all from start to finish."

He settled down in his chair, took another long dram of his whiskey, and then told me the following tale:

"The card game was coming to an end. As well as the general and myself, present were a couple of other military types: Lord Kitchener, fresh from his victory in Sudan; Frank Milton, the general's old aide-de-camp; and young George Montagu, nephew of the Earl of Sandwich—and before you ask, yes, the general delighted himself by serving a round of sandwiches to the heir to Sandwich. Thought himself awfully clever. Dreadful man.

"Anyhow, as I say, the game was nearing its conclusion, and it had taken all my skill and self-restraint not to fleece the lot of them of all the money in their pockets, but I was hunting for bigger game tonight and wanted them all in a good mood. So, I folded when I should have called and let them all feel rather more accomplished players than they are, particularly the general, whose good humour I most needed.

"At about eleven, we all took our leave. Or rather, I should say, the others took their leave. I doubled back immediately after saying goodnight, knowing that the window in the front room was still open—"

"Why was it open?" I interrupted.

"Because I had arranged for it to be opened, of course, Bunny. Halfway through a hand, I complained that the room felt a little close, and of course all these Men of Empire, big game hunters all, used to cold nights in the Sahara, were hardly going to admit to a little effete cricketer such as myself that they were feeling chilly. Thus, the window was thrown open, even as the fire roared. Allowing me, a little later, to slip back into the drawing room and secret myself in a side closet until the house was all asleep.

"I didn't have to wait long. Most of the staff had long since retired. After twenty minutes or so, it was clear that no one stirred, so I let myself out and made my way to the library, where the general keeps his diamonds on display. He had shown them to us all earlier that evening, boasting of the maharaja he had filched them from. I was in the room, and had just got the case open, when it started . . ."

He paused then, and I saw that he was gripping his glass tightly. So tight, I was afraid it might shatter in his hand. I reached out and took it from him. "What started, AJ? You can tell me," I said as gently as I could muster.

"The screaming, Bunny. The screaming."

Over several more drinks, Raffles recounted to me what happened next. That the silence of the night was savagely interrupted by violent screaming; how he, instinctively and with a selflessness and courage that speaks well of him, had run towards the source of the screams—the general's bedroom at the top of the building.

Raffles was, of course, an intruder; if he was discovered, he would have had to answer hard questions as to what he was doing in another man's home long after he had been seen to leave, but none of this caused him hesitation.

Someone was screaming in mortal terror, and towards that terror, Raffles ran.

"I got to the top of the stairs just as the servants below began to emerge from their quarters; the screaming had reached a horrific pitch, and where before there had been decipherable words—'help,' 'stop,' and the like—now there was only the formless howling of a creature in torment. And then, just as I laid my hand on the general's doorknob, more horrific still, the screaming stopped.

"I threw the door open. The room was in darkness, save for the moonlight through the open window. The general appeared to be alone, standing with his back to me, sort of hunched over, with his head hanging down, dressed only in a dark-red nightdress. I stepped towards him, and he half turned to greet me—which is when I realized that he wasn't hunched, not exactly. His neck had been broken, and his head was hanging, barely attached by torn skin and sinew to his neck."

I considered. "The pyjamas. His pyjamas were not of red cloth, were they?" I asked.

Raffles shook his head, kindly, pleased that I had picked up the scent. "No, Bunny, the pyjamas were not. They were a light, baby blue. Rather dapper, to be honest. But they had been stained red by the copious amounts of blood flowing freely from the general's neck."

"He had been beheaded? How?"

"Not quite, not beheaded, but pretty damn close. Ripped. As far as I could tell, whoever had done this had attempted to pull the general's head off his body. Gripped hard and simply pulled it loose by the application of constant, relentless traction. Rather as one might pull the cork from a bottle, or the wings off a fly. That was why he had been screaming, and that was also why the screaming had so suddenly stopped.

"There was clearly nothing I could do for the fellow, he was dead before his body hit the ground. That he had still been standing when I entered was simply the last spasms of his nervous system, as you will sometimes see a rabbit or a pheasant thrash about even after a kill shot.

I ran to the window to see if I could catch sight of his assailant—and . . ." He ran dry.

"And?" I pressed him.

"Well, I saw something, Bunny, but I'll be damned if I can tell you what it was. I just about made out a shape climbing down the outside wall of the general's home. But not in the way you or I might descend a wall, if we had to. Not by means of rope or careful use of drainpipes and windowsills."

"Then how?"

"He sort of slid down, head first, using his arms and his legs in equal measure, and then, when he was still some distance or more from the base, he leapt!"

"To the ground?"

"No, that I could just about fathom, but instead he pushed himself off from the building, propelling himself outwards towards the boundary wall, which was fully thirty feet away. The fellow seemed to soar rather like a bat, but even so, didn't quite make it all the way but instead grabbed on to a bough of the mighty oak and, using the momentum and the elasticity of the branch, proceeded to whip himself the further distance over the wall, and then he was gone. Like some creature from the foul imaginings of that Stoker fellow."

My head was spinning. "You think it might have been a vampire?"

He looked at me now with something approaching pity in his eyes.

"No, Bunny, not an actual vampire. I've had a scare tonight, but I haven't lost my senses, and neither should you. I don't know exactly what I saw climb down that wall, I don't know what sort of man can twist another's head nearly off and then leap twenty yards into the night air, but I'm not quite ready to throw out all of my wit and reason, and I'd ask you to stay with me in the land of the possible for a little while longer."

"'When you have eliminated the impossible, whatever remains, however improbable, must be the truth,'" I recited, still reeling from all I had been told. Raffles wasn't amused by this.

"I will thank you," he said coldly, "never to quote that overrated dilettante in my presence."

~

The next morning, of course, the papers were all full of the general's spectacular murder. Each headline was more grotesque and sensationalist than the last.

MASSACRE IN MAYFAIR

HORROR STRIKES IN GENERAL'S HOME:
LOYAL SERVANT OF EMPIRE MEETS GRIZZLY END

BRUTAL MURDER: PANIC IN MAYFAIR, SPECIAL DETAILS

IS JACK BACK?

Raffles, who had spent the night in my guest room, was much recovered the next morning. Indeed, he was entirely himself. He reviewed the papers with a contemptuous expression on his face, particularly the last one. "Jack! How lazy are these newspapermen. It's been two decades since the Ripper struck, he'd be geriatric by now, even aside from the fact that he favoured female victims and a rather different modus operandi."

"I imagine they don't know the details. The police, I'm sure, are keeping things under a strict veil of secrecy," I ventured.

"Good luck to them! It will take a better man than Mackenzie to stop the maids or the butler from talking about what they found last night. It will drive those of them who aren't there already to drink, I tell you that."

Mackenzie was the inspector who had, for some years now, made it his personal mission to capture the elusive "gentleman cracksman," and his inability to deliver on his charge had endeared him to us. He was an energetic fellow, but of limited intellectual capability, and whilst he harboured some suspicions that Raffles might be the cracksman, he had failed to corral any hard evidence to support his hunch, and it had thus far not been difficult to bamboozle and fool him.

"Would you like me to come with you to the police?" I asked. "I should be happy to help provide some explanation for your presence in the house. Perhaps we say you left your gloves or similar—or rather than being inside the house, you could say you witnessed the intruder from the street, leaping over the wall?"

Once again, the eyebrows tut-tutted, but out loud, Raffles said not a word.

"Raffles, we are going to tell the police what you saw, are we not?"

"What on earth would be the point in that, dear boy?" he asked, lighting a cigarette.

I didn't like it when he called me "boy," but I knew he meant nothing by it, and there were more important issues to focus on. "There's been a terrible murder. It's your—our—civic duty."

"Thieves don't have civic duty, Bunny. We exist on the other side of the ledger. Takers, not givers. I thought you would have figured that out by now."

"In the normal course of things, Raffles—but this is different. This is beyond our usual sphere."

He gestured to the newspapers on the desk like a magician inviting me to choose a card from a rigged deck.

"Even assuming there was some way to tell my story without implicating myself, Bunny, there would be no purpose to it. What can I give the police by way of actionable information? I didn't see the intruder's face, I have no idea as to his identity, I didn't actually see him kill the general. He was gone from the room by the time I got there.

"All I have to offer is that an unexpectedly agile individual climbed a tree and disappeared into the night. No, the police will do nothing useful with that. We'd find a rash of headlines about villainous circus acrobats and trained troupes of murderous mandrills next—no, no earthly use to anyone."

"An acrobat! Raffles, but surely that would explain things; it could be an acrobat from some travelling Eastern circus—somebody that the general had wronged whilst on a tour, perhaps? He does—did—after all have something of a reputation as a brute in the field, unafraid of using artillery to break up demonstrations and the like."

Raffles took a deep inhale and regarded me as if I had finally said something of value.

"Bunny, my dear fellow. What an original thought." This praise was unusual enough that my breast may have swelled a little from pride.

"You think I am onto something?"

"When you have ruled out the merely ridiculous, then whatever remains, however preposterous, will be what appears in the papers," he said, lighting a second cigarette. "I give that one for free, Bunny, to you and your beloved detective!"

~

It is perhaps appropriate at this juncture, before we proceed much further into the dark heart of this narrative, for me to tell you a little of myself. For if I am asking for your trust in accepting this outlandish tale as true, then it is meet and proper that I extend some of that trust in kind and have you know something of me.

Very well, then. Let us begin with an admission. "Bunny" is not my real name.

It is simply what Raffles calls me. A sobriquet he has given me partly as a sign of the affection that exists between us, but more, I believe, as a tribute to a past comrade of his, now lost, Captain Harry "Bunny" Manders.

I never knew Manders, but from his service record, it would appear he was only an average soldier, never any good with a gun and a fool with horses.

He was killed at the Battle of Talana Hill, along with dozens of other British infantrymen under the command of Major-General Penn Symons. Penn Symons, it is worth saying, was also a fool, a military moron, ordering close-up tactics against long-range rifles at Talana Hill, and hence exposing his men to mass casualties. His men, including Bunny, who, not given to disobeying orders, marched his way to certain death.

In his obituary of Penn Symons, the then under-secretary for colonial affairs, who went on to play such a significant role not only in this tale but in world history, noted his "energy and enthusiasm" and his popularity. The under-secretary says nothing about his ability, and further records that the principal reason for Penn Symons' quick rise up the ranks was the persistent and unfortunate death of his superior officers.

Perhaps Bunny and Penn Symons had something in common—poor soldiers but good chaps, good friends. Bunny, certainly, was such a friend to Raffles: loyal and faithful, for the better part of a decade, the two of them had been partners in crime, rifling through jewel cases and safe-deposit boxes in many a daring exploit. Then they signed up together to serve in Africa, where Bunny paid the ultimate price. Raffles, I believe, loved Bunny in the way only men can love, and now remains loyal to his memory by bequeathing his nickname to me.

Or possibly he simply couldn't be bothered to properly pronounce my real name. Which leads us to the question, if I am not Bunny, then who am I?

My name is Lieutenant Balvinder dev Singh, alumni of Government College, Lahore, where I was schooled in Latin, philosophy, mathematics, and English literature; late of the 2nd Patiala Infantry; assigned by His Highness, the Maharaja of Patiala, at the request of the British, to serve an auxiliary role in the Second Boer War, honorarily discharged and, at the time of this narrative, thirty-six years of age, unmarried, and a pupil barrister at 9, Stone Buildings, Lincoln's Inn.

I stand six foot two inches tall and weigh fourteen stone. I wear a full beard and, until my service in southern Africa, a turban. On my third day in the field, a bullet pierced my turban and gave me an unscheduled haircut, and thereafter I swapped my headdress for a helmet. I am a Sikh still, but the Guru would not want me dead. Like many of my countrymen, I am, above all else, pragmatic.

Sikh? Turban? Balvinder?

Yes, dear reader, you have found me out. I am not a white man. You didn't get that from "hullabaloo" and "pyjamas" and the fact I would not have been welcomed at the gambling table of an imperialist general?

Very well, then, let me spell it out: I am a Sikh, an Indian, a subcontinental. I am also a former soldier, a lawyer-in-training, and for the past three years (and I acknowledge that this third career sits somewhat ill at ease with the preceding two), an amateur thief, assisting Raffles when opportunity permits in his campaign to separate the upper echelons of British society from their valuables.

If any of that gives you pause as you hold this slim volume in your soft hands, if you feel that you have been misled in your purchase, that you have embarked on this tale of derring-do under false pretences, then I quite understand. Return the book to your local bookshop; I am sure that the bookseller will grant you an exchange or credit. Or if you wish to go further in show of your disgust, feel free to throw it into the fire or, better yet, rip out its pages and use them for your necessary needs after water closet business.

No? You have decided to continue with me, despite knowing what you know? Very well, then, you have been warned. Let us continue.

In the days that followed, London society spoke of little other than the general's gruesome murder. Raffles, the only man who had actual knowledge of the crime, was the one person in all the city who did not speak of it. He didn't mention that night again; indeed, it seemed almost as if he had blacked out the memory—too unpleasant to consider, and so best forgotten. Even as the police investigation spun its wheels, he refused to share with them what he had seen. This, to me, was an abdication of basic moral duty, but when I said as much, Raffles was unmovable. He remained of the opinion that he had little knowledge that would be of use to the authorities, and that the personal risk that he—and I—would run if he did reveal what he knew was too great to be countenanced.

As the days grew into weeks and no leads were found, the conversation of this great and turbulent city eventually moved on. As did Raffles, who quickly reverted to his usual routine of daily indolence, weekend cricket house parties, and quietly plotting our next "job." It seemed as if, in all of London, I and I alone remained obsessed with the mystery of Fitzwilliam's murder. I cannot explain why it stayed with me so, except to say that I have always had an interest in mysteries and a strong inclination that justice should be served. I fully admit that this inclination sat ill with my nocturnal life of crime, but the theft of a few jewels seemed to belong to an entirely different kettle of fish than a violent murder.

However, whenever I brought up the events of that fateful night to Raffles, seeking greater detail, he waved me away, telling me mockingly that I should apply the methods of the Great Detective to the problem.

Which was, though I did not admit it to Raffles, precisely what I had been doing.

It turns out that being apprenticed to a master criminal has certain secondary advantages. Having the experience of helping Raffles plan and execute burglaries of elaborate complexity, I was well placed to think through the questions of motive, means, and opportunity from the perspective of a criminal.

So it came to be that I spent my days sketching plans, not of our future robberies but of this monster's foul murder, scanning the papers to see what their latest speculations were and building out my own theories. As the weeks went by, discussion of the murder left the front page and travelled by gradual increments into the depths of the small print. On one occasion, I'm ashamed to admit, I even bought tickets to a travelling circus, and spent a fruitless, if enjoyable, few hours poking around the monkey cages, commiserating with a poor chained Indian elephant, and even ingratiating myself into the company of lithesome acrobats so that I might pepper them with specific and technical questions, which they found quite bemusing. Later that evening I watched them spin and whirl with such dextrous skill and unexpected beauty that I found myself thinking that I must return, and next time bring Raffles with me.

I was becoming increasingly haunted by the Grand Guignol of the scene that Raffles had described, and its details would conjure themselves unbidden into my dreams. Again and again, in the hours between dusk and dawn, my unconscious mind would find itself invaded by headless military men, crawling *vampyr*, and tumbling oriental acrobats.

Looking back at it now, from the distance of some four decades, I wonder if this growing obsession within me was motivated more by a sense of justice or out of a sense, however vague, that the general's killing was part of something far bigger. Whatever my motivations, and for all my feverish work, however, I got nowhere, and from my discreet inquiries, neither had the Yard.

The case had more or less been given up on, and the world continued to turn. I was, if I am being honest, a little relieved to admit that I, too, would have to put the investigation away and return to my normal life of law studies during the day and some light burglary with Raffles in the moonlight.

~

Karma, in Sikhism, is a concept related to but different from that understood in the Hindu tradition.

To the Hindu, and by extension to those here in England who, if they know anything of it, from Kipling, Arnold, Carus, and the rest, believe Karma to be a mystical thing: a supernatural precept which decrees that what you do in this life determines how you come back in the next, as an evolved human or as a dog or a gnat.

To the Sikh, Karma is a much more practical and immediate force. It concerns what we do in our lives and the consequences in the here and now. Comparisons may be drawn to the theological distinction between Catholics and Protestants; where the papists maintain that both faith and good works are necessary for one's salvation, the reformers believe heaven may be found by God's grace alone.

To my mind, the more precise analogy is to Sir Isaac Newton's third law: *Actioni contrariam semper & æqualem esse reactionem*—to every action there is a reaction equal and opposite.

Which is all to say, just when I had given up on my detective games, and perhaps because I had given up, and because Raffles had not come forward, and because the police had no leads, and because of the horrific Karma of all of this, well—that's, of course, when the universe moved in reaction to our failure, to our indifference, to our incompetence and selfishness.

The mysterious assailant struck again, this time in a way so horrific, so blatant, and so close to home that even my friend Raffles couldn't walk away from it.

CHAPTER 2

Feasting with Panthers

I had been looking forward to being at Mapperton again. To walking its wild lanes and gazing into its spectacular skies.

The house, located in Dorset and home to the Earls of Rutledge, is one of the finest examples of the English country manor, an artful blending of Tudor, Stuart, and Georgian styles, nestled in two thousand acres of formal gardens, woodland, and farm.

The house was a none-so-subtle reminder of the power and wealth of the English, when even a relatively minor aristocratic scion could live in a palace worthy of a maharaja. I was a callow youth then, my head too easily turned by luxury and pleasure. That said, I looked forward to our visits to Mapperton for one principal reason above all others: the Hunt.

The current earl and his sons were all great sportsmen. The earl had spent considerable time in the savannahs of Swaziland, where he had achieved the rare distinction of bagging each of the "Fatal Five," the big game of that dark continent. Back here in his native England, denied such exotic targets, he had instead focussed his sporting energies on training his boys in the shooting of grouse, the bagging of rabbit, and the ancient art of deer stalking. The estate's wild woodlands provided admirable landscape in which one could train one's senses and skills against those of these beasts. It was not tiger hunting, but it was the best that England could offer, and I was glad to be invited.

Or to put it more precisely, I was glad that Raffles had been invited, and that he had included me in his entourage. The earl's hunting parties were elite events, gatherings of the wealthy and powerful at which alliances were forged and business was done.

For myself, sitting as I do so far below the salt line as to be beneath contempt, would never normally be included in such rarefied company. Even Raffles' inclusion was a concession to his fame as a cricketer; he was here not as one of them, but as a shiny novelty, essentially the entertainment, brought to bat and bowl for show. He both knew and resented this. Indeed, to his perverse mind, this provided sufficient moral justification for whatever theft he might choose to perform whilst on the premises, and the prospect of some sport of his own more than any love of hunting informed his decision to accept the invitation.

So it was for different reasons that Raffles and I were in eager anticipation when, early on the Friday morning, earlier than any other guests, our hansom entered Mapperton's long, elegant drive-way. Out of such happy contemplations, we were both shocked to see a gathering of police carriages, and a veritable force of men surrounding the entrance to the great house.

We both reacted simultaneously, leaping from the cab and breaking into flat runs towards the house. Whilst I cannot say which of us had our feet on the ground first, I will report that despite my being the younger by a decade, we reached the front door together, I out of breath, he focussed and barking inquiries at the pair of callow-faced constables who had moved to bar the door.

"No one is to enter, sir—order of the chief," pronounced the first. "No one is to see until the bigwigs from London get here," confirmed the second.

Raffles looked them up and down and chose his mark, the younger of the two. "You know who I am, lad?"

"Yes, sir. Mr. Raffles, sir. My pa took me to see you get your century against—"

Raffles smiled indulgently; for all his resentment of the upper classes fetishising his accomplishments at cricket, he took genuine pleasure from the appreciation of a common man who loved the game.

"Very good. Then know also that your superiors will not penalize you for letting me in at this time. I have from time to time been of some little assistance to the police, you see. Inspector Mackenzie of Scotland Yard has had occasion before now to confide in me in some of his most difficult cases . . ."

This was a somewhat inventive claim for Raffles to make. Certainly, we both knew Mackenzie of the Yard, but our relationship was less that of collaborators, and more of investigator and investigated. The only cases in which the inspector had cause to "consult" Raffles were burglaries bearing the hallmarks of the Gentleman Cracksman, and his interest in Raffles was not as an ally or confidant but as a prime suspect. That he had not thus far been able to prove his case did not make him our friend, but our very frustrated adversary.

Not knowing any of this history, and caught between their protocols on the one hand and Raffles' celebrity on the other, the constables looked at each other, uncertain. I could see that the younger and most junior was pale-faced and drawn, and was persistently dabbing at his mouth with a soiled cloth.

"What happened to your colleague, Constable? He seems a little the worst for wear?" I inquired of his fellow.

"Tompkins is the one what saw 'em first, sir. He was first on the scene. Took him a little unexpectedly. The rest of us had a chance to prepare ourselves. He's only nineteen, sir."

"I quite understand. Tompkins, go round the back. Ask the cook to make you some black tea. Darjeeling, if she has it, with a squeeze of lemon. A hot cup and you'll be much restored." I combined the concern of a matron with the commanding tone of a superior officer, and the lad responded accordingly, looking at his senior for permission, and quickly slipping away when it was given.

The constable looked at me as if for the first time. Raffles' primacy had meant that he had not focussed on me till this moment, but now that I had engaged with his suffering junior, and done so with care and authority, he saw me as a kindred spirit. An interesting side effect of expressing compassion is that it creates space for its reciprocation. "Thank you, sir. He's just a boy, as I said. Shouldn't have seen what he saw today. None of us should, we're simple local coppers, sir. We rescue cats and have a word with the village blacksmith when he has a few too many on a Friday night. This sort of thing doesn't happen in Dorset."

"No. But it happened in London before, didn't it?" commented my friend Raffles, taking the type of intuitive logical leap that only true artists are capable of. "It happened in Mayfair to General Fitzwilliam. And now it's happened here."

The constable looked at Raffles in shock.

"How could you know . . . ?"

"As I mentioned," my friend Raffles intoned dryly, "I have had past occasion to be of service to the Yard. You've described what you found here to your superiors, I presume?"

"Yes, sir. We used the telephone in the house, sir! Every station has one now, sir, all very modern. Instructions heard down the phone from London loud and clear, sir. They are sending the top man, sir, with strict direction that nothing is to be touched till he arrives."

The constable's sense of self-importance at having use of the modern contraption of the telephone was as touching as it was revealing of his inexperience. Raffles knew exactly how to play him.

"We wouldn't touch a thing. Would we, Bunny?"

I raised my hands to indicate obedience. The constable considered, and then, overwhelmed by the combined forces of class, charm, celebrity, and compassion, he stepped aside and gestured for us to proceed unaccompanied through the great door to confront whatever we might find within.

~

I will keep brief and factual my description of what we saw in the dining room. There is already sufficient terror in the world that to dwell on it more than is necessary is the sign of either perversion or cruelty, and I hope to the gods that I have little propensity for either.

Insofar, however, as the brutal detail is relevant for your understanding of what is to follow, I must set it out clearly:

The Earl of Rutledge and his two adult sons, the Viscount Hollingwood and the Right Honourable Rupert de la Tour, had been dead for some hours. Rigor mortis had set in, and their bodies were taut in the final paroxysms of death.

The elder son, Hollingwood, a handsome if slightly hard-featured man in his mid-twenties, who I had last seen on the back of a fine horse, was the first we encountered as we entered. He had been stripped of his clothes and positioned on his back on the dining table with his limbs extended to their most extreme positions, so he took the form of an X.

When I say his clothes had been removed, I must unfortunately stress that I mean all of them; nothing had been left to conceal his manhood. But that scarcely mattered, for what drew your eye was not the fellow's privates but the fact that his ribs had been cut down the centre and pried open, and the contents of his chest had been removed. Like a carved turkey he served as the centrepiece of the table. His arms were splayed wide, and I noticed that his right arm stopped at the wrist, the hand having been removed.

Sitting on opposing sides of him, propped up in a facsimile of life, were his father and his younger brother, Rupert. A lad who in life I remembered as being blessed with dark, curly hair, a large, handsome head, and a sweet disposition, but who had now been posed, with his eyes cut out of his head, his mouth open as his left hand shoved into his open maw a large morsel of meat. On closer inspection, this "meat" was revealed to be a ventricle of his brother's heart. Rupert's right hand, like his brother's, was missing.

The father, on the other end of the table, had fared no better than his unfortunate offspring. His head had been removed completely at the neck, and placed on his own plate, screaming soundlessly as his own left hand shoved a fork deep into the soft matter of his brain. My subconscious knew before I saw with my eyes that his right hand, like those of his sons, had been severed at the wrist and was nowhere to be found.

I am not a man easily shocked. My long years of duty in the theatre of war have inured me to the brutality man is capable of and to the degradation that violence works on the human form. Nevertheless, I confess that in that moment, the horrific spectacle before us shook me to my very core and I wanted nothing more than to run screaming from that foul room and join poor Tompkins in a cup of hot chai. My fists clenched and unclenched, my mouth ran dry, and somehow from some deep part of me, the words of the *Japji Sahib*, most holy of Sikh prayers, came unbidden to my stupefied tongue:

> *Ik-Onkaar Sat Naam*
> *Kartaa Purakh Nirbha-o Nirvair*
> *Akaal Moorat Ajoonee Saibhan*
> *Gur Parsaad*

For those who require a translation, a crude one might read:

> *There is One Universal Creator God.*
> *The Name is Truth.*
> *The Creator, Without Fear, Without Hatred.*
> *Timeless Being, Beyond Birth, Self-Existent.*
> *By the Guru's Grace.*

Though that captures little of the poetry of the original of this prayer, said at the moment of death, to guide the departed's soul to merge with the divine. I knew not what divinity the earl and his boys might have aspired towards, or if the grotesque and incomprehensible manner of their murder might allow it. I knew not if I even still believed in *Onkaar*, but it gave me some small comfort to say the words.

Raffles, in the usual run of things, had little sympathy with religion, whether that be the Christian faith or what he regards as my pagan customs, but he did not interrupt me as I chanted the words, instead lighting a cigarette, and I saw that even he was shaken, as it took him three attempts before he could hold the flame steady long enough for it to catch.

Only when his cigarette and my scripture were complete did we meet each other's eyes. In my expression was posed a question, and in his came the immediate answer: What was laid before us did indeed represent a foul progression of the killing of General Fitzwilliam that he had witnessed three months earlier in Mayfair.

"This is of a piece with what I witnessed before. The same inhuman strength, the same torturous mutilation of his victims, but this is an escalation."

"An escalation!" I exclaimed, not for the first time frustrated by Raffles' habitual understatement. "This is more than that. The entire male line of a grand family, wiped out, and in such a fashion! Surely also, this cannot be the work of a lone assailant, however strong, this must be the outcome of a co-ordinated attack?"

"You did not see what I saw, Bunny. The creature who tore Fitzwilliam's head from his neck had strength aplenty. To my mind, the chief difference is that this time the assailant is not satisfied with murder but seeks also to leave a message. A message written in flesh," he intoned dryly.

"But what message?" I asked. "What is the possible meaning of this grotesquerie?"

Raffles was about to answer when he was interrupted by a commotion outside. We heard a firm and commanding voice and plaintive responses from the local constables and the fast-approaching footsteps of a group of agitated men.

"The inspector is here," I surmised.

Raffles nodded. "Not a word till I say, Bunny. We need to play this carefully. That clot Mackenzie will be so over his head here as to be dangerous."

And the door opened and a furious police officer entered the room—shouting as he walked. *"Why . . . Why? Why?!"* he demanded of the men dancing around him. "Why is there a *cricketer* in my *crime scene?*"

We looked at the newcomer in surprise. For it was not our old adversary Inspector Mackenzie at all. The person who stood before us was a far superior figure. I recognized him from his frequent appearances in the newspapers: his features pinched and ferret-like, his hair always fine, now thinning, but neatly combed—the intensity of his manner, suggesting someone who had risen to the top of his profession through will and determination as much as by any native aptitude.

That full intensity of character was now directed at us.

"I ask again, why is there a *cricketer* in my *crime scene??!*"

We were in the presence of Commissioner Sir Gaston Lestrade.

Famous since his beginnings as a fledgling detective in the 1880s and 90s, when he had found himself charged with handling some of the strangest cases in the brief history of the force and who, recognizing that he was in over his head, had sought the counsel of a then unknown consulting detective. Now, two decades later, Lestrade had been elevated to commissioner and overall head of the Metropolitan Police.

Banished to a side room, and kept under the close if somewhat bashful observation of none other than young Tompkins, Raffles and I were, it was made clear, to wait for Lestrade until he had completed his inspection of the dining hall. He would deal with us later, we were assured, in a tone that did much to indicate that we were, in the most charitable estimation, a low-priority inconvenience and, at worst, an active impediment to the investigation.

Prevented by the presence of the officer from discussing any matters of sensitivity, Raffles and I were left to puzzle things out separately and in silence. Or, I should say, I was: Raffles, displaying once again his infuriating ability to relax in the most inhospitable and stressful of circumstances, stretched out on a Regency sofa and, placing a kerchief over his face, fell immediately asleep.

I could not quite imagine how he did it, and nor, it would seem, could Tompkins, who gazed at the quietly snoring Raffles with utterly unconcealed incredulity.

"I don't reckon I'll ever be able to sleep again, sir. After seeing what I've seen today."

"No. I understand you there, lad. I feel much the same. But Mr. Raffles here, well, he's cut from unusual cloth."

"Quite, sir. He must be."

At this shared understanding of our common and quotidian humanity, so in contrast with the unique nature of my companion, the young officer and I settled into a companionable silence.

From time to time, over the long hours that followed, there would be a flurry of activity. Additional teams of investigators arrived, these dressed more like scientists than police, in white coats and bearing medical equipment. There was an individual whose job seemed to consist of spreading graphite powder over all the hard surfaces with a fine brush and then photographing his results. Tompkins revealed on questioning that this gentleman worked for the Police Fingerprint Bureau, though what precisely the function or jurisdiction of this organisation was, he could not say.

Later still, proceedings were interrupted by the arrival of the rest of the hunting party, who were quickly turned away with minimal explanation by the police, and I noted also that the household staff were being detained *in situ*, doubtless for further questioning.

In between the moments of intense activity, or at least those apparent to me from my rather limited perspective, were long stretches of nothingness, and I was left to speculate in circular and repetitive fashion as to the best course to take when the superintendent eventually turned his attention to us.

My mind whirled in unhelpful spirals with each thought linked like a centipede to the ones preceding and succeeding it: Why was Lestrade himself taking personal charge of this crime? Terrible though it was, surely the on-site investigations should be left to active service detectives, rather than an elderly administrator, however famed his earlier exploits? What should we share with Lestrade about Raffles' knowledge of General Fitzwilliam's murder? It was our duty to be forthcoming, but could we do so in a way that would not place suspicion upon us, either of our actual criminal pasts or, as likely and far worse, of involvement in these terrible crimes? Was there a way to balance our moral obligation with the legal jeopardy that revealing the truth might bring upon us? I searched my mental case notes for some legal theory that might square this circle.

Above all: What were the motivations and intentions of the shadowy and ominous adversary who had now, within the scope of mere weeks, murdered four of the wealthiest and most powerful men in English society, and had done so in a manner so terrible and terrifying as to beggar the imagination? All these thoughts and more spun together in my troubled mind, merging and meshing, until there were no distinct thoughts left, but simply a spinning vortex of confounded anxiety.

After some hours, an ambulance trolley arrived, and one by one the bodies were removed on a gurney. I was inevitably reminded of my war duties, and noted the efficiency and compassion with which the morgue workers dispatched with the earl and his sons. There was a sacred trust in this duty, to be the first to bear the dead from their place of death, and these men discharged it with honour.

Only after this sad task was complete, and with the sun now setting behind Mapperton's exquisite but now rather sinister seeming woodlands, were we summoned to our audience with the commissioner.

~

The late earl's study was less a place of learning and more a display cabinet for his many hunting conquests. Trophy after trophy adorned the walls and shelves of the room, birds and fish on the smaller shelves as well as some native English beasts—but pride of place, in the room's centre, was given to the proof of Rutledge's success in bagging the Fatal Five.

A bull elephant's tusk, a rhino's horn, and the mounted heads of a buffalo and a leopard adorned the walls, and finally the skin of a magnificent lion was spread across the central table, its mane cresting high above the surface. Before I could complete my inspection of these impressive trophies, Lestrade entered, and without ceremony or greeting sat himself behind what would have been Rutledge's desk and lit a small cigar.

"Well?" he demanded. "What the bloody hell have you two got to say for yourselves? Why were you here, and what do you think you are up to, and is there one good reason I shouldn't put you in front of the magistrates straight away for interfering with an official investigation?"

I looked at Raffles, uncertain as to what tack he would have us take. As ever, he was the picture of unruffled calm.

"I'm sure you are aware, Lestrade, that my colleague and I were invited guests of Rutledge . . . of the late earl. We simply arrived a little early this morning for the weekend's festivities and so were on the scene before you."

"Yes, I know all that, but that doesn't explain why you bamboozled the local boys into letting you in against my express instructions. Have you no common sense at all? Wading into the scene of the crime like that—you could have destroyed valuable evidence!"

"Bunny and I know how to conduct ourselves. Did your investigations reveal any disruption or interference?" Raffles' block shot was one of his most effective stratagems at bat, and he was utilizing it here to good effect.

"That is hardly the point. You had no business—"

"Sir Gaston, Commissioner. What Raffles means to say is that we have information pertaining to this matter that is not public and might be of assistance. We wish to help."

I'm not sure which of us was more shocked to hear the preceding come out of my mouth. Raffles spun on his heel and looked at me with surprised annoyance, whilst Lestrade's rodent head swung towards me suddenly, his nose twitching as it appraised this new target.

Perhaps I was most surprised of all. I have grown accustomed to letting Raffles set the agenda in all our professional dealings, content in these matters to be the supporting act to his leading man. However much that posture suited me for the day to day, however much I was prepared to suppress my own instincts when we were engaged in our petty thieving, this was a different matter altogether. People were dying, and we were already culpable for not having come forward earlier with what we knew.

Whether Raffles saw it or not, there was only one course of action left to us, and I was taking it. He saw the determination in my eye, and ceded the floor, but with a final warning: "Hop carefully, my dear Bunny," said Raffles so softly that only I could hear. "Hop very, very carefully."

The inspector turned his penetrating eyes on me. "Mr. Singh. What is this information? If you have anything that can help the police in this matter, it is your duty and obligation to divulge it at once—"

"Yes, sir. But, sir, there is one legal doctrine that I feel the need to point out first—"

He looked like I had presented him with a steaming turd. It is one of the great ironies of our time that the men of the police force have precious little knowledge or reverence for the very laws they are charged with upholding and still less for us lawyers, charged with the interpretation and application of those laws. For my part, I was glad I had paid good attention in my lectures, though I was putting my learning to rather different use than I had anticipated.

"Legal doctrine? What hair-splitting, needle-dancing infamy is this? A man and his sons are dead, hunted and butchered like so many guinea fowl, and you are here talking of legal niceties?!"

"Nemo tenetur se ipsum accusare," I said, and let the phrase hang in the air between us like a piece of unexploded military ordnance.

I fancy I saw Raffles' smile. "Very good, Bunny, well played, old boy," his expression seemed to say, and I knew I was on the right course. This was not a view shared by Commissioner Lestrade, who quickly proved himself less of a linguist than he was a detective:

"Neno tantur . . . What the devil are you saying, is that Hindostani? Speak English, man!"

"My colleague, Lestrade, is, in fact, speaking Latin. Legal Latin at that, you see, Bunny is currently preparing to take his bar exams. Perhaps they leave such things out at the police academy in these modern times, no matter, no matter. Bunny, could you provide the commissioner with a translation?"

"No one is bound to accuse himself," I explained, "a long-standing ecclesiastical and common law tradition, enshrined in the Evidence Amendment Act of 1851 and the Criminal Evidence Act 1898—the essence of which is no person may be compelled to provide any evidence if said evidence might incriminate themselves."

Lestrade's fury now was reaching incandescent levels.

"I know the law, you jumped-up pair of . . . Wait, you believe yourselves to be incriminated in these foul murders?"

Raffles took the next shot, as we two were now aligned on both objective and methodology and, like a partnership of batsmen, were working in perfect synchronization.

"No. Absolutely not. You see, Commissioner, my colleague and I do have certain information and insights that we believe might be of use to you in this investigation and in the connected murder of General Fitzwilliam, in both of which our involvement is purely that of witness and concerned citizens. The circumstances in which we obtained that information, however, those are, shall we say, open to misinterpretation. Therefore, before we give you our information, we will require certain assurances that nothing we say that might, however tangentially or inaccurately, seem to incriminate us in any *other matter* will go beyond you. We confide in you and only you, and we ask that you keep fully distinct and private the confidences we share except only where they directly assist you in the investigation of these murders. Are these terms acceptable?"

Lestrade's ferret-like features became all the more pronouncedly animalistic as he considered our proposition. Like many who have ascended through ability rather than birth to the corridors of power, he had a keen sense of his own worth and of the relative worth of others, and he clearly chaffed that a dark-skinned foreigner and an amateur cricketer, however famous, were dictating terms to him.

He looked back and forth between me and Raffles. You could see him working through the implications and assessing his options, clicking through them like a human abacus. The warring impulses were at work within him. On a personal level, he resented Raffles and my very existence. On the other hand, he was a professional and he wished to solve the case before him, and his long association with the Great Detective had perhaps conditioned him to the idea that an outsider's perspective could be valuable in shedding light on the most confounding of cases.

Eventually he leaned back in the chair and, with great self-control, took a deep breath and with a much-altered tone, mixing patronage, disgust, and man-of-the-world resignation, spoke as follows:

"Tell me what you know. You have my word I have no interest in whatever . . . indiscretions, or rank private immoralities, your information might incidentally reveal.

"Such things, whilst repulsive to me personally, are beneath my professional notice, and no charges will be brought pertaining to such matters. My focus on this case is on catching the butcher behind it, and that is all. I trust that sets your minds at ease, so now proceed to tell me whatever it is you claim to know."

Raffles and I looked at each other, and I could tell that he was suppressing the desire to laugh. The policeman had considered the evidence carefully and come to a completely incorrect conclusion. Far from realizing that he had here before him the great Gentleman Cracksman, responsible for a string of the most daring burglaries of the past decade, whose takings included the Melrose diamonds, an original Velázquez, and the Belvoir pearls, the same master criminal who his underlings had been assiduously if ineffectively tracking for years now and who his lieutenant, Inspector Mackenzie, in particular, had made it his life's work to apprehend, he had instead leapt to the conclusion that the illegality we were at pains to conceal was that of the practice of gross indecency, of acts of the Greek sort—of unseemly love between men.

On reflection, I can see how the commissioner dropped into this particular gaff. The shadow of Oscar Wilde, the Disgraced Playwright, after all, still cast its long, grey cloak over our city. Indeed, a phrase of Wilde's came to my mind at this moment "feasting with panthers"—he had used it in a rather different context, but it seemed to fit the monstrous tableau we had confronted in the dining room.

I shook my head to clear it of such unhelpful thoughts and turned my attention back to the present moment, where I could see Raffles and the commissioner regarding each other in silence, each considering how to proceed. The commissioner sat with pursed lips, his piece said, waiting for Raffles to respond. Raffles, for his part, sat still, his sensual mouth twisted into a half-smile, leaning forward, on the edge of a decision.

Something in his expression reminded me of what would have been the final link in the commissioner's chain of faulty logic. There have been, even since I have known him, certain rumours of Raffles' late-night proclivities . . . That is to say, rumours about Raffles' own romantic inclinations have circulated amongst those given to society gossip. I am confident that these are idle and baseless slander, purely the malicious speculation of those who Raffles had offended with his quick wit and careless manner, but on this occasion, it appeared that the rumours were working in our favour.

Raffles had clearly reached the same conclusion. His expression changed, and animation flowed through his face like water, and suddenly he radiated gratitude and shame in equal measure, playing the part of the secretive sodomite to perfection.

"Commissioner, you are a man of exceeding good sense, and if I may say, of Solomonic discretion and judgement. It is rare and refreshing to see someone capable of keeping their eye so firmly on the big picture and not being distracted by irrelevant details. We should be honoured to confide fully in you and trust that our information, such as it is, shall in your capable hands be transmogrified into the gold of deduction and lead to the swift apprehension of this evil criminal."

Lestrade smiled, pleased to find himself back in control of the situation, and seemed almost to purr with joy, a tabby cat being assiduously stroked by its mistress.

"I did not get to where I am by being distracted. Now, come to the point, please, we have wasted enough time. What do you know that sheds light on this dark matter?"

"Very well," said Raffles, reclining back into the deep leather chair and lighting a cigarette. "Let us begin at the beginning."

CHAPTER 3

You Have the Watches,
We Have the Time

Late that evening, on the train journey back to London, Raffles was uncharacteristically quiet and withdrawn. I could not blame him: Our time at Mapperton had been filled with such horrifying revelations that my head was quite overflowing with riddles and speculation. Add to what we had seen, the very real risk to our personal reputations and liberty that sharing our information with Lestrade engendered, and we each had much to consider. Thus, it was that we rode the train for more than two hours in an intense silence, each engaged with our own separate but parallel preoccupations.

Perhaps because of the bloody carnage we had witnessed that day, I found my mind drawn to our time serving together in the war, when last I had seen the human body subjected to such cruel indignities.

I realize some clarification is necessary on that last point: When I say I "served" with Raffles in the Second Boer War, I do not mean that we fought shoulder to shoulder, still less that we shared barracks. Neither of those things would have been permitted.

Raffles was a sergeant major in Paget's Horse battalion, a fine cavalryman riding within a unit of 120 of his brother soldiers, all of them drawn from London's ruling classes. Barristers, bankers, and gentlemen of leisure. I doubt not that he fought valiantly, for Raffles, as you have seen, does not want for bravery, but he fought for the most part from astride a steed, whilst I saw the war from the mud. And whilst his tool was a bayonet, mine was a stretcher. Despite my combat experience in my native Punjab, the British had decreed that I, and nearly ten thousand of my fellow Indians, were fit to serve in their war, but not to actually fight alongside them.

No, this was a White Man's War, betwixt the Brits and the Boers, yet fought on African soil and with such a contingent of Indian auxiliaries. What is an "auxiliary," you ask? Nothing more than a ten-shilling word for a collection of tuppenny jobs: We were the drivers, grooms, cooks, and water carriers, or in my case, a stretcher-bearer, dashing unarmed through gunfire to collect the British wounded and return them to the relative safety of the medical tent.

"Relative" being the operative term, as few survived the tent either, even minor injuries often becoming life threatening as the result of infections or botched surgeries. Making my job as a courier of injured men from one fatally dangerous place (the battlefield) to another (the hospital) as pointless as it was full of jeopardy. But I fear I have veered somewhat off topic. Forgive me, having been denied a horse of my own during the war, I tend to mount hobby horses aplenty when talking about it.

That also you perhaps should know about me. I am not a man short of opinions, nor one shy to share them, a character trait which London society seems to find ill-matched with my status as a foreigner and a dusky-brown foreigner at that. Which is, I suppose, how I have ended up with Raffles as my closest companion. Since the day I pulled him from underneath his dead horse, and returned him to the medical tent with a broken leg, he has done me the courtesy of treating me not as an uppity Indian but simply as a fellow adventurer, a brother in arms. As long as I do my bit when he needs me, and have a whiskey ready when he needs that, Raffles embraces me quite completely, he takes me as I am, as a whole man, accepting both my complexion and my complexities.

So it was that when we pulled into Waterloo station, at a little after nine o'clock in the evening, I asked Raffles what his intentions for the night were. I imagined that perhaps he would suggest we decamp together to either his rooms or mine, to talk and drink and make sense together of all that had happened.

"I can release you from any obligation to me this evening, Bunny. I shall not be requiring your company. Let us make sure to regroup in the next few days."

My face must have expressed my disappointment at this statement, as he laughed in his kindly cruel way and continued. "Don't look so hang-dog, old fellow, you're a Bunny, not a bloodhound! We've done a good day's work, and there is nothing else for us at this moment. I need to shake all that death and gore out of my system, and my remedy is best pursued alone."

"What have you in mind?" I knew Raffles, at times, was capable of indulging in narcotics to refresh himself, and he knew well that this practice did not gain my approval, but I felt the need to at least inquire as to my friend's plans. He smiled, a half-smile of secret sin, and said only:

"I need to howl at the moon like an Alaskan wolf and run free for a little. I'm sure you have needs of your own. Let us each in our way replenish our energies over the weekend, and thus restored, we can once again apply ourselves to the matter at hand. Why don't we say breakfast at the club on Monday, eh?"

With that, my friend raised the lapels of his coat and, with a small but warm smile, turned away from me, like a bat into the night, and was gone, doubtless to some opium den or back-street gambling establishment where he could indulge his need for stimulation.

So it was that I found myself wandering the streets of London alone, trying to make sense of all we had seen and learnt that fateful day.

～

Once our terms had been accepted, Raffles had clearly and concisely shared with Commissioner Lestrade what he had witnessed weeks earlier at General Fitzwilliam's home in Mayfair.

Through the telling, as the light in the room gradually shifted from the cold brightness of a winter's day to the darkening shadows of the afternoon, Lestrade sat attentively, making a few small notes in his pad in virulent peacock-blue ink. Where he felt Raffles had glossed over some detail or another, he requested elaboration in clear and direct terms. On our general arrangement, he was as good as his word, and asked no questions pertaining to why it was that Raffles had been in the general's house at such a late hour and after all the other invited guests had long left. I could see though from a barely visible arch of an eyebrow that he was drawing further incorrect conclusions about the general's taste in sexual companions.

For his part, Raffles gave his account straightforwardly and without adornment or editorialization. My friend possessed a clinician's gift for relaying a narrative with precision and clarity, but so extraordinary was the tale in its essentials, including a description of a being of apparently superhuman agility and strength, that I braced myself for a violent and incredulous reaction from the commissioner.

None such came. When the tale was done, Lestrade withdrew into silence for several moments, his face characterized with a deep inner reflectiveness. Clearly something we were telling him was resonating with his own theories, or with other evidence in his possession. Something in the man seemed to relish collaboration, and once again, I detected the residue of the Great Detective's training. Lestrade seemed to think better with an audience, to enjoy the act of performing his reasoning out to the stalls, and so it was that we were granted a front-row seat. Lestrade rose and, gathering up his coat and hat, left the room with a fierce determination, gesturing for us to follow him. We strode behind him out of the house and into the garden, and cutting through the formal gardens, we quickly found ourselves heading into the woods.

"Rutledge and his sons were last seen by the staff yesterday at four," he explained as we walked. "They requested that the cook make them a camp supper and explained that they wished to walk the grounds in preparation for the hunt this weekend. Apparently, such a course of action was their habit and provoked no surprise from their servants.

"Nor was it found surprising that the trio did not return by sunset, nor by the time the staff themselves were retiring for the evening. Jarvis, the butler, assures me that his lordship and his sons often spent the night sleeping under the stars, striking camp, making a fire, and telling stories of their time in Swaziland."

"They were attacked in the grounds, then. Not in the house?" I surmised.

"Precisely," responded Lestrade, as we navigated a particularly robust thicket of pine trees.

Raffles nodded, his quick mind processing the information: "That would explain how no screams were heard. If they had been murdered in the house, like the general before them, then the entire household would have been awakened and the alarm raised much sooner. This way, the killer had time to kill them and then to transport them into the building and arrange them in that macabre diorama we discovered."

"Not killer, but killers, surely, come and see—here, it was here at this very spot where they were attacked. We could not understand from where, but hearing what you have just told us, I think I see how it could have been done."

Lestrade had led us to a clearing in the woodlands, a circular space perhaps thirty yards across, with several felled trees that could serve as the crude structure of a campsite. Indeed, this was how the space had been used; we saw laid out a military-style canvas tent, three bedrolls arranged around a fireplace, where a kettle was suspended on a makeshift cooking range.

This, then, is where the party had set camp for the night, content to sleep beneath the stars on rough ground whilst playing at being great hunters, whilst their feather-beds in their ancestral mansion house lay empty only a few hundred yards away. Such are the unfathomable ways of the rich.

Alongside the camp gear was a collection of hunting rifles, each of which had been systematically destroyed, broken in pieces, metal and wood shattered and splintered. I looked at the sundry pieces of the weapons, once miracles of engineering, technically advanced tools of death, now so much firewood and shrapnel, snapped in twain by some monstrously strong hands, as a child might snap a twig.

"No gunshots were heard?" asked Raffles.

"Several were. But nothing was made of it. They were, after all, out hunting . . ." responded Lestrade.

"But what force could have taken them here?" I asked, perplexed. "Three of them, all able-bodied and experienced hunters, armed, and, in the earl's case, at least a seasoned veteran of many bloody wars. On their own ground, two hundred yards or less from their home. Who could have surprised them here? And with such speed and strength as to kill them all outright? It must have been a savage and overwhelming ambush, of multiple assailants!"

"Am*bush*," said Raffles, "that's precisely the point. Your Latin will come in helpful once again, Bunny old boy. No? Let me do this one, I still remember a bit from school days . . . 'ambush' comes from *imboscāre*—or 'to lie in wait in the woods'—they were surprised from the trees."

I suddenly saw how it was done. Raffles had been a half step ahead of me, but I had caught up now. Lestrade, however, was lagging behind. "What can you mean?" he asked, peering around into the thick undergrowth.

"Look above you, Sir Gaston," I urged him, pointing up to the canopy. "From high above, in the branches of these mighty trees, there was the villain's hiding place." Lestrade adjusted his gaze as I intended, and Raffles picked up the explanation:

"Good English oak, Scottish pine, maple—there are a dozen places to hide up above. The assailant waited patiently, a hundred feet or more above their heads, waited till their guard was down and they were falling asleep, I'd warrant—and then dropping down, like a particularly lethal variant of manna from heaven, he came."

Whatever Lestrade lacked in the speed of his reasoning, he made up for in the alacrity of his action. Barking orders, he directed the men to procure ladders and ropes, and over the next several hours, a search of the trees nearest to the campsite was carried out.

It was slow work. Country policemen are surprisingly ill-trained in the art of tree-climbing, but eventually, the third tree ascended proved our theory correct. A magnificent silver birch revealed itself as the hiding place of the murderer. On one of its broad branches, fully seventy-five feet above the ground, a perfect vantage point of the campsite was found, and carved into the branch, a series of fresh gashes from a hunting knife, clear evidence of an assailant passing their time and waiting for their moment to arise.

Once this was found, I could clearly see in my mind's eye the moment of attack. The strange, agile creature that Raffles had encountered at General Fitzwilliam's scaling the tree in its inhuman, lurching style, observing silently from its elevated hiding point, and then at the moment of maximum vulnerability, leaping down, from branch to branch, with freakish strength and speed, and taking its victims unaware. The hunting knife which scored the tree was first murder weapon and then, later, artist's brush as the assailant assembled his grisly masterwork.

That the murderer in the two incidents was the same seemed now without question. Only one possessed with the near-supernatural agility that Raffles had witnessed could have surprised Rutledge and his sons from above. Yet, beyond that, I struggled to imagine what possibly linked the two crimes, the one sudden, apparently unmeditated, the other so carefully constructed and meticulously executed.

In all the horrors and uncertainty of war, the one thing that every soldier knew was who the enemy was. Here, we were taking casualties but did not know who we were fighting. This was a perversion of warfare. This was not what I had expected to encounter when I had taken the decision to move to London.

~

I said earlier that my and Raffles' friendship was forged in the fields of war, and whilst there is truth in that statement, it is not the complete story. It would be better to say that our friendship began in the veldt, through the circumstances of the war, but it was cemented here in the city, through our shared choice to live a life of crime.

My decision to move to London after the conclusion of the war, rather than returning to the Punjab, was a choice not arrived at lightly, but only after much consideration. I suffered from homesickness, of course, and was desirous to be reunited with my family. However, my experiences in the Boer War, my friendships with men from England, and the tales I heard of the great capital had engendered in me a curiosity that demanded satisfaction.

Accordingly, I wrote to my father to inform him of my intentions and ask his blessing. I did not ask for, nor expect, practical support, but I hoped that he would be sympathetic to my desire to better myself and explore the world before returning home, and perhaps even proud of my admission to study law at so prestigious an institution as Lincoln's Inn, so it was with some sadness that I received his reply, which I translate here:

> *Balvinder, Jaan**
> *Your letter came as a great surprise to your mother and I. We are glad, of course, that you have concluded your military duty without injury and have been warmly anticipating your return to your home.*
>
> *To learn, therefore, that you have chosen to delay reunion with your family in order to sojourn in London was an unwelcome revelation. We are at a loss to understand your motivations in doing so. You speak of "experience" and "opportunity." These are new words to us. The words you fail to use are "duty" and "obligation"—those are the values with which we raised you. Perhaps they have been washed away by the winds of war, or they grow*

out of fashion with your friends, but they have sustained your family and your culture for generations, and they will sustain us through this new trial.

Balvinder, you are a grown man, your decisions are your own, yet this course of action displays a degree of self-absorption that we did not anticipate in our firstborn. I grow old, your mother grows old, the farm requires much work, and your siblings cry in vain for their big brother.

Perhaps we will be here when you choose to return, perhaps we will be as last year's grass.

Remember us as you pursue your "adventures" in London.

Your Father

*The term signifies "darling," though does not have the feminine connotations of that word in English.

So it was that when I arrived in the capital, in the summer of 1902, I was an unmoored man, cut loose from family and my past, and with only my admission letter to Lincoln's Inn and Raffles' address at The Albany with which to navigate the city.

I found myself temporary quarters in a boarding house in Bethnal Green, conveniently located for the Inns of Court, and populated by many other recent immigrants, from India, Africa, and with Hebrews, such as Seth, who hailed from Poland and the Baltic states. The quarters were neither spacious nor pleasant, infused with a malodorous stench in the hot summer months, but there was a companionable feeling of community, and since much of my waking hours were spent at the law libraries, my requirements were simple.

I commenced my studies at Lincoln's Inn, and found to my delight that I was not the only student from the colonies seeking admittance to the bar. There were several other Indians, as well as one negro, Sylvester

Williams, a young man from the island colony of Trinidad, whose ambitions outstripped all of ours, determined as he was to one day be attorney general of his (he assured us) soon-to-be-independent island nation. Together, we formed our own small island, a group united by colonial experience marooned amongst our white associates, connected as much by history as by late-night study sessions and communal meals.

My greatest concern was securing income to support my tuition fees, books, robes, as well as the cost of my lodging and other expenses. I quickly discovered that few of the roles available to a former soldier of Indian heritage, recently arrived in London—security guard at the docks, fish porter at the market, night waiter at a late-night Hindoostan cafe—paid sufficiently to meet my needs.

Late one night, struggling to make notes on the case of *R. v. Pear* (it concerns a horse that may or may not have been stolen) by the flickering light of my last remaining candle, my need finally overcame my reluctance, and I put the casebook aside, and turned my pen instead to entreaty. I wrote to Raffles, informing him that I had recently arrived in London, and expressed a desire to resume our past acquaintance, reminding him, in terms I hoped were subtle, of his promise to help me situate myself and of my need for a well-paying occupation.

I had low expectations, fully imagining that whatever camaraderie had existed between us on the battlefield would wither away now that we were returned to civilian life. Raffles was an important figure, possessed of fame and fortune, and there seemed little rational reason why he would go out of his way to be of service to a low-ranking auxiliary from a faraway war. That said, I also knew him to be a man of honour whose life I had saved; surely, he would not abandon me now?

I was delighted to receive a response by return post, a brief missive that read simply:

> *B—The city glows brighter with you in it. Meet me at Claridges at 10pm tonight and we shall see what we shall see—AJR*

I arrived at Claridges at the appointed hour, dressed in what passed for my finest suit, an all-black affair in thick, coarse wool that I had acquired at a second-hand establishment at the Temple, suitable for attending lectures but little else, and was seeking vainly for the confidence to approach the imperial doorman at the grand entrance when a familiar voice sounded behind me.

"Bunny. Marvellous to see you."

I spun, to see Raffles, cashmere overcoat, carelessly thrown over evening dress, the diamond studs in his white shirt front glimmering in the moonlight. He shook my hand warmly and then surprised me by pulling me into a brief embrace.

"Can it be? The Indian Rabbit has come to England. How glorious. What fun we shall have."

He released me and, looking around, made a gesture with his head for me to follow, and set off down a side road. I followed, confused but glad to see him.

"Are we not having a drink? Is Claridge's no longer on the agenda?"

"Oh, plenty of time for that, dear chap. The drink is the reward after the job."

"Job?"

"Yes, indeed. You expressed a desire for remunerative work, did you not? Well, to your wish, I flock, like the veritable genie, fresh from the lamp."

He turned down a further side street, and increasing in pace, we walked north towards the area of London I now know to be called Hatton Garden, but at the time was simply a collection of cobbled streets and anonymous small shops to me.

"You see the third shop on the left there, number sixty-seven?" Raffles asked—I peered into the gloom and identified the premises to which he gestured, a small shophouse, the "shop" section on the ground floor and a modest residence upstairs. In elegant gold lettering on the glass front, I read the words "S. Bawrowski, Gems & Fine Watches." A CLOSED sign hung from the door handle.

"You see, Mr. Bawrowski has a watch that I sent in for repair, but he's only gone and taken his wife on a summer holiday and won't be back for weeks. That puts me in a bit of a pickle."

"Do you need the watch so urgently? Do you not have another?"

"Oh, plenty of watches, old fellow. But not like this one. This one is an Audemars Piguet in twenty-four-carat gold, with a ring of delightful little diamonds marking every five-minute interval."

"Oh. I see." I didn't, of course.

"Oh, indeed, and to complicate the situation, the fact of the matter is, the watch isn't mine—"

"Oh?" I repeated, feeling more stupid by the moment.

"I borrowed it from a friend of mine, dear old Monty Devereux. Monty leant it to me to wear to Queen Charlotte's Ball, vain fool that I am, I thought it would look rather fine with my ruby studs, and then, I scratched the thing! Just a teeny-tiny scratch, but I couldn't return it to Monty like that. I was trusting this fellow Bawrowski to polish it out, so I could return it without Monty being any the wiser, and now he's dashed gone on holiday and the watch is stuck in there. You see the problem?"

"Yes, quite. An annoying predicament."

"More than annoying! Urgent! I'm seeing Monty tomorrow, and if I don't have his watch, he's going to be frightfully annoyed with me."

"But what can be done?"

"Ah, you've arrived at the nub of the problem, dear Bunny, with the perceptiveness and precision that are the hallmarks of your character. That is the very question, and the answer is that I'm just going to pop into the shop and get it back."

"You have a key?"

"I do indeed. I am a regular customer of Bawrowski's, and indeed, I believe he sees me as something of a personal friend, as far as a man of his persuasion—he is a Hebrew, you understand—can have a gentile as a friend, and he has long trusted me with the key to his premises."

"Oh, how excellent. The problem is solved!"

"Almost. But I need your help."

"Of course, anything I can do—"

"Your task is the easiest of all. Stay here, keep an eye on the shop, keep a look out up and down the street, and if you see anyone coming, whistle. Can you do that for me?"

"Yes, of course, but . . . I don't understand, what am I looking out for?"

"Oh, Bunny, you charming innocent. I forget how new you are to London. Just imagine how this looks: It's late at night. I'm a man in dark clothes, rifling through the drawers of a jewellery shop in Hatton Gardens. I have a key, of course, but how am I to explain how I came by it? It is practically inevitable that some cloth-headed policeman will jump to the wrong conclusion, presume nefariousness, and then we're wasting our evening explaining ourselves to the local magistrate. It would get straightened out in the end, of course, but by that time Monty's watch would find itself snug in a safe-deposit box down in Scotland Yard till Bawrowski returned from the South of France."

"Oh. Yes. I see how that would be . . . awkward."

"Precisely so. All right, ready—here we go—"

With that, Raffles crossed the street, pulled something from his pocket, and quickly started to fiddle with the door lock. There seemed to be some problem with the key, or perhaps the lock was stiff, because it took him a few moments of jiggling to get the door open, and once within, he shut it behind him. I saw a lit candle within and could see the shadow of my friend systematically searching through different shelves in the establishment.

Remembering my charge, I shifted my focus from the shop to the street, identifying all possible routes of approach and switching my focus at periodic intervals back and forth, back and forth. It was a quiet night and there was little footfall. I heard laughter, and peering into the dark, I saw a young couple exiting a nearby pub, she leaning close to him, and them walking, linked arm in arm, a little uncertainly, in the opposite direction.

I crossed to the opposite side of the street, to ensure I was covering all angles, and started to imagine possible ways to distract a policeman or nightwatchman should one appear. I found, to my surprise, that I was quite enjoying myself. The thrill of the enterprise, the heightening of my senses in the cold night air, brought back the sense of mission, thrill, and common purpose that had been omnipresent in our war days, but in this instance with far less imminent danger of having a bullet lodged in one's skull.

Just as I was beginning to wonder why it was taking my old colleague so long to find the watch, he appeared by my side again, silently and with such stealth, that despite my having been on high alert, I did not notice him till he was upon me. "Well done, old fellow. Now, quick, step, let's get ourselves that drink."

~

Later, in his apartment, Raffles mixed us both whiskeys and soda from a heavy crystal decanter, offered me a cigarette, and lighting one for himself, threw his long frame back on an elongated couch and blew a cloud of smoke into the air. "Mission accomplished! Our first of many, I hope."

"May I see the watch?" I asked, most curious to see this rare artefact that had caused us such trouble. Raffles raised an eyebrow in an expression I would come to know well.

"Of course, of course." He rose, crossed the room to where he had hung his coat, and reached his hands deep into its pockets. I heard a rattling sound of metal against metal, and was surprised to see Raffles' hands emerge, holding not a watch but fists full of glistening gems, rings, necklaces, and other fine pieces of jewellery.

He brought his haul over to the central table and laid it out in front of me. I looked on incredulously, first confused, then with a growing and painful realization that I had just assisted in a burglary.

I was about to reproach Raffles when, with a casual flick of his wrist, he threw something at me, my native reflexes were activated, and I caught it. It was a broach, small but heavy, finely wrought from woven gold, in elaborate patterns in the Kundan style that seemed to me likely to be of Indian origin, and in its heart a beautiful deep-red ruby, glistening in the glow of the electric light.

"It's worth easily two hundred and fifty pounds," said Raffles softly. "My fence won't give you its full worth, of course, but we should manage around one thirty-five. That's your share for your role in tonight's little job."

I looked at him, my jaw agape, my heart beating fast. My weekly rent was six shillings. The cost of my entrance fee to the Inn had already depleted all my salary and pension from the military. A hundred and thirty-five pounds was a year of expenditure, comfortably, and Raffles had thrown it to me as casually as he might skip a stone across a pond.

I looked at my friend, and he held my gaze with his. Nothing was said, but everything was clear, this was a moment of choice, a branching path in the life I was to lead. I considered it carefully.

I could see my father's face, full of judgement and reproach. I could hear my grandmother's sitar, plangent, painful, and beautiful. I looked out of Raffles' window to the glittering lights of this extraordinary city, where behind every door lay infinite possibility. I considered the arrogant face of my pupil-master at the Inn, the condescension of the white students. I looked around Raffles' study, in which things of beauty competed for my attention, and I considered how much easier it would be to study if I had a chair to sit in and a lamp to read by.

My hand closed around the broach, repossessing it for my people from whom it had been taken, and I met Raffles' eye. "Was there ever a watch?" I asked, settling back into the deep upholstery of the sofa.

"What watch?" he asked, and then refilled my glass with whiskey.

～

My recollections, fond or otherwise, were interrupted by the call of a baying newsboy crying, "Read all about it, 'Earl of Rutledge dead in gruesome attacks'!" I could see from the sensationalist tone in this usual staid paper, and from the long line at the newsstands, that London would be talking of little else this weekend. I joined the line, bought a copy of every paper available, and, finding a convenient park bench, settled myself to read them all closely.

CHAPTER 4

Raga Mala

I had made my way through six newspaper articles on the murders, each more sensationalist and ill-informed than the last, when I was distracted from my review by the sound of some stray notes of music carrying on the night air. Not just any music but a distinctly Indian tune, a raga, the cyclical building block of so much Indian classical composition in both the Hindustani and Carnatic traditions.

My grandmother had played the sitar, and much of my childhood was spent at her feet, marvelling at the dexterity with which she plucked music from its strings. To hear these notes of home here in London was both surprising and joy-imbuing to my anxious soul.

I looked around me to discover that my meanderings had brought me to the outer edges of Kensington Gardens just across from the Royal Albert Hall. I checked my watch; it was a little past the hour of ten. Surely too late for a concert to be in progress?

I followed my ears and found that the music came not from the hall itself but from a building opposite, more precisely, from an open window on the second floor, seeping through the cool night air to my hungry ears. The building itself, a wedding cake–shaped edifice in red brick and limestone, loomed imposingly before me and resembled a mansion block of apartments, or perhaps doctors' surgeries—then I saw the signage:

Royal College of Music

Musical students in this august British institution, in the centre of London, were playing a raga, a piece of Indian classical music? This day seemed full of puzzles. I pushed at the door and proceeded within.

Making my way up the stairs, I quickly located the source of the music, a studio at the end of a hallway. I hesitated for a moment at the threshold, but having come this far, I resolved that I would complete the exercise and entered.

It was a large room, a rehearsal space I later came to understand, with wooden floors and a central raised dais. On this dais were three musicians, a tabla player, one on sitar, and a young lady who was playing the violin.

The tabla player and the sitar player were both men, and both Indian. Malayali, if I took them correctly with the distinctive shining dark hair and round faces of their people. I felt warmth towards them at once, for whilst they were not Punjabi, not of my linguistic or religious tribe, and many thousands of miles and even more cultural distance separated our homelands of Punjab and Kerala, here in London we were unquestionably kin, it being a strange rule of travel that the farther one goes from one's home, the more enthusiastically and wholeheartedly one feels towards people who, if encountered in one's native land, one would likely ignore entirely.

The violinist, sensing my presence, paused her bowing and turned to look at me. Unlike her compatriots, to my eye she was English, with startlingly pale skin and thick brown hair, which she had tied back severely, so as not to interfere with the playing of her instrument.

Her face was expressive, a wide mouth and wider eyes. Her beauty was penetrating, it struck one with physical force. She looked like a painting by Rossetti, though her expression spoke to a more practical disposition than one suspected was possessed by those diaphanously clad ladies.

"Pray, do not stop on my account . . ." I wasn't quite sure how to proceed. "I . . . I heard . . . I came . . ." I trailed off, not finding the words to explain myself.

The violin player looked at her colleagues with a question in her eyes, and they both made barely noticeable gestures of assent. Thus appointed spokeswoman for the trio, she turned to me, and with a voice of high status but unexpectedly low register, spoke thus:

"Sit, then, and listen. We do not object to an audience. But pray, sir, do not fidget!"

Nodding my acceptance of her terms, I looked round for a chair. Seeing none, I came to a quick decision and removed my coat and hat and folded myself cross-legged down onto the ground, as I used to sit as a boy at my grandmother's knee. Something in the childishness of my posture seemed to amuse her, and she turned back to her colleagues, counted down from three, and they resumed their rehearsal.

~

For those unfamiliar with Indian classical music, I am forced to say a few words to attempt to describe what I experienced that evening. "Attempt" because, whilst I recognize that some description is necessary, I know also that no true description is possible.

Perhaps I should not be too hard on myself and say that the fault lies not with my literary prowess (or lack thereof) but with language itself. Words are unequal to the task of describing music, because music begins where language leaves off. Music is the alternative to language in those moments when no words are adequate. It is the language for things unsaid and unsayable: for grief, for hope, for spiritual transcendence, and for love.

Sufficient, therefore, to say that Indian classical music has, in its cultural origins, some overlap with European tradition. Both grew out of religious practice: A raga may function like a sung Latin mass to elevate the soul, to bring the audience-congregation closer to God.

The multifarious gods of India, however, are radically different to the singular deity of the Anglican church, and their stories far more varied and multistranded. Hindu religious narratives, in particular, which inform much of Indian musical tradition, are not constrained by such linear constructs as beginnings, middles, and ends; instead, they cycle and spiral in intricate repetition as the universe itself cycles from creation to destruction and back again, for all time and for all that is beyond time.

As it is with our gods and our stories, so it is with our music. Ragas, whilst obeying strict rules of tonality and melody, are not rigidly constrained by the staves and bars of musical notation, but are built with space for copious improvisation, so much so that no one can say with any certainty at the beginning of a performance how long that performance may last. Songs loop and dive, turning back on themselves and weaving intricate, repetitive, and cyclical journeys before resolving. There are legendary tales of musicians who played not for hours but for days, taking their audiences on rhapsodic odysseys that changed them forever.

Such it proved for me that evening, as I sat, for how long I knew not, surrounded by the warm waves of familiar music. I was buoyed, enveloped by the warmth of a forgotten sea, my body and my very soul nourished and cleansed by the ebb and flow of rhythm and melody, even as the tones of the sitar and violin scrubbed my brain clean of all fear, doubt, and unease.

～

A sharp sound, like the retort of a distant rifle, startled me, and in a moment, I was on my feet and on my guard. The room was dark and unfamiliar. I spun round, trying to get my bearings, but slipped and fell. The floor was recently polished and slippery, and for that my feet had not prepared.

I hit the ground, attempted to get up, slipped, and fell again, but this time my descent was rudely interrupted by laughter. Not cruel laughter, but a genuine, unmediated guffaw, though an unusually musical one that seemed to ascend and descend the scale even as it built in intensity.

"I'm sorry," said a familiar woman's voice. "I shouldn't laugh, but my goodness, you spun like a giddy top! Are you alright?"

I lifted my head to see her. My fears were confirmed. It was the violinist. She stepped down from the dais, and walked halfway towards me, her laughter fading and concern animating her face. The last vestiges of confusion fell from my laggard mind, and I realized what had happened.

I had fallen asleep. Stupid, cloddish, doltish Balvinder. Calmed like the savage creature of the play by the charms of the maiden's music. I had been sprawled here on the floor of a rehearsal room at the Royal College of Music, doubtless snoring like a sick dog, whilst this mysterious beauty and her companions laughed at me. The "rifle shot" which had woken me had simply been the snap of a music stand being put away.

Her companions? Where were the Malayalis who had been playing? I looked around for them, and she, understanding intuitively the question in my mind, answered—

"Arvind and Anand left a little while ago. It was my turn to lock up. They were most hesitant to leave me with your sleeping form, saying it was improper for a lady to be left unaccompanied with a strange Indian man, but I pointed out that I had rehearsed alone with each of them on many occasions, and they had little answer to that. They wanted to wake you, but I said you looked like you rather needed the rest. Why did you, by the way?"

Even her spoken voice was musical, each word a separate note, plucked from an exquisite instrument. Slowly, carefully, not quite trusting myself to speak, I rose to my feet. "It has been a challenging day. I apologize for falling asleep. It was most disrespectful."

"We took it as a compliment."

"How so?"

"We were playing around with *Shankarabharanam*. The raga's theme is tranquillity. It seemed to work on you." She laughed again, that big, musical laugh that in anyone else I would have found offensive but in her, somehow, was charming. I found myself laughing too, and there we were, two utter strangers from different worlds, linked only by a melody, laughing together, alone in a darkened room.

We stopped at the same moment, and then we were suddenly aware of the strangeness and inappropriateness of our situation. She spoke first: "It is late. I should get home."

"Of course, of course. I apologize again, and I am most grateful to you for—"

"It is late," she repeated, and her lilting accent burred stronger in her soft yet insistent tone. "Late, and dark and dangerous. Will you not be a gentleman and escort me to the safety of my home, or must I walk alone through London streets, and with mysterious killers on the loose and all?"

～

The moonlight flooded the streets like a drunkard's spilt drink, its giddy fumes rising off the pavement and confounding our senses. It was an October night, but I do not believe that either of us were conscious of the cold as we walked and talked through the streets of Kensington towards what I took to be her family home in Mayfair.

Her name, it emerged, was Maud Adler. Born in Tipperary, in Ireland, she had been a musical prodigy who won a scholarship to come to the Royal College in her ninth year, had started performing at the age of thirteen, and subsequently toured the world. Playing her violin throughout the United States of America in the august company of the Boston Symphony Orchestra and as far afield as Australia.

More recently, her tours had taken her to India, where she had encountered the Carnatic tradition, and on her return to England, and to the Royal College, she had gone about sponsoring students from the subcontinent, determined to bring Indian music to a Western audience.

She laid out for me her contention that Indian and European classical composition complemented one another, which from a position of relative ignorance, I was happy to agree with.

Leaving aside music for the moment, we spoke a little of the matter that was dominating the weekend newspapers—the murders of the Earl of Rutledge and his sons. Perhaps to impress her, I let slip that I had been present at the scene of the crime, and after expressing initial disbelief, she listened intently to my account. I was careful to omit the most horrific details, but she reacted not with disgust but thoughtfulness, interrogating me with a precise focus not on the salacious details of the crime but on the purpose of it.

"What could the motive be for such a terrible deed? Why would someone do this?" she asked, and there I found myself unable to answer, and also surprised to realize that she was the first person to ask what now seemed a most obvious question. Neither Lestrade nor Raffles nor myself had raised the matter of motive, both being entirely preoccupied with method, the *how*, not the *why*.

It was this insight, when combined with her extraordinary biography, that moved me to express my admiration, or at least I tried to: "Your cultural attainments and intellectual prowess would be remarkable in anyone, Miss Adler, but in—"

"In what? Step careful, Mr. Singh. Do not disappoint me by saying 'in a woman.'"

Which was, of course, precisely what I was about to say, but sensing in my companion a strong strain of Wollstonecraftian philosophy, this notion I have heard described as "feminism," I quickly parted from my planned statement. "I was going to say, in one so young."

She smiled, perhaps not quite believing me, but willing to pretend she did.

"We are not so far apart in age, surely?"

"I am fully thirty-six."

"And I, eight and twenty. So there is not much in it."

"Thus, you make my point."

"How so?"

"Well, I have an eight-year lead in this world on you, and yet when I compare our relative accomplishments, I am but a mewing babe."

She turned on me, her eyes shining but her mouth stern. "You have fought in a war?"

"In several."

"You have saved the lives of your fellow soldiers."

"When it was possible to do so."

"How many languages do you speak?"

I paused. This was not a question I had been asked before, and I had to count in my head. "Punjabi, Hindi, English, obviously. Some basic Afrikaans, even more rudimentary Zulu. I read Urdu and a little Sanskrit, and I can find my way around a Roman statute book."

"We'll call that six. You were born in a village in the Punjab, but now live in London?"

"Yes."

"And you are currently preparing for your bar exams?"

I realized that I had told her more about myself than I realized on our short walk. I nodded, sensing the direction of her argument, no longer trusting myself to speak. "I would say we have both travelled a long way from our beginnings, Mr. Singh. But now, here we are, arriving at the end of this particular journey."

I must have looked confused, because she clarified with a backward shake of her head.

"This is where I live. Thank you for escorting me."

She opened the ornate door of a mansion block of apartments and stepped within. I found myself suddenly deathly, urgently afraid that I might never see her again.

"Wait," I said, knowing not what justification I could offer to that demand. She turned, framed against a warm internal light.

"Yes?"

"Your name. Your last name. Adler. It is familiar to me?"

It was, and I had been attempting to place it during our walk, but that was not what I wished to say. Given that I could not begin to say what I wished to say, I was content to say anything, any nonsense that might keep her from closing that door and retreating into the warm and impenetrable interior of her family home.

"You are thinking of my cousin Irene. She had some fame as an opera singer, and then cropped up in one of the popular accounts of the Great Detective's cases. She hates that people remember her for that, and not for her music. She's lovely. She lives in Boston now, with her terribly handsome and even more wealthy husband."

Irene Adler. Yes, that was it. But the information brought me no comfort, as I was beginning to realize that, for me, the younger Miss Adler and not her notorious relation would always be "the woman."

As if reading my mind, Maud stepped back out onto the step for a moment, and in a gesture so simple and so terrifying in its unconventionality, she reached out a hand towards my face and laid it flatly against the thick hair of my beard.

"It is an article of your faith, is it not, to never shave?"

I found I dared not to speak. I would not move my jaw against her hand, lest it cause her to remove it. I dared not even breathe. I would maintain this connection, forever, if we both must be turned to stone to do it. I tried to nod with my eyes. She seemed satisfied with my answer.

"I wonder, Balvinder," she said, using my given name for the very first time. "I wonder which of us, the Irish woman or the Indian man, the artist-turned-educator or the warrior-turned-lawyer, I wonder which of us is more constrained by empire, by the society of the English—and which of us is the more free?"

She stepped back, her hand breaking contact from my face, and I found myself able to once again inhale. I had no answer to her question—the very asking of it went deeper into things that I thought I understood—but now realized I had never even properly considered.

Seeing my confusion, she smiled. "Why don't you come by tomorrow afternoon and take me for a picnic in the park and we can discuss it?" And, having made this characteristically audacious suggestion, she turned and crossed the threshold once again, closing the door behind her.

CHAPTER 5

Our Client, the Imperialist

This volume is intended as an account of matters political and historic. I included in the previous section some detail on my first encounter with Maud Adler because she came to play an important role in the events that follow, but there is no need for me to detail what else passed between us over that golden weekend, and accordingly I will put aside such personal matters and return to the main narrative.

The following headlines greeted me at the newsagents on Monday morning:

War Declared on Aristocracy

"None of us are safe"—
England's Greatest Houses in a State of Panic

Grotesque Murder of Earl of Rutledge Part of a Wider Pattern, Sources Revealed. Foreign Agents Suspected.

Mysterious Assailants Bring Terror to England

Fenians Strike Back?!

I read the accompanying articles with alacrity, but once again found little new information contained within. It would appear that the nation's journalists, having been denied fresh findings, had spent their Saturday nights industriously producing sensational puffery.

Save for alleging an unspecified and vague "conspiracy" to unattributed "police sources" and unsubstantiated implications of a "foreign threat," the pieces brought no new information to the matter, and, indeed, with the exception of *The Times*, failed for the most part to make the obvious connection between Fitzwilliam's murder and the events at Mapperton. Further, none of the accounts contained accurate details. Whilst all spoke in general terms about the "mutilation" of the victims' bodies, no description was given of the specific horrors Raffles and I had discovered. No reference was made, for example, to the fact that each of the victims was missing his right hand.

Nevertheless, the articles, however ill-informed and inaccurate, seemed to be having an effect. As I made my way to the Garrick Club for my pre-arranged breakfast with Raffles, it was clear to me that the mood on the streets was tense and that the general population of London was bracing for new attacks.

The Garrick Club, named for David Garrick, the greatest actor of the last century, was one of several to which Raffles belonged, and his unquestioned favourite. The club was much favoured by the artistic classes and also by politicians and others keen to be seen to patronize the arts. Since Raffles thought of himself, both as cricketer and as thief, as an *artiste par excellence*, it was unsurprising that this was his preferred haunt.

Also, the breakfast provided by the Garrick was really rather good, and I arrived with a hearty appetite and savoury anticipation. Frustratingly, despite it being several minutes past our arranged time of meeting, Raffles had yet to arrive, and because I was not a member myself, I was reduced to waiting for him in the entrance hall.

You see, I was only here as Raffles' guest, and no guests are to be admitted without an accompanying member in good standing. Despite the fact I was well known to many of the staff, including the young lad working the front desk, I was obligated to loiter patiently, doing my best to maintain my good mood as a series of members pointedly averted their gazes from me as they passed through the antechamber and into the inner sanctums beyond.

Perhaps it was the weekend of heady conversation with Maud—I mean to say, with Miss Adler—or perhaps it was the newspaper articles that were so keen to blame "foreigners" for the atrocities, but I found myself more conscious than usual of the way these members of the Garrick, these so-called gentlemen, viewed me. These were some of London's most prominent citizens, and also some of its most imaginative ones. Playwrights, authors, composers, singers and the like.

Many were known to me personally, from past dinners and long evenings at the club as Raffles' guest. In his company, I drank with them, talked of politics and the latest plays, debated the day's news, and sympathized with their private woes and tribulations. If, at times, I had felt myself somewhat lost in their maze of references, I believed I had, on the whole, discharged myself adequately, kept up with their witticisms and insights, and in those moments, I felt myself to be, if not their friend exactly, at least a welcomed guest to their company.

Standing in the cold hall now, however, where even men whom I had known in their cups were averting their eyes from mine as they walked past, I came to understand what I should have always known. These men tolerated me only because of my association with Raffles. I was not their friend, not even worthy of recognition when alone. They would take the slightest excuse to break with me. The realization filled me with a mixture of despondency and fury.

To compound the matter, my hunger was rising to intolerable levels, and my stomach began to rumble with such ferocity that I convinced myself the entrance clerk could hear it from across the hall. Damn and blast Raffles for his delinquency! Did a man's word to his friend mean nothing—was breakfast not a solemn promise in these degenerate times?

I was reduced to glaring furiously at each club member as they entered, defying each, in turn, to meet my eye. Somewhat to my surprise, though, the very next man along smiled broadly on seeing me and extended his hand.

"Bunny, isn't it? Good to see you, fellow—what are you doing out here?"

I realized I had been glaring at Jimmy Barrie, the celebrated Scottish writer, who had, only last year, achieved remarkable acclaim with his play about flying fairy folk. Barrie was a sensitive soul, one who despite his fame and wealth always had a childlike softness to him, and who had always displayed a gentle and respectful curiosity about my life in India.

To be sure, Barrie had his peculiarities, and Raffles was capable of being quite cruel about him, gossiping mercilessly as soon as the author left the room. The subject of the gossip was the married Barrie's association with Mrs. Llewelyn Davies, an equally married woman with five boys who the author had rather unconventionally befriended.

I, however, was most fond of the gentle Scot and so was immediately consumed with guilt for having mentally grouped him with the other men of the Garrick. I explained quickly that I was waiting for Raffles.

"Out here—in the lobby? Why?" His tone was genuinely confused; all his great powers of imagination could not conjure up a reason for my behaviour.

I explained it gently: "I'm not a club member, Jimmy. It is not permitted—"

Barrie's eyes widened in moral horror at my social predicament. "What? Nonsense. I *am* a member, and you shall be my guest till that laggard AJ arrives. We shall break our fast together. You will be better company than the morning papers, which seem to be full of nothing but this terrible business with Rutledge and his poor boys."

With a nod to the doorman, he whisked me into the coffee room, where a table was quickly found for us. I felt good about this development. To have Barrie embrace me so warmly gave me comfort about my social standing and made me feel less dependent on Raffles as my only sponsor in this world. We both ordered the kedgeree, and I was positively salivating in anticipation of its arrival.

Barrie, however, had his mind on other things than the food. He immediately brought up the matter of the Mapperton murders and asked my opinion on the subject. I hesitated. I had begun to realize that talking openly of Raffles' and my involvement in this matter was unhelpful. Thankfully, I was saved from having to lie to Barrie by the arrival of our orders.

The fragrant aromas of curried haddock, boiled eggs, and buttery rice filled my senses, and my stomach thrilled in excitement. I grasped my fork and lifted the first bite to my mouth—only to be interrupted by the arrival of a waiter at the table. Neither Barrie nor I acknowledged him at first, both fixated on the feast before us, and doubtless assuming he was simply there to refill the teapot or some other similar duty; however, the boy cleared his throat, and it was revealed that he bore a note. Barrie reached for it instinctively, but to our mutual surprise, the waiter explained in tones of strained incredulity:

"For Mr. . . . Singh, sir."

I took the note, recognizing immediately Raffles' hand.

Summoned to Whitehall. Colonial Office. Come at Once. AJR

I looked at this brief missive in complete confusion. What could it mean? Barrie regarded me with a quizzical eye, and I sensed, for the first time, that underneath all his kindness and solicitude hid the mercenary soul of a writer, for whom every experience presented opportunities from which to craft his fiction. Even in my agitation, I could perceive his careful study of me, his literary mind doubtless reducing my expression of confusion into a few choice and clear sentences. Would I now appear in some future instalment of Peter Pan's adventures, transmogrified into a junior member of the pirate crew?

This, however, was not the time for such speculations. I rose, made my apologies to Barrie, said a regretful goodbye to the kedgeree, and, running out of the club, hailed a cab. Raffles needed me.

~

The Colonial Office building, located just off Charles Street, is an imposing affair. If you were to imagine a modern castle, complete with porticos, imposing balustrades, and armed guardhouses, then you come fairly close to an image of the building that loomed in front of me.

How could it be other than imposing? It was from this place that the populations of more than half the globe were ruled: from Canada to the Caribbean; from the Cape Colony on the southernmost tip of Africa to the veiled protectorate of once mighty Egypt; from the farthest antipodes of Australia and New Zealand to Malaya and Singapore, Hong Kong and Burma. All those millions of souls and their labour, their livelihoods, their freedoms, and their destinies were controlled by those few within this building.

We lived in a world of puppets, and within these walls sat the masters.

I looked up at it with awe and apprehension filling my empty belly. What on earth was I doing here? Why had Raffles been summoned, and who was I to cross this threshold and enter the very belly of the leviathan, this mighty bureaucratic beast that had somehow conquered my brave and unconquerable people?

"Mr. Singh. Here we are together again." The voice was soft but firm.

I spun round to see the pinched face of Commissioner Lestrade smiling humourlessly behind me.

"Come along, then. It is best not to keep one's superiors waiting." Linking his arm into mine, he marched me forward into the building, the doors opening at his nod, functionaries bowing and scraping as the great man strode confidently up a grand marble staircase and through the inner halls towards the place of our meeting, whilst I, like so much jetsam and flotsam, was carried in his wake.

The commissioner's presence obviously pointed to this visit being related to the murders at Mapperton and of Fitzwilliam. As we walked, I attempted to extract some context from Lestrade, quizzed him as to why this had now become a matter for the Colonial Office, but he brushed away my queries with a rather theatrical "all will be explained."

I suppose, in a way, it was.

We found Raffles in an antechamber, waiting impatiently for us, though none but me would have known it. Outwardly, he was as composed and calm as he ever was, but I could tell from the set of his jaw and the tapping of his fingers that he was much agitated by the circumstances.

I went to his side, hoping for a moment in which we could compare notes and arrive at a mutually agreed-upon plan of action, but the presence of Lestrade made that impossible, and no sooner had we made mutual greeting than a bespectacled secretary appeared from nowhere and ushered the three of us into a banquet-hall-size meeting room with walls clad in dark mahogany and an unbroken row of windows overlooking the street. As we entered, Raffles leaned into my ear and whispered in dry tones: *"Lasciate ogne speranza, voi ch'intrate."* All hope abandon, indeed.

Two others were already within, sitting together on the far side of the massive conference table that bifurcated the room. Both were elderly men, with greying hair and the marks of age on their faces. I took a step into the room and then came to an abrupt halt as I recognized them and a sudden lightheadedness came upon me, forcing me to steady myself by leaning on Raffles.

My experience in war and my criminal exploits had both put me in situations of real danger, and I am not a man easily unsettled. Even when confronted with the grisly discovery at Mapperton, I flatter myself that I had played my part with competence and calm.

In this moment, though, I was like a child confronted with a pair of mythological creatures. A dragon had appeared before me belching flame and sulphur, accompanied by a unicorn, and all I could do was gape in wonder. Because I knew who these two men were.

The shorter of the two was a friendly-featured chap, a little heavier than perhaps he had been in his prime, who was in the process of clambering to his feet with the aid of a stout wooden walking stick; a smile of recognition blossomed on his face as he extended his hand to Lestrade.

His companion, by some distance the taller, remained stretched out in his chair, his legs akimbo before him, the top of his head balanced on the headrest, apparently asleep. I knew his appearance from the papers, of course, but he looked different now from the familiar public image. He had grown gaunter in his advancing age, and the celebrated aquiline head now loomed larger than ever, dominating one's impression of him. His great, noble skull was disproportionate even to the considerable length of his body; his hair was scraped back severely and tightly lacquered, not a strand out of place. This was done, one suspected, not out of vanity but out of a desire to minimize distraction, to have nothing interfere with his keen senses, not even his own hair. He turned towards me then, his eyes snapping open. They were not an old man's eyes but keen and piercing, and I felt them bore into me as I was subjected to the cold appraisal of his legendary intellect.

Helplessly mesmerized, I stood in silence, observing him observing me, his attention darting from my hands to my cuffs, my trousers, and then to my boots, and then back up to my face and beard. How strange, I thought, that in the priorities of his inspection, it is my face he looks at last, but doubtless he has his methods.

Having made his appraisal, he turned away and, seeming to lose all interest in me, stretched and yawned. I was devastated. To be found interesting by him would have been the highest praise possible. To be so dismissed was hard to take.

Raffles, who knew my obsession with this man only too well, observed my despair with a detached amusement. He could have mocked me, as he had so many times before, but in this moment, I felt my friend's support as he grasped my shoulder firmly. "We are together in this," his grip said, and I was reassured by that.

Lestrade, who had blithely missed the subtext of the moment, now declared himself host, and was busy making introductions: "May I present to you AJ Raffles and his companion, Mr. Balvinder Singh. Gentlemen, it is my honour to introduce two men who need no introduction, Mr. Sherlock Holmes and his colleague Dr. John Watson."

For those reading this in some distant future, where the Great Detective's legend has faded, I should perhaps make some attempt to explain the strength of my reaction upon meeting him.

I had first read Dr. Watson's colourful accounts of his and Holmes' adventures in India, where they were widely available, not only in English but also translated into Urdu. First came *"Ajīb Sāzish"* ("A Strange Conspiracy"), based on the case of "The Red-Headed League" and adapted by Muhammad Muhsin Faruqi, and then *"Khoon-Naba-e-Ishq"* ("The Bloody Torrent of Love") based on Dr. Watson's *A Study in Scarlet*. I devoured these, and they quickly put me on to the English originals, which I read and re-read with a devotion that others in my family reserved for the writings of the Guru.

Holmes' impossible feats of deduction, his insistence on the primacy of logic, his constant willingness to answer the call for his king and country, and the unquestioning loyalty that he and his friend and chronicler had to each other came to lodge themselves permanently in my imagination, shaping my young mind.

Since moving to London, much to Raffles' chagrin and constant mockery, I had made a particular point of following Holmes' and Watson's exploits in the press and of learning all I could of the Great Detective's methodologies and practices.

Why, you might ask, should I, a former soldier and current thief, hailing from the Punjab, maintain such a deep and childish fascination with the methods of a British consulting detective, however celebrated? What had his world to do with mine?

On one level, the answer is surely obvious. In my nocturnal work with Raffles, I am a criminal. Holmes is the greatest opponent of the criminal classes the world has ever known. It would be logical for me to study him, if only to be more certain of how to best evade him and his lesser counterparts.

Yet, as I have already disclosed, my interest in Holmes both predates and goes far deeper than that. I had not before this moment subjected it to a full interrogation, but looking back now, I see with clarity that I was obsessed with Holmes because of what he represented: He was a force for order, for logic, clarity, and balance, qualities that were absent in my young life. Holmes demonstrated the capacity of a singular mind and an uncompromising will to bring about justice and fairness in a universe that cared little for such things. In my culture, people are what they are born to be. Holmes' unwavering determination to invent a role for himself in the world was, in and of itself, inspiring.

Consider the following hypothetical: If, by some accident of fate, I had been born not in the Punjab but in Shropshire. Born not to Indian parents but to English ones. If that were so, then what would change?

That alternative Balvinder—let us call him Barry—would have fought in the war as a captain in the cavalry, like Raffles, not as an unarmed auxiliary, carrying a stretcher. Barry would be a member of the Garrick in good standing, able to enter at will and order kedgeree with wild abandon. Barry would be free to love who he wished to love and to marry whom he would. I would be the conqueror and not the conquered.

That was not my reality. I was Balvinder, not Barry, and fate and chance had dealt me a different hand, and I played it best I could. I knew nothing of Holmes' family or background—but I wondered what his destiny would be if he had been born in Calcutta, not London; Salman, not Sherlock.

Would Salman Holmes have lived and died in a slum, achieving nothing of note? Would his exploits have been limited to solving the Case of the Missing Chapatis and the Matter of the Mysterious Mongoose? Or would, as I suspected, his unparalleled intellect, his *sui generis* gifts have ensured that he would always have become that which he is: a man who, by the utilization of his singular powers, made his country stronger and safer, and bent the arc of history to his purpose; a fixed reference point of certainty and order in a chaotic and contingent world.

None of which philosophical meanderings did I express to him in that first meeting, for no sooner had Lestrade spoken his introductions than we were joined by a sixth man, who entered the room already in the full flow of speech. Speaking in a clear and oddly captivating manner, not to any one of us, but to all of us at once:

"Ah, excellent. You have all met and made yourselves known. Very good, gentlemen. Allow me to explain why I have summoned you here, and of what utility you may be to your government and to your country. Or, in your case, Mr. Singh, I suppose I should say to your *adopted* country. Yes, adopted country, very good, very good. Sit down, sit down, I require your attention, and I rather you didn't all loom above me so as I set out the situation."

Our host, as we took him to be, was a small, slight personage, a full head shorter than me, and I was not the tallest in the room. He was perhaps five foot six and, as I say, modest of build with narrow shoulders and womanly hips. Whilst young—I put him as my junior by perhaps half a decade—he had a certain natural authority about him, seating himself without hesitation at the head of the enormous table. Though physically diminutive, the fellow had a soldier's bearing, a man unquestionably of action and courage.

What was most notable about him, as I've already alluded, was his speaking voice. Aristocratic in its accent, yet without the nasal quality that many high-born men of the period affected, he was possessed of a remarkable instrument: clear, musical, and resonant, and capable of producing a seemingly endless flow of words, which he appeared to select as much for their melody as for their meaning, and which continued unabated, even as he produced and lit a cigar. Somehow he had perfected the trick of being able to inhale and speak simultaneously and without impediment:

"As you are all aware, the Earl of Rutledge and his sons were brutally murdered in their home last week. You are also by now doubtless aware that that incident is not a solitary one but part of a broader pattern. Mr. Raffles here was the sole witness to General Fitzwilliam's murder, some weeks past, and has provided us with details that make clear there is some commonality of, shall we say, *style* in these crimes."

At this, Dr. Watson turned and stared openly at Raffles. Holmes made no movement, having inclined once more in his chair, with his eyes staring at the ceiling above. Our host continued his narration, comfortable now that he commanded our attention:

"What none of you are aware of, the new information that I must now impart to you, is as follows . . .

"These two are not the only incidents. Far from it. There have been a series of other attacks on other distinguished sons of Albion, occurring not only here at home but also across our dominions. In Egypt, we lost an assistant counsel to a bombing; in Bechuanaland, a district commissioner to what was first thought to be a wild animal attack but was subsequently revealed to be a murder: the man's hands were cut off at the wrist, a detail, I understand, which was replicated at Mapperton. The aide to the resident in Uganda was bitten by a cobra of a species native not to Africa but to India, whilst a chief magistrate in Zanzibar, by all accounts an excellent outdoorsman, was found dead in a trap designed to catch wild boar. These attacks go back several years and were not previously believed to be connected, but rather isolated local accidents or one-offs, but recent events have suggested to our intelligence services that there may be a link between the murders abroad and those at home."

The minister's voice now took on a rolling oratory that underlined the grave import of his words. "We believe that there is a deep conspiracy at work, a shadowy network of assassins that encompasses the entire globe . . ."

"I'm sorry, Mr. Under-Secretary, but did you say you had some *new* information for us?"

This interruption came from Holmes, who had drawn his attention away from his close inspection of the ceiling and was now regarding our host with undisguised impatience.

The under-secretary for colonial affairs (as I now understood him to be) seemed most put out by the interruption. "Eh, what? My good man, I am giving you the information!"

"You are telling us nothing that I do not already know. All the cases you mention have been well documented in the press, and I have taken a note of them. That they are connected is a matter of obvious inference. If you would have me be of use to you, either rapidly get to the heart of the matter, or if you have nothing new to impart, then pray, stop wasting our time and allow me to make my own inquiries."

The under-secretary blinked a few times in silence. It was clear that he was unaccustomed to being addressed in this way, and was considering his response. He drew on his cigar again for comfort. It was a huge Havana that quite dwarfed his small hands—making him seem even younger than he was. Like a schoolboy trying on a hat of his father's to affect a simulacrum of adulthood. The man-boy sucked on his cigar again and nodded sagely a few times and then, having calmed his nerves and decided on a response, rounded the full force of his personality on Holmes.

"I was told you were unusual, Holmes. I was warned of it. I am delighted to discover it to be true. I am also a connoisseur of the unusual, a collector of experience. We have that in common, you and I. So, then—what conclusions have you drawn? What motivates this web of assassins and terrorists? What is their cause, their animating ideology? Eh?"

"Is it not obvious?"

All of us had been utterly transfixed by this back-and-forth between the under-secretary of colonial affairs and Mr. Sherlock Holmes, between the junior minister, whose limitless self-confidence seemed to exist quite independently from any actual accomplishments, and the grand old detective, whose own self-certainty came from decades of being consistently correct, that it took us all by surprise to realize that this last statement had not come from Holmes but from elsewhere in the room.

I looked around to determine the source—first to Raffles, then to Lestrade, and then at Watson. To my surprise, all of them were staring at me. As were, to my escalating discomfort, Holmes and the under-secretary, who now rounded on me, his cigar serving as an extension of his pointing finger.

"You have something to add, Mr. Singh? Is the matter as transparent to you as it is to Mr. Holmes? Are you also a . . . uh . . . Great Detective?"

I looked to Raffles in my confusion, wishing him to explain what was happening. He shrugged at me, and it slowly dawned on me that, once again, my mouth had spoken unbidden and the obnoxious phrase "Isn't it obvious?" had come not from one of the others but from my own lips. Now the entire company was turned to me, waiting for an explanation of my most unfortunate ejaculation. I took a deep breath.

"The assassins are a cadre of anti-imperialists. People who hate the empire and all its works."

The under-secretary nodded sagely. "Go on . . ."

"The victims are either agents of empire, soldiers or administrators tasked with enforcing Britain's will abroad, or in the case of Rutledge—have profited from empire. In Fitzwilliam's case, both were true. He was the officer in charge of some of the most brutal subjugations of uprisings in India, and he also was a . . . collector, I suppose you could say, of Indian jewels."

It was most disconcerting to have all of them listen to so intently; even Sherlock Holmes was paying me what appeared to be a significant proportion of his full attention.

"Go on," repeated the under-secretary, leaning forward hungrily on the desk.

"The nature of the killings. The early ones seem purely functional, but as they progress, one gets a sense they are . . . designed . . . to be symbolic."

"Symbolic?! What do they symbolize?"

"Take the case of the cobra bite. To import an animal native to India to kill an African administrator makes a statement about solidarity. They are telling us that they are united in their opposition to Britain's imperial forces, that a blow against one of us is a blow against all, and will be avenged. That is their meaning. As for the man killed in an animal trap, he—like Rutledge and his boys—was being hunted as the English hunt big game . . . and this obsession with the removal of the right hand of the victims . . ."

"Yes?"

"It is a reference to what the Belgians did in the Congo Free State—a brutal punishment meted out on rubber tappers who failed to meet their quota."

"A reference?!" The under-secretary had gone quite red with anger. "They would attack us with a metaphor? How dare they! Worse, how dare they equate the integrity of an Englishman with the sins of that filthy Belgian butcher?"

The room went silent for a moment. My heart was beating heavily. My mind had been puzzling on the question of motive since Maud had raised it on Saturday, and I had given voice to conclusions even as I reached them. Then Watson turned to Holmes. "Is he correct, Sherlock?"

Holmes considered for a moment, and then, with a tiny gesture that caused my heart to leap with unexpected joy, gave his concurrence: "That the motivating ideology is anti-imperialism? Almost certainly. I had come to the same conclusion, though I took the rather shorter route of observing that there was no other reason for us to be having this meeting in the Colonial Office with the under-secretary of colonial affairs. Should the government's agents have determined that the common factor in these attacks was, say, financial, then we would be sitting at Number 11 Downing Street meeting with the chancellor of the exchequer, or perhaps with the president of the Board of Trade; should the motive be personal, it would have remained the purview of Lestrade here. No, we are sat in this great department of state for the very reason that Mr. Singh describes; these are acts of organized terror, perpetuated by those who would be free from what they perceive, however irrationally, as England's imperial yoke."

The under-secretary smiled wryly at this. "I was warned you were a character, Holmes. Very good, I am no stranger to character myself. Allow me to set forth some truly *new* information, that which I am confident will interest you. This morning, this department received a letter purporting to be from an organization behind these crimes, putting the British government on notice of their perfidious intention to create greater carnage."

With this, he produced from a file a short typewritten note, which he proceeded to read aloud. To my great surprise, what he read was not a demand or a conventional warning but instead lines of verse:

> *What if the breath that kindled those grim fires*
> *Awaked, should blow them into sevenfold rage,*
> *And plunge us in the flames; or from above*
> *Should intermitted vengeance arm again*
> *His right red hand to plague us?*
>
> *When all this comes to pass on England's shores*
> *Inquire not why your Empire was destroyed*
> *Instead express surprise that it had been—*
> *For so, so long, permitted to subsist*
> *At all.*

The opening stanza was, of course, drawn from *Paradise Lost*, but it was the second and final verse that I couldn't quite place, though it seemed familiar to me, and I said as much. The under-secretary exploded at me with a ferocity greater than he had previously displayed: "Familiar?! Of course it's bloody familiar, it's from Gibbon, you imbecile, *Decline and Fall!* Mangled into blank verse and mashed together with the Milton. It would appear our terrorists have poetic pretensions."

"Literary critique aside, Under-Secretary," said Holmes dryly, "the meaning is clear: This is a threat of escalation on a dramatic scale, but do we have evidence that the note is genuine? That it indeed comes from those we seek?"

Churchill smiled at this and picked up a small wooden box from his desk. "I'd say so." And handed the box to me. "Open it, Mr. Singh, perhaps you'll find the contents also *familiar*." He packed a sneer into that final word, his fine vocal instrument apparently as effective in schoolyard taunts as it was in grand rhetoric.

I opened the box. Inside it were three hands, each severed at the wrist and stained dark crimson from their own blood. One hand a piece from each of the earl of Rutledge and his two sons.

His red right hand.

After the grisly box had been taken away and we'd all had a drink from the under-secretary's private store of whiskey, the conference resumed, and lighting a fresh cigar, our young host made clear at last his intentions in summoning us.

"You all now understand the nature of the problem. Well, then, you will appreciate the urgent need for a solution. This note and the accompanying . . . package . . . represent between them a clear threat. Whoever is behind it has made abundantly explicit their intention to mount an even more serious attack. One where there may be mass casualties. We must take this seriously and act with all due urgency. They have considerable resources and are legion. How else could they strike in so many places all across the globe?

"My view is that what is needed is a mass mobilization of resources; we will meet force with superior force and put an army on the streets of London, placing an iron shield around our people, and round up any and all suspects."

"How would you identify suspects?" inquired Raffles softly.

"We will follow your colleagues' good advice, of course, and start with people who look like they harbour some misplaced animosity towards the Crown or the empire."

"What do those people look like?" I asked, immediately fearing the answer.

"Why, Mr. Singh, I would say that, in many cases, they look rather like you." The under-secretary's threat hung in the air for a long moment, and I saw in my mind's eye, the rounding up of all Indians and Africans who had come to the great city of London and called it home, an image of guns being fired on unarmed crowds, so common in the colonies, but now brought home to the capital. I looked at Raffles in fear and apprehension, not knowing what could be done to avert this terrible outcome.

"Commissioner Lestrade, do you agree with this course of action?" asked Raffles, still speaking in a quiet undertone as if we were whispering in the back row of a funeral.

Lestrade cleared his throat and looked distinctly uncomfortable. "With all respect, Minister, I believe this is a matter best left to the civilian authorities. Thus far, we are dealing with a handful of murders, not a mass attack. A deployment of the type you describe will cause panic amidst the populace. I have nothing but the utmost admiration for the good men of the army, of course, but the military is a blunt object, and I believe what we require here is a blade, not a cudgel. A fold of blades, perhaps, such as we have assembled in this room."

My heart beat fast at this unexpected statement, and I believe I would have interjected in shock had not Raffles caught my eye with his own. Lestrade was still talking—"hear him out," my friend's eyes said to me.

"Mr. Sherlock Holmes and Dr. Watson, of course, have served their country before in matters of supreme delicacy and importance, and so we ask you gentlemen, please, one further time, to step into the breach.

"As for you, Mr. Raffles—I have assured the under-secretary that you and Mr. Singh are possessed of unique insights that may prove valuable to the investigation. Working under my supervision, of course, and with the full resources of the Metropolitan Police, I believe the four of you will give us the best chance of catching these criminals before they can make further mischief."

Having spoken his piece, Lestrade subsided into silence and fixed his eye on the under-secretary, a man decades his junior but nevertheless his superior in this matter, awaiting a ruling.

It was not long in coming. The under-secretary looked at us each up and down and then, perhaps a little begrudgingly, nodded his consent. "Very well, Lestrade, I will give you the rope you ask for, but it will be a short one. Gentlemen, you have one week to achieve some result in this matter. In that time, you will have the full support of my office and of His Majesty's government. Whatever resources are necessary, whatever expenses accrue, be assured you have *carte blanche*. But I tell you now, should your dirks not prove effective in that time, then I shall not hesitate in wielding my cudgel and will deploy the army in such numbers as that London shall feel like occupied territory and God beware any who work against our purpose.

"Now, go with God, and come back when it is done. Should you be successful in this matter, you will have the thanks of a grateful nation, and more than thanks—I have with my authority to pay a very healthy reward for the satisfactory resolution of this matter. Get to it, gentlemen!"

With those imperatives given, we were ushered out of the grand room and ejected out into the pale winter sunlight of Whitehall, blinking like babies, new to the world and still coming to terms with the awful responsibility with which we had been charged.

CHAPTER 6

Tea for Two and Two for Tea

It was the detective who suggested that the four of us—Lestrade had remained at the Colonial Office for a private conference with the under-secretary—should become better acquainted. "A successful collaboration will be dependent on our ability to work effectively together, and that, in turn, will depend on a certain amount of familiarity," he commented, nodding to the good doctor, who immediately set about hailing a cab, which quickly transported us to The Savoy.

In short order, we were seated at a discreet table in the corner of the large dining room. Again, Dr. Watson had made the arrangements, and doubtless being familiar with Holmes' preferences in these matters, he had requested a seating situation that afforded us privacy without drawing undue attention to that desire for privacy. It was neatly done.

Until the ordering—and the waiter—was out of the way, we restricted ourselves to innocuous small talk including, to my surprise, a spirited debate between Raffles and Holmes as to which of 1899 or 1897 was the superior year for Left Bank Bordeaux. (They agreed to disagree with good humour and accepted the sommelier's recommendation of a bottle of excellent Burgundy instead.) Once these matters were dealt with and I was, at last, able to sate my hunger on a venison chop, only then did the real conversation begin as we turned our attention to the urgent task before us.

"This is quite the matter we find ourselves thrown together in," commented Raffles by way of overture. "But let me assure you, gentlemen, you may rely on me and Bunny to discharge whatever part falls to us with all diligence and care."

I thought it was a commendable sentiment, and well said, but it seemed to dissatisfy Watson, who, frowning, turned to Holmes as if for permission, but getting no guidance from his friend's impassive expression, blustered ahead nevertheless. "Very good of you, old chap. But if you'll forgive me . . . The thing is, that, well, Sherlock, that is to say Sherlock and I are rather accustomed to working alone in matters of this nature.

"To be totally honest, if we are to get to the heart of things, I some-what fail to see what expertise it is that you bring to the situation? I mean, Sherlock is the world's foremost consulting detective, and I have a certain experience through my long association with him . . . but you two, I mean, excellent fellows and all that, I don't doubt, but what specifically do either of you have to offer by way of relevant experience to this bloody business? That's what I want to know."

Watson had worked himself up into quite a simmer to get all that out, and despite his slur on our collective contribution, I found myself feeling sorry for him; clearly it pained him to speak so frankly, but he took it as his duty. Further, I had to concede that I could see the good doctor's point. From his perspective, what the devil would a cricketer and a pupil barrister have to offer to a team designed to guard against a terrorist group set on doling out bloody death to representatives of His Majesty's government?

Watson's perspective was, of course, incomplete. As you, gentle readers, are well aware, Raffles and I, in fact, were in possession of knowledge and skills that sat far outside the realm of most men, and were of the utmost relevance to the task in hand. As we had demonstrated in our painstaking explication of the scene of the attack in the gardens of Mapperton, our hard-earned experience of planning and executing complex criminal endeavours gave us a singular advantage in retracing the steps of these blaggards.

Who, after all, is better placed to catch a criminal mastermind than a pair of accomplished criminals?

Add to our daily lived experience of means, method, and motive, obtained and applied in the course of dozens of daring burglaries and deceptions, the undeniable fact that Raffles had seen the murderer up close, and it was clear we were uniquely placed to assist with the matter at hand.

The issue, therefore, was how were we to convince Holmes and Watson of this utility without disclosing our illegal activities? Lestrade's misbelief that Raffles and I were a pair of posing sodomites had provided sufficient cover for our disclosure of what Raffles had witnessed of Fitzwilliam's sorry end, but it would be of little use in enfranchising us to the detective and Dr. Watson.

All this ran through my mind in the same fraction of a moment that it took Raffles to raise his eyebrows, but before either of us could respond to Watson's challenge, Sherlock Holmes smiled, not unkindly, and spoke softly.

"My colleague has, with his usual good sense, arrived at the threshold issue in this matter. That said, Watson, I would hazard the opinion that there is more to Messrs. Raffles and Singh than might appear at first glance. At least to the first glance of those untrained in the art and science of deduction. Allow me to elucidate, and by doing so, I believe I will both set your mind at ease and save our new friends the need to explain themselves, and thereby convey our conversation more swiftly towards our shared purpose.

"You have heard, have you not, my dear Watson, of the celebrated 'Gentleman Cracksman'? The thief who exclusively targets members of high society, relieving them of their prized jewels, their irreplaceable pieces of art, their family silver, in the most baffling and impossible of circumstances?"

Watson turned to his old friend, assuming an expression that seemed to me much practiced, a studied blankness and a set of his shoulders that indicated keen anticipation. I realized that he was preparing to be politely astounded. If Holmes noticed this, he made no indication but continued blithely.

"He to whom no locked room is impenetrable, no security system adequate, who taunts the police with little notes and keepsakes left at the scene of every crime? The very fellow who, on one notable occasion, succeeded in the theft of a priceless Fabergé egg by the clever contrivance of having himself locked into the bank vault which contained it?"

Holmes' fingers danced in illustration as he told his tale, and he seemed to me more, in this moment, to be some master conductor of a storied European chamber orchestra than an investigator of crime.

"One has to admire his audacity. In fact, the Gentleman Cracksman must be a very remarkable fellow indeed, for he has kept his identity an utter secret for almost a decade now and remains at large: undetected, unknown, and uncatchable, an endless frustration for the Yard . . . You remember, of course, Watson, that Inspector Mackenzie, at his very wits' end, has pleaded with us from time to time to take on the case, in an advisory capacity?"

Raffles and I looked at each other; this train of thought was shortly to arrive at a dangerous destination, but we knew not how to see it off. Watson was bubbling with a charming mixture of anticipation and frustration. He knew too well from long experience that his companion was about to astound him with some casual feat of deduction, and he was working his grey matter frantically in an attempt, almost certainly futile, to anticipate where this was going.

"I am aware of this 'Cracksman,' of course. I'm afraid, though, I don't see his relevance to the matter at hand?" Watson hazarded, and for the first time, I wondered how much of his dullness was true, and how much was a performance for Holmes' benefit.

Holmes smiled widely, taking a somewhat unkind pleasure, it seemed to me, in his friend's slowness.

"Do you not? Surely, Watson, it should be obvious that the Cracksman must be a member of the very fashionable circles of society which are his hunting ground. That he must himself be one of the elite on whom he preys. How else is he to be afforded such regular and easy access to the valuables he so desires?

"Once that deduction is made, then it was a simple matter of cross-referencing. Which guest was consistently present at the time and place of the burglaries bearing the Cracksman's unique signature? To answer *that* question, all that was required was a few quiet afternoons with the society press. As I suspected, only one plausible name emerged consistently."

Watson looked at Holmes, then at Raffles, then back at Holmes, his jaw slowly descending till it nearly grazed the gravy on his plate.

"No . . . surely . . . but . . . you?" Having said this much, Watson decided that silence was the better part of discretion, and sat back in his chair and drained his wine glass.

For my part, I dared not turn my head towards Raffles, dared not make even the slightest movement, lest it was taken as confirmation of Holmes' theory. This was not my secret to share, and it had to be Raffles' decision as to what was said next. I held my breath for an eternity of anticipation until I heard Raffles' dry chuckle.

"Well played, Holmes. But a carefully thumbed copy of *Tatler* would hardly suffice as proof before a magistrate at the Old Bailey."

"Do you deny it?" asked the detective, casually, carelessly even.

"I do not dignify it with either denial or confirmation. I merely state that what you claim as evidence would be of little use in a criminal trial." Raffles looked Holmes defiantly, eye to eye, two prize hounds, circling each other. Watson and I looked from one to the other, each of us as tense as shipping cable. Holmes, for his part, seemed utterly relaxed—

"You are surely correct in that, so it is fortunate that I have no intention of disclosing my deduction to the authorities, nor of taking the matter any further. I mention it now simply so we are all clear between us as to where we stand and that my friend Watson understands the specific skill set that you and your . . . accomplice, if I may use that word, without causing offence, bring to our shared enterprise."

Raffles lit a cigarette and, as he exhaled, smiled. "I am sure we are grateful to you for your discretion. May I ask one question?"

"Certainly—" Holmes spread his palms wide, like an obscure technical journal laid open, legible but incomprehensible.

"You say that the police have come to you, to ask for your assistance in the matter of . . . of the Cracksman's exploits?"

"On more than one occasion."

"May I ask why you declined to work on the case?"

This was a question on which I also was most curious. Holmes considered for the slightest of moments, and then gave his answer, even as he accepted a cigarette from Raffles.

"Perhaps when I was younger, I would have taken it on. I was building a reputation for myself then, and there may have been some small cachet in apprehending such a clever and high-profile criminal. These days, however, in what we may safely call the twilight of my career, my priorities differ from what they once were. Due to the small measure of fame I am forced to endure thanks to Dr. Watson's little potboilers, each day's postbag brings with it a dozen offers of remunerative but pointless puzzles from up and down the country and all stops abroad. I must of necessity be selective.

"My preference is for work that presents a significant challenge, that engages, perhaps even taxes, my faculties, that energizes my old soul and gives some colour and some interest to the pale shade of grey that otherwise permeates daily existence. Failing that, the case must at least be of objective importance. Matters of moral significance, puzzles on whose resolution the national interest depends, or, at the very least, matters of life and death.

"We must all have some methodology in choosing how we spend our time, particularly as time becomes an ever more limited resource, and these are mine. A dandy stealing trinkets from other dandies? I'm afraid that simply did not rise to the level of serious consideration."

I waited for some mighty eruption of prideful annoyance from my friend, who I knew would take poorly to this suggestion of his relative insignificance. In the event, only a quiet "I see" emerged. Raffles was surely wounded by the detective's condescension, but he gave no outward sign of it; his sense of dignity would not permit Holmes the satisfaction.

Holmes continued unhesitatingly, taking Raffles' smile at face value.

"Nevertheless, I am glad to have your assistance in this manner. Your deficiencies as an adversary become more akin to virtues in an ally. The two of you, I take it, have been working as a team? Please, Mr. Singh, there is no need to deny it. Clearly you are highly capable players in your chosen domain. As such, you will have skills that we can use: safe-cracking, the coaxing of double-locked doors and other matters of the locksmith; I assume you are equally well versed in forgery and disguise and in the principal tools of the confidence trade. You are both ex-military, and in excellent physical condition, so I will take it as a given that you will display bravery in a fight, have a certain facility with firearms, and that you will not grow reticent should violence need to be done. These attributes will, I am certain, prove themselves of the utmost utility as we navigate the dark paths ahead of us."

Raffles and I looked at each other, pleased at this positive and clear-sighted assessment of our value to the task ahead.

I felt it was time I contributed to the conversation and, clearing my throat to get the table's attention, addressed myself to the detective: "Mr. Holmes, this demonstration of your powers is remarkable. You are all the legend says you are. I believe I speak for both of us when we say that whatever poor skills we have are at your disposal in this matter."

Raffles frowned a little at my perhaps overly florid praise of Holmes, but inclined his head in agreement with the broader point.

"Capital!" said Holmes, clapping his hands unexpectedly, creating a sound so loud that a lady at an adjacent table turned to investigate the matter, but then lowering his tone and leaning conspiratorially forward, Holmes proceeded more circumspectly:

"The first question to address is the strange and thus far complete overlap between your . . . between the Cracksman's putative targets and that of our anti-imperialists."

I was confused at this at first. "Forgive me, Mr. Holmes, can you expound your meaning?"

"Certainly. I refer to the extraordinary confluence that your most recent two targets for burglary—I assume there were only the two, though I suppose there may be others I am unaware of—also proved to be the targets of our terrorists. Not only that, but both you and they choose the very same day, or in the case of Rutledge, the same weekend, on which to strike. Surely this strikes you as strange and worthy of investigation?"

Raffles and I looked at each other once again, suddenly and painfully aware that the detective was now regarding us as suspects in this matter, an implication much darker than the one we had been seeking to avoid. Raffles went ice cold, and in an even voice asked, "Are you making a further accusation, Mr. Holmes?"

Holmes smiled. "Not as yet. But we owe it to ourselves to interrogate this matter, do we not?" He did not wait for a response, instead taking our shocked silence as permission:

"Very well, let us interrogate it. There are three possibilities. Firstly, the matter is one of pure and utter coincidence. I believe we can dismiss that for now. For you and the assassin to have crossed paths once by accident is of course possible, but for it to happen twice in so short a period is surely suggestive. Or as the playwright might have put it, to lose one victim may be regarded as a misfortune, to lose two begins to look like carelessness . . .

"Secondly, there is the possibility of collusion. That cracksmen and the anti-imperialists co-ordinated in this manner, that there is a dalliance of sorts between you, as your objectives, if not identical, are at least overlapping. Or perhaps Mr. Singh's native sympathies mean that your objectives have expanded from mere theft to more political ends?"

I felt my bile rise at this baseless accusation but could think of no words with which to rebut it. Thankfully, my friend Raffles, as ever, knew exactly what to say; his voice an exposed blade, he carved the following words into the conversation:

"Holmes, if you are accusing me of treason to my country, then your-so-called powers are so much poppycock and have ruinously misled you. Whatever my . . . habits when it comes to personal property, my loyalty to king and country is both unshakeable and unquestionable.

"You talk of blood and loyalty, Holmes, yet of the four men at this table, you are the only one not to have served your nation in battle, not to have bled on foreign soil, not to have risked life and limb in the grand and brutal cause of empire. So step very carefully, sir, else you make an enemy of us after all."

I found myself moved to speak, to address this slander, though to do it to my childhood hero took a considerable stiffening of my sinews. "Mr. Holmes, further, we have heard today from the under-secretary that the crimes on English soil were predated by a series of similar assaults spread across the far colonies. Surely you do not suggest that we had any involvement . . ."

Sherlock raised a conciliatory hand. "You both speak most eloquently. Raffles, my dear fellow, I do not doubt your honour, though I believe that, in my own way, I have been of some little service to the Crown. It is Balvinder, however, who is the more persuasive. For he speaks of facts, rather than indignities. That you came forward to Lestrade with a full account of what you had witnessed that fateful night in Mayfair is the strongest evidence for your innocence in this matter. You took a real risk of being implicated by doing so, and there was no conceivable gain to either of you. And, of course, you could not have been involved in the crimes in India or Africa. As it happens, the imbecile Lestrade jumped to a quite felonious conclusion, but that is his affair. The problem with these career police officers is that their minds end up too often in the sewer in which they are forced to work; it is our job to occasionally remind them to look up at the stars, eh?"

I noted with surprise Holmes' second allusion to Wilde. I was beginning to understand that his subtle mind had interests far wider and more varied than Watson's popular accounts had led the general public to believe. Not simply a cold, analytical machine, Holmes was a man who clearly immersed himself fully in the currents and pulse of our time. For the moment, though, his focus was tight and clear—

"As I say, your actions in coming forth, and your assistance to Lestrade in demonstrating the likely means of the murder, indicate a genuine desire to help apprehend the assassin, for there are no other motivations that align so cleanly with that course of action. No, I think we can rule out collusion. That, of course, leads us to the third and final possibility. Watson, what say you?"

Watson had been frowning ferociously through this exchange. Measuring carefully his companion's analysis against Raffles' protestations and working, in his own methodical and dogged way, towards a conclusion. He looked up now, clearly pleased to be offered a chance to contribute. "The third possibility . . ." he began, extemporizing a little for time as he gathered his thoughts. "The third possibility can only be that there is an overlap in the selection criteria of our adversary with that employed by . . . by the Gentlemen Cracksmen?"

His voice went up a little at the end of the sentence, turning a proposition into a question, seeking his colleague's endorsement of his theory. It was quick to come:

"Capital work, Watson, you really have got the trick after all this time. Yes, that is precisely my conclusion. Whatever mix of factors had led our friends here to land on Rutledge and Fitzwilliam as ideal targets for a little light thieving, and to alight on the particular days in question as being most promising for infiltration and, shall we say, extraction—that same analysis must have been carried out by our assassin or, more like, by his superiors. It is that analysis that we must now apply to anticipate their next move. This is how our new friends will add such great value to the project we are together embarked on!"

Watson glowed a little there, seeming genuinely pleased to have earned Holmes' approval. His mood quickly turned serious, though as we looked at each other then, understanding clearly the outline of the task before us, he appeared pleased to be once more united in the cause. Which is when the detective added, as an apparent afterthought: "And, of course, we must not forget Mr. Singh's unique ability to effectively serve as our agent behind enemy lines should such a course of action be needed."

I had my mouth full of hot tea at this point, and I fear I may have swallowed it too suddenly at Holmes' statement and descended into a coughing fit that was only arrested by Dr. Watson's strenuous slapping of my back. When I recovered, I turned my attention to the man whom I admired above nearly all others and found myself demanding of him—

"I'm sorry, Mr. Holmes, but what precisely would you have me do?"

"Mr. Singh, as the under-secretary so crudely pointed out, we must concede that it is at least possible, if not likely, that the ringleaders of this terror organization are not white men but members of the colonized races? Both their motivations and their methods suggest as much. And whilst the murders here in England are possessed of some intriguing features when it comes to means, those in the colonies are straightforwardly the work of household and office staff who have access to their masters in moments of unguarded repose. *Ergo*, the murderers are likely some combination of native folk: African, Caribbean, and, in all likelihood, Indian.

"Accordingly, your inclusion in this little team has some specific utility. In cricket terms, which I am sure Raffles here will appreciate, I would say you are our 'ringer'—in all probability, the most valuable player we have. For you will be our guide to the inner psyches of these men, offering insights that would never occur to the rest of us. As a colonial subject, as one to whom 'empire' has been inflicted rather than as a beneficiary of it, you will have unique perspective to offer us as we delve deeper into this matter; and yes, should we need someone to infiltrate the organization against whom we strive, then how fortunate we will regard ourselves in having someone of your complexion on our side. Do you not agree?"

~

I was left to puzzle on the implications of Holmes' words as the conversation went on, and the rest of the luncheon was spent sharing notes and working out in detail our next steps of action. Raffles described once again his encounter with the mysteriously agile assassin in Fitzwilliam's home in Mayfair, to the accompaniment of Watson's amazement and Holmes' precise analytical questioning.

We compared our theories of the brutalities at Mapperton—it emerged that Holmes and Watson had spent all of Saturday there, at Lestrade's invitation, performing their own inspection of the crime scene, and had come to much the same conclusions as we had, though Holmes had some additional questions for Raffles:

"This matter of hiding in the trees. Is it a methodology you have employed yourself?"

"From time to time. People tend not to look up," responded my friend. Holmes nodded in agreement.

"Quite so, but here is where I differ from your analysis. I believe we are dealing with multiple assailants, not just the one."

"You have evidence of this?" I asked.

"The overpowering of three well-armed men and the transport of their bodies surely speaks to a group rather than an individual, does it not?"

Raffles shook his head. "You did not see the . . . individual I encountered as he tore the head from the shoulders of a man in peak physical condition. This murderer has strength to spare."

"Yes, of course. But then what would explain the cigar ash I found on the opposite side of the clearing?"

Raffles' eyes flashed annoyance. He did not appreciate being played in this way.

"You could have mentioned that earlier."

"Forgive me, I perhaps enjoy my little theatrics too much. John has somewhat spoiled me in this regard. Nevertheless, a full ounce of Cuban ash, suggesting that someone—someone with expensive tastes—was waiting in the shadows. This man was the superior, unless I am very much mistaken, waiting for his assassin or assassins to do their work, and then stepping in. I think the master is the man we must find, not his dog. And with some urgency, before he fulfils the promise of his poem and strikes again. Do we agree?"

Having demonstrated his superior grasp of the situation, Holmes proceeded, with the calm confidence of a general who has weathered many campaigns, to dole out our assignments. As he had intimated earlier, the assignment given to Raffles and I was to identify likely further targets of the assassins.

To do this, we were to apply the very methodology that Holmes had employed to identify Raffles as the Gentleman Cracksman: cross-referencing. We would go through all the most notable political and military figures of the empire currently in Great Britain and evaluate their residencies with our practiced eye, probing for opportunity. From this analysis, we reasoned we would at least arrive at a shortlist of probable victims, venues, and dates that our mysterious adversary would find irresistible and could begin the setting of a trap.

Whilst we worked at this, Holmes was to pursue his own line of inquiry. He offered no elaboration on it, and it was clear that he would only reveal his methods when it suited him to do so. In any case, we agreed that Dr. Watson and I would act as go-betweens, meeting regularly to update the other with our respective groups findings and to discuss the next course of action.

Before we went our separate ways, I asked Holmes one final question that had been nagging at me. "The under-secretary for colonial affairs. Our client in this matter. He is a singular individual. But one perhaps too keen to see brute force as the only solution to any problem."

"Indeed," agreed Holmes. "It is something of a family trait, as you will surely appreciate."

I was baffled at this comment, finding myself now cast in the role of Amazed Recipient of Holmes' pronouncements. "You are mistaken, Mr. Holmes, for I have no knowledge of the man's family."

"Oh? I am surprised. His father, after all, has had some considerable impact on your native country."

"His father? Who is his father?"

"Your tenses need correcting, for the man has been dead these past ten years. But you surely would know of him, as he was a notable, some would say infamous, secretary of state for India in the 1880s, when you would have been a young man there."

I frowned, trying to connect this information with the unusual individual we had met today. The secretary of state for India when I had been a student had been a hard-line imperialist, openly disparaging of Indian nationalist politicians, and who had gone on to launch a bloody war of conquest against Burma, presenting that once proud kingdom as a vassal to Her Majesty Victoria as a "New Year's present," as he callously put it.

I suddenly remembered his name, and hence realized who our client, the current under-secretary, was. "You are speaking of Lord Randolph Churchill, so this fellow is his son . . . ?" My face must have shown my utter shock, for Raffles could not restrain himself from laughing out loud.

"Oh, Bunny! You mean you didn't recognize him? He cut quite a figure in the veldt, don't you remember? Crusading-journalist-turned-combatant. Getting shot up on trains and taken as prisoner by the Boer—and then escaping, and having escaped, writing of his exploits in fevered missives to the papers, making himself the star of his own fiction! Ridiculous young scamp he was back then. Still, young Winston seems to be finding his bearings."

"All of thirty years old and an under-secretary of state already. There are people who say he will be prime minister soon," commented the doctor.

"Yes," said Raffles, his face beaming a broad smile, "but most of those people are his mother!"

How the others fell about laughing at that, and, in an affectation of sophistication, I joined them, though, in truth, I knew nothing of Under-Secretary Churchill's mother or political prospects, but the laughter served to unify the four of us, and it was in such good humour that we went out into the London day, no longer strangers but now a team, united by common purpose and determined to triumph against our unknown but doubtless formidable adversary.

CHAPTER 7

Private Lives

Or so I thought. Raffles, as was so often the case, had ideas of his own.

As we walked together, I asked him when he wished to embark upon the first stage of our project, and he looked at me as if I had proposed we single-handedly lay siege to the Port of Gibraltar or embark on an expedition to the moon.

"'Project,' dear boy? What can you mean?"

I gaped at him askance. "Why, the very matter that Holmes entrusted us with, not twenty minutes ago. The creation of a shortlist of potential targets—before these murderous ruffians make good on their threat and strike again."

"Oh. That." He seemed a little disappointed in me. "I don't think we need to bother too much about that, do you? I don't really see myself as an aide to that contemptuous old hack. Let him do his own busywork."

For as long as I knew Raffles, he never lost the capacity to surprise me, so changeable was he in his moods and affectations, so mercurial in his alternation between resolution and dissolution. At this moment, I was unable to discern if he was merely goading me, or was serious in his intent.

"But, Raffles!" I protested. "We agreed, did we not? We have been given a most grave and potent responsibility and a demanding deadline by Under-Secretary Churchill . . . This is a matter of national importance . . . ?" I stumbled forward, attempting to make my case. "I know that you were put out when Holmes cast aspersions . . . but surely you do not mean—"

"Why do you care so much, old boy? It's not even your nation, is it? I mean, not really."

He said this last softly, with no trace of cruelty in his tone, yet his words cut me so deeply that I found that I did not trust myself to respond, lest I say something so intemperate that it would forever damage our friendship. Instead, I nodded stiffly and, wishing him a good day, set off for my rooms, doing my best to ignore the dark clouds that followed me down London's cold streets.

~

The next morning, I woke determined not to have my course of action decided by Raffles. If he wished to play the petulant schoolboy, I was under no obligation to do the same. I took this matter seriously; I had done so from the moment he had arrived at my door in disarray and confusion, telling his grisly tale. I had been intent from the start to do whatever I could to assist in this matter, and if I had allowed myself to be temporarily dissuaded, I was now once again on the road of the righteous.

My resolve, I should explain, came from something more than my own sense of morality; I had been given an official commission by a minister of state, and an assignment by none other than the Great Detective. My adopted country and my childhood hero had entrusted me with a task of the greatest importance; it fell to me to act to prevent a great tragedy. Further, if we did not discharge our obligation in the time frame given, then I knew that Churchill would, in unleashing the army, do much damage to not only civil society as a whole but specifically to the members of the Indian and African races who had, like me, come to London seeking a better life. This prospect instilled in me a unique terror and provided a tribal motivation to act.

Damn and blast Raffles and his insouciance and disdain! My friend saw all of life as a game, to be played for advantage and amusement, and for too long I had been content to follow his lead and cock my snook at the world. I had joined him in sniggering behind our sleeves at the stupidity of those who invited us into their homes, unaware that we pillaged them for sport. These recent tragedies, however, made me feel newly ashamed of my past behaviour. Violating the trust of our hosts for our own purposes felt too close to the modus operandi of the vicious killers whom we were now tasked with stopping.

So it was out of a mixture of determination and guilt that I sat down at my desk that morning and began my research. I admit I took some childish pleasure in organizing myself, writing the heading "Case Notes" on a fresh jotter and then dividing my notebook into sections: "Suspects," "Potential Targets," and "Clues." I even wrote out the Great Detective's dictum about the impossible and the improbable and placed it centrally on the mantel above my desk as a constant reminder to apply his methods.

That done, though, I found myself struggling to know where to start. Holmes had urged us to "think as burglars" and itemize homes or other locations that we would judge easy pickings. The trouble with this approach was that it proved insufficiently selective. I was confronted with an excess of abundance. There were so many great houses filled with wealth, and we had already burgled so many of them as to make this shortlist not short at all, but too long to navigate.

I decided to try a different approach, beginning instead with the social calendar. I reasoned that I should assemble a list of the principal events of the season, as thus far the assassin had chosen social gatherings as their entry point to their targets.

The logic of this seemed compelling, and indeed Raffles had often used a similar methodology when planning our own lawless transgressions. The rich and powerful of this country are not generally easily approachable. Their grand houses are built to be impenetrable—the old saw about an Englishman's home being his castle arises from the truth that, for the elite Englishman, their homes *are* castles.

Whilst at play, however, the wealthy, curled darlings of our nation become more vulnerable. Both by virtue of the fact that, in quest of their pleasure, they venture forth into public spaces, and in equal measure because by inviting their peers into their homes, they transform castles into palaces of indulgence, to which access is easy and targets plentiful.

After a busy morning, which necessitated a trip to the local newsagent, I had made a comprehensive study of *Tatler*, the society pages of *The Times, The Sketch, Country Life, The Illustrated London News*, as well as of my own meagre stack of invitations (or, if I am being honest, Raffles' invitations that he had sent to me to respond to in my role as his *de facto* social secretary). I assembled a representative list of events which I judged to be likely targets. Starting with this very week, I made an annual calendar of the most likely events.

21 October—Centenary anniversary of the Battle of Trafalgar. Lavish celebrations were scheduled in Trafalgar Square, including the decoration of Nelson's Column, to be attended by the king and all his ministers.

15 November—Season reopening night of Prince's Skating Club, Knightsbridge. Where the most fashionable lords and ladies would put on their skates and enjoy uncrowded ice.

6 January 1906—Twelfth Night celebrations at Chatsworth House. Hosted by the most ambitious of ladies, the "Double Duchess," Louise Cavendish.

11 February—Hunt Ball, presided over by the Master of the Hunt at the Savoy Hotel. A grand affair, with the heads of slain beasts being prominently displayed as trophies.

13 March—Charity Ball for the Royal Free Hospital, hosted by Lady Randolph Churchill. I noted that this event was being hosted by none other than Under-Secretary Churchill's mother, so he would certainly be in attendance.

10 May—Queen Charlotte's Ball. The annual tradition when debutantes curtseyed to the long-dead queen's birthday cake at Lansdowne House.

15 May—Opening night of the Colonial and Indian Exhibition at Crystal Palace. Complete with grand orchestral performances and to be opened by Churchill's boss, the secretary of state for the colonies, Lord Elgin, and attended by members of the royal family.

I could have continued indefinitely. On 12 July, the Earl of Wemyss was to host the Stanway House literary gathering, and I saw that my erstwhile breakfast companion Jimmy Barrie was scheduled to give a reading, whilst the science writer H. G. Wells was to preside over parlour games and amateur theatricals; on 17 August was the annual Taplow Court house party "The Souls" circle—a weekend of debates, poetry readings, and cricket matches of the so-called Souls group of intellectuals to which Raffles was usually invited to play.

I looked at the list, exhausted by the act of assembling it and overwhelmed by its sheer opulence. Even so summarized, it was an intimidating affair, a never-ending merry-go-round of pageantry, pomp, and circumstance that comprised the everyday life of an upper-class dandy.

Further, what I had noted here barely scratched the surface: These were only the most visible, the most high-profile events. Every night, up and down the nation, dozens of smaller but no less lavish affairs were thrown in private houses, hotels, and clubs.

This was what it meant to be to sit at the apex of the richest, most debauched nation on earth. To feast on culture, frippery, sport, and the finest comforts that the world could produce and your far-flung empire could channel back home. To live a life of utter indulgence, dancing from one celebration to another, pausing only to sleep.

I found my mind thrumming with conflicting impulses. Disgust and repulsion vied in my bosom with rapacious enmity and desire. I found I envied these people even as I despised them.

Somehow I had become distracted and forgot my purpose, which was not to pass judgement on the English aristocracy but to protect them. But how was I to do that? Each and every one of these occasions would be awash with potential victims, and whilst they all presented challenges to an infiltrator, it was clear to my criminal eye that a determined assailant could find ways past any defences.

My list provided so many clues as to be not a clue at all. Frustrated at my wasted work, I took the pile of society papers and threw them with fury into the bin. Before I could determine what new approach might prove of greater utility, my front door knocker sounded, breaking my concentration. Secretly grateful for the interruption, I descended my narrow staircase, two at a time. I was certain I would find Raffles on my step, both because I did not have many friends who would arrive unannounced and more because he had surely by now seen the error of abandoning his duty and had returned to me to lend his considerable gifts of instinct and intuition to our mission.

I threw open the door with a wide grin on my face, and my arms open to greet my friend, only to see before me a most unexpected guest, Miss Maud Adler.

~

As I have said before, it is my objective in setting out the particulars of this matter to share with the reading public an important narrative concerning the true nature of Britain and its relationship with its colonies and dominions that would otherwise remain too little known. It is my hope, in so doing, that my part in these matters, what I did and why I did what I did, will be better understood and my small role in history may be given its proper due.

Nevertheless, this is not a personal memoir. I feature in the narrative because I was a participant in this affair, not because I have any desire to aggrandize myself or share my private business with the world.

Certainly, it is not my intention to write here of matters of the heart.

Yet it is impossible to tell this story without also, to some small extent, telling the story of myself and Maud Adler, because it was Maud's insights on the matter, and then later, her actions, that helped to bring the matter to its bloody and climactic conclusion.

Forgive me, my love, but I must betray your trust and expose you to the world. I do so not lightly, but because if they are not to be condemned to repeat the mistakes of the past, they must first know the truth, and you, my Maud, you were a beacon of truth.

At two o'clock on Sunday, the night after I first met Maud, I found myself, at her express invitation, once again at the door of her home in Mayfair.

In my arms was a heavy basket containing the provisions for a picnic. Not owning a suitable hamper, I had visited first at Fortnum & Mason to purchase the same along with a collection of potable foods, including several of their celebrated Scotch eggs, a varied range of preserves, a selection of cured meats, a variety of English cheese, and some newly bottled Pouilly-Fumé which I trusted would accord with Miss Adler's taste. I may have been a little excessive in my purchases, seeking in the exercise to distract from my own nervousness.

For, whilst I was not a total beginner in matters of the heart, the current situation seemed to me fraught with uncertainty and danger. In my youth in native India, I had enjoyed some small popularity with women, but that had been years ago, and other than one drunken and much regretted visit to a night house in the Haymarket, my years in London had been chaste ones. Certainly, it had never occurred to me before this moment that I would come a-courting to the family home of a high-born English lady, and I strongly suspected that my reception at the hands of her father would not be a positive one. What English father relishes the prospect of a dusky Indian ex-serviceman appearing as a suitor to his daughter, even as unconventional, well travelled, and artistic a daughter as Maud Adler?

It was with some relief therefore when, upon my ringing the bell, the door was opened not by an angry paterfamilias with a musket, and not even by a haughty maid, but by Maud herself, who, casually inspecting the hamper, deemed it most charming, and tucking her slim arm into mine, indicated that we should head north towards Hyde Park.

She was dressed in a simple white blouse with a high collar, a white skirt that flowed freely in the wind, and the ensemble was completed by a straw hat with a crimson ribbon fastened around its brim. There was nothing expensive or opulent about her clothing, no frippery, no high fashion or fastidiousness, yet to my eye, she was the very pinnacle of elegance, and when the sunshine caught her, she shone as if lit from within.

We talked easily as we walked, as we had the night before. I found myself wondering, not for the last time, what it was in her that allowed me to talk so freely, without concern of judgement or misunderstanding. It was as if the light of her soul caused my shadow to cleave itself from my body and scuttle away, leaving me to walk free and unrestrained. Even the dark thoughts of murder and mutilation passed from me, and it was as if we lived in a different, better world than the one I usually inhabited.

We ate by the waters of the Serpentine. I laid out a blanket to protect her skirt and unpacked my carefully selected provisions, hoping they would meet with her approval. To my relief, they did, and she ate with a hearty appetite and complimented my selection of wine. I confessed I knew little of vintages and vintners but that I was endeavouring to learn, under the supervision of my friend Raffles.

"Is he a good friend?" she inquired, and I found myself relieved that she did not appear to recognize the name "Raffles" or have any knowledge of his fame as a cricketer.

"He is my best friend," I responded without hesitation.

"I am glad to hear you have good friends, Balvinder. In these dark times, we all need good friends. I shall be your friend, if you'll have me." This was her way of speaking, you understand: directly and without concern that she might be misinterpreted. Maud was always categorically herself at all times.

"I would count myself lucky, Miss Adler."

"Maud, please, Balvinder, now that we are friends, we must use each other's Christian names."

"That is, I am afraid, impossible," I said firmly.

"Why?" she demanded, and there was a play of laughter in her voice, as if we were engaged in a game, the rules of which were known only to us.

"Well, for one thing, Miss Adler, I am not a Christian."

She looked upset at first, afraid that she had caused offence, and then reacting to the twinkle in my eye, she laughed heartily, and then, using her hat as a club, beat me around the shoulders. A stern-looking governess, walking past at that moment with two young sisters in her care, saw us and tutted a sound of disapproval. Which only had the effect of making Maud howl with laughter and beat me further.

Later that afternoon, she requested I walk her to the Royal College, where she intended to spend the afternoon at practice. As we approached the majestic dome of the Albert Hall, I found my heart grow once again heavy at the prospect of parting ways.

There are in my culture those who, finding themselves in love with God, choose to spend their lives in service at our *gurdwaras*, devoting themselves to the role of *sewadars*, holy volunteers. I imagine that part of their motivation in doing so was that they could not bear the idea of being separated from God's presence, and for the first time, I knew what that fear of absence might feel like, for I knew with a certainty that I seldom possessed that I would give anything to be in Maud Adler's presence for the rest of both our natural lives.

The clarity of that knowledge was shocking to me, but if I was clear about my desire, I was also clear that it would remain unfulfilled, for no union was possible between the two of us. It was not that interracial marriage was illegal, or even unheard of. Indeed, at the turn of the century, the most rarefied heights of society had gathered to celebrate the union of Prince Victor Duleep Singh, son of the maharaja of Punjab, and Lady Anne Coventry, daughter of the ninth earl. The marriage had gained the blessing of Victoria herself, the wise queen intervening when Lady Anne's own parents sought to forbid the match.

So such things were possible, but I was no royal and could not in good conscience demand of Maud the sacrifices that an association with me would surely require her to make. Nor, come to that, was it a one-sided problem. My own family would never accept a white bride for their eldest son. We would be forever caught between two worlds, accepted by neither, scored by all. What kind of lover would I be to demand that the object of my love suffer such an existence?

Possessed of this knowledge, I turned to her and blurted out unprompted, "But this cannot be!" To which, she, with perfect reasonableness, inquired what the devil I was talking about.

Fool that I was, I attempted to explain my concerns, all the time acutely aware that even having these concerns was extraordinarily presumptuous. It was arrogant for me to claim to know what Maud's intentions towards me were. Yet in that moment, I could not help myself, so strong were the feelings that gripped me that I spewed it all out in a long speech.

I detailed my growing feelings towards her, my intemperate hope that she felt the same, and my simultaneous certainty that those feelings were best left buried and forgotten, lest we, by defying the norms of our respective cultures, break the promise of her bright career against the anvil of society's disapproval.

I told her in terms definitive that we must forget whatever powerful passion we had inadvertently stirred in each other, and put our love aside in the name of pragmatism and good sense. I grew quite emotional as I made this speech, moved by the scale and scope of my own sacrifice.

She listened to me speak for some time with a studiously neutral expression on her usually voluble face. When I finally came to an end, my mouth dry and my eyes wet, she reached for my hand and squeezed it.

"You are a good man, Balvinder Singh," she said, "but you are also a fool."

I found myself thinking that perhaps I had spoken too ornately, too delicately, and that in my attempt to spare her feelings, I had failed to express myself clearly.

"You wouldn't understand," I said as gently but as firmly as I could.

"Why not?"

"Maud, you are talented and beautiful and bright and deserve the finest of futures," I declared, "but you have lived a protected, cosseted, comfortable life—you know little of how this world treats its outsiders, because you are, yourself, born to power and privilege. You cannot see what is plain to me, that an association with one such as myself would test that status to its very limits. Your own people would turn their faces away from you. You would be an outcast from the very society you seek to better through your music."

"My people?"

She had gone very still, and her white skin seemed practically translucent; beneath its surface, a burning redness radiated out from her, her inner light growing darker, angry.

"The English, I mean," I said, feeling the need to clarify.

"Balvinder Singh. I'll say this the one time, and the one time only." And her tone changed, her accent broadened *"I. Am. Not. Foocking. English."*

The crudeness of her language shocked me to my very core, but I was still confused, and my face must have shown as much.

"I'm *Irish*, you foocking ijit! And don't you ever forget it again."

Then she slapped me hard across the face, and disappeared into the bowels of the building before I could say another word.

~

My readers will be perhaps baffled how I, an apparently educated man not unschooled in the nuance of London society, had made such a basic mistake. To clarify: Maud had told me that she had been born in Ireland, but I had not given the matter much thought. For the most part, she spoke without an Irish accent but in the plum round vowels of the English upper classes, and she lived in Mayfair, most elite of London districts. I had taken the location of her birth simply as a geographical fact, not a political one. How wrong I had been to do so.

I stood on the step, speechless and in shock for some little time, my face smarting red. Perhaps I considered going in after her, but then some smarter part of me must have taken hold, deciding retreat to be the best strategy. I left Kensington and headed directly to Bloomsbury and the British Museum Library.

It being a Sunday, the library was, of course, shut, but in my past visits, I had befriended several of the assistant librarians, and finding one of them engaged in his own weekend research, I cited an academic emergency, and I was able to persuade him to give me access. I chose a thick volume entitled *Ireland: 1494–1868* by an Irish historian who rejoiced in the name of William O'Connor Morris as well as a shelf full of papers by other writers. I settled down, my cheek still recalling the blow that Maud had dealt me, and began to read.

Six hours later, my cheek was no longer stinging but now was lit with the hot flush of shame. What an ignorant fool I was! A "foocking ijit" was, in fact, the accurate descriptor. So perfectly did Maud's memorable phrase fit me that I was grateful that, as a Sikh, on my death, I would be cremated and not buried. For if I were to ever have a tombstone, it was now clear that on it would be carved the words BALVINDER SINGH—A FOOCKING IJIT OF THE HIGHEST ORDER.

I had known next to nothing of England and Ireland's long and painful history. Nothing of the nearly six-hundred-year course of invasion, subjugation, and humiliation of Maud's nation and people at the hands of the English; nothing of the sectarian violence, the systematic cruelty, and the assault on the Catholic faith. None of this had been taught to me at school in India, and none of it mentioned in my legal studies. Centuries of uprisings and centuries of brutal suppression, systematic, authorized, *official* theft of the island's wealth, leaving its inhabitants in unspeakable poverty and a million or more to die in the horror of the great famine.

I had, in my untutored stupidity, viewed the United Kingdom of Great Britain and Ireland as one homogeneous entity, whole and complete unto itself. I was vaguely aware of the growlings of Irish Home Rule but had assumed that to be largely a matter of politics fought by MPs in Whitehall, not the righteous cry of a people seeking to regain control of their nation.

I saw also in my reading an uncomfortable echo. So much of what had been done to Ireland over the past few hundred years, I could see, was now being done to my homeland. The locations of the crimes were thousands of miles apart, but the methods, tools, and motivations seemed almost identical. The lessons learned in Ireland were being applied in India to terrible and powerful effect.

It was therefore a different, chastened, questioning version of myself that emerged from the library, and it was that version that would the next day draw the conclusion that so impressed my colleagues: that those behind the recent assassinations were anti-imperialists.

What I had not, could not, mention to Holmes or Watson, or to Under-Secretary Churchill, and even less to Raffles, was that I was beginning to feel some sympathy for them. This was why Raffles' casual gibe at me, that England was not really my nation, had landed so hard. Because for the first time since landing on these shores, I was beginning to question that it was.

All this confusion of identity and loyalty had been swirling in me, but was suddenly wiped clean from my mind when Maud appeared at my door and replaced with a far more bowel-clenching, blood rising, immediate, pressing, and personal flavour of confusion.

What was Maud Adler doing at my home?

~

I turned to ask her this question, but she was already halfway up the flight of stairs, heading towards my study, and I was reminded of Raffles' casual assumption of rights over my house. I looked out into the street to establish if the neighbours had taken note of my visitor, and seeing only a smug pigeon, shut the door and followed her up the staircase.

"Maud, I must apologize—"

She held up her hand to my face, her palm flat towards me, like a schoolteacher silencing a rambunctious pupil.

"I have a question for you, Balvinder Singh."

"Ask it. Anything."

"What is the status of women in the Punjab?"

I sensed that she was testing me, and to buy time, I parsed out her question in my mind: *Status.* Most would consider the word derived from the Latin, but the root *sthā* is, in fact, also found in Sanskrit: to stand, to stay, to be situated. Where are women situated in the Punjab? Where would Maud Adler be situated? Where, come to that, was I situated in England?

Oh, what was served by this relentless questioning of things? Could we not leave things alone, unexamined just for a moment? Even as my brain whirled around the nestled questions, I found myself speaking, giving a surface answer to a deep question.

"In my culture, women are venerated as mothers, sisters, wives. Women are treated well, enjoy privileges and freedoms—"

"Freedoms?"

"Certainly."

"Are women free to be, say, musicians?"

I felt on more comfortable ground here. "Of course. My own grandmother was most accomplished at the sitar."

"Did she play for her private pleasure or for paying audiences?"

"For her own pleasure, of course, and for that of her family."

"Why 'of course'?"

I stuttered a bit; the answer was so obvious, I struggled to articulate it: "It—it—it would not be proper. She was a woman of high caste, from a good family . . . She was my grandmother!"

And then I realized the trap Maud had laid for me. But she did not attack. Not yet. She was content to play with her prey a little longer, an artful tiger enjoying the terror of the deer.

"Are there no Indian women who perform music publicly, then?"

I searched my memory. "No, there are . . . but they are . . . women of the court."

"What does that mean?"

I felt danger all around me, there were teeth lurking round her every word, yet I could not stop myself from responding.

"Courtesans."

She smiled sweetly, as if all she wished was clarity. "And what does that mean . . . ?"

"Whores." I was angry now and I spat the word out. She did not seem to notice, as she smiled still, but her smile was sharp.

"Actual whores, or just treated as whores because they dare to perform in public?"

"I don't know. I was only ever at court briefly, when my father had business there. Does it make a difference?" I felt very afraid.

"I imagine it would, yes. For them, I mean. Strange, is it not? How men need to categorize women so. If you're afraid of us, we become witches to be burned. If you desire us, then we're whores to be bought."

"I would never call you by either of those names."

"Because you don't fear me? Or because you don't desire me?"

I don't remember crossing the room, then it was only three or four paces between us, and suddenly I was no longer by the door but by her side. I grasped her by the waist and picked her clean off the ground, holding her aloft so we looked at each other eye to eye. I don't know why I did such a thing, save that I felt a powerful need to take control of the situation. Maud exhaled sharply as my grip squeezed her, but otherwise made no sound, and instead met my eyes with her own fiery stare and, reaching out, gripped my shoulders in her hands, so we were locked like two wrestlers about to commence battle.

"I wish to apologize for not appreciating your true Irish nature, and for my ignorance of the history of your people," I said, with a formality that seemed to sit strangely with our current state of physical intimacy.

"Damn right," she responded, speaking low, her jaw set.

"Having spent much of Sunday at the library engaged in research on the 'Irish question,' I see now that I was a fool and making assumptions that were disrespectful and patronizing." I seemed to be trapped in the mode of a letter writer to *The Times*.

She was in my arms still, and cocked her head to one side. "You spent the day doing research? The British Museum Library is not open on Sundays," she said. I nodded in agreement.

"Not usually, no. I can, however, be quite persuasive when necessary."

"Oh. Can you, now?"

Something in her softened, and her grip on me shifted slightly, transitioning from battle stance to embrace. Until this moment, the only time our skin had touched was when she had put her hand on my face, the first time in tenderness, and the second in anger. Both times, she had initiated the contact, and I had been the recipient. This time I was the instigator; I had seized her, seeking to reverse the positions. I would not be prey any longer, but predator. This was wishful thinking, because holding her tight, I found I did not know what to do next. I was no tiger, but a house cat which, having lost the instinct of its ancestors, did not know what to do with its captured prey.

That was my first mistake, for Maud Adler was no mouse but an apex predator, and leaning into my face, in what I mistook as a tender gesture, she suddenly bit down hard on my lip, drawing blood. The shock made me release her, but she did not fall, tightening her own grip, wrapping her legs around my waist for purchase. For a moment, I was acutely conscious of the strength in her, her arms and legs tightly muscled from hours of standing practice at her instrument, the delicate lines of the tendons in her neck bisecting her prominent clavicle, and of her softness also, as her chest pressed against mine.

Then she bit me again, this time with full ferocity on my neck, and I screamed like a child in pain.

We fell forward, onto my desk, shoving aside the output of my morning labours, and, now in a frenzy such as I had never before experienced, I reached for the neckline of her dress, and . . .

No. I have said this would not be a personal memoir, not a recounting of the most private moments of private lives, and I stand by my word. Whatever pleasure it gives an old man to remember himself and his perfect love as they once were, in the first flush of their heat, I shall not waste your time or despoil her dignity by recounting it here.

Enough for you to know that, on that afternoon, Maud Adler and I, an Irishwoman and an Indian man, decided that we were no longer content to live as passive subjects of an empire that had occupied and despoiled our homelands; we would no longer be the colonized, no longer victims, no longer would we live as chattel or vassals of the crown; we would cease to play the part of exotic curios, existing only for the amusement of the English, conforming to their norms and constrained by their customs.

No, we would stage our own small defiance against centuries of subjugation, if we were to stand here in London, if we chose to be situated here in the heart of the empire, then we would also choose to stand together, and claim our own status. We would live free as our full selves, we would live as man and wife, and give not two ripened figs what the ijit English and their foocking society might make of it.

CHAPTER 8

A Regular-Type Life

It was later that day, and I was in my galley of a kitchen boiling water and adding herbs to it. Maud had passed comment that she missed authentic chai and had thus far failed to find the right mix of spices in London with which to make it. I very much wanted to surprise her with my own private concoction, the ingredients of which I had carefully obtained from the spice merchants who plied their goods down by the docks. Accordingly, I boiled water and into the bubbling pot threw in whole pods of cardamom, black pepper, and cinnamon, cloves, a peck of closely chopped ginger, and a sprinkling of star anise.

The satisfying aroma steamed from the pot and danced around my little kitchen, and I warmed my best teapot to serve as a receptacle.

Balancing my offerings on a tray, I made my way back up the stairs, where my little suite of rooms, bedroom, guest room, and study sat adjacent to one another. I was surprised to find the bedroom where I had left her empty, and the lady seated at my desk in the study, carefully inspecting the scattered detritus of my morning labours. She had gathered my notes, newspapers, and other research materials and was making notations herself, her brow furrowed as she unconsciously chewed her lower lip in concentration.

In normal circumstances, being acutely conscious of the secrecy of my assignment, my first instinct would have been to take the papers from her and make up some story as to their provenance. This instinct was, however, somewhat muted by the fact that Maud was performing her investigations in a state of complete and utter nudity, having apparently neglected to reclothe herself in my absence.

"Maud—what are you doing!"

"Is that my tea? Good lad, bring it here."

"Never mind the tea! You can't be in here . . . like that . . ."

"Why? Is someone likely to burst in on us? Do you have a secret butler who lives underneath the floorboards?"

"No, we are quite alone, it is just . . . unseemly."

"You didn't seem to mind it so much earlier."

"That was . . . different . . . Please, Maud . . ."

I cast around and saw an old dressing gown of mine and, picking it up, threw it onto her, as one might use a net to catch a wild beast. She caught it and, with an exceedingly distracting shrug, put it on.

"Suit yourself, you silly sausage, now can I have my chai?"

Calming down somewhat, I remembered my purpose and poured out two steaming cups, and for a moment, we sipped in pleasant silence, except for her purrs of approval of the beverage.

Once she had drained her second cup, however, Maud quickly returned to the matter at hand. "You're investigating this beastly business with the Mapperton murders, I see. I thought there was something strange about you having been at the crime scene . . . Now it all makes sense. It's grand you being an amateur detective as well as a lawyer, fella. Though I've been looking at your workings here, and I think you might be missing a trick, if you don't mind me saying."

I was speechless until I remembered my foolishness and vanity in labelling the files in the manner of Holmes—or rather in the manner I imagined him doing, having never actually had the opportunity of inspecting his papers—and could see how Maud, finding my "Case Notes" files and combining them with my intemperate boasting about having been at the scene of the Rutledge murders, and quickly jumped to a conclusion that was, whilst adjacent to the truth, incorrect.

I was about to protest and find some way to explain when she continued. "I say, do you think there is some connection to anti-imperialism here?"

I was flabbergasted by her question. Maud, based on nothing but my notes, had somehow spontaneously jumped to the same conclusion that the world's greatest detective and the collective intelligence of the British government had reached. That I had also come to the same conclusion did not lessen my appreciation of my beloved's brilliance; indeed, it enhanced it. Perhaps it is part of human nature to value most in others the very skills and attributes one values in oneself. In any case, struck by the skill and speed of Maud's deduction, I immediately decided that to dissemble from her would be fruitless and, indeed, that there might be much to gain in enlisting her keen intelligence to the task that had been defeating me. Certainly, without Raffles there, I was in desperate need of a collaborator to move this matter forward.

So, as we consumed a second pot of chai, I described to her the meeting at the Colonial Office, the findings of Under-Secretary Churchill, the ominous warning received, and the race against time we were now engaged with. I flattered myself that she was a little impressed that I had the trust and confidence of the Great Detective himself, and I was also pleasantly warmed to discover that she also had read Dr. Watson's case accounts, albeit not with the same obsessive fascination with which I had studied them.

My tale told, our chai drunk, Maud sat back contemplating all we had discussed, and then, as rapidly as before, I saw conjecture and conclusions flash across her eyes. "Bal, we should consult with the Anti-Imperialist League."

The organization was unknown to me, and my expression must have said as much, because she continued. "It's American, my cousin wrote to me about it. It's new, but already terribly influential. It was founded in protest to the United States' annexation of the Philippines, and a lot of important people are involved with it. Mark Twain, for one."

Now I was even more confused. "You believe that the author of *Adventures of Huckleberry Finn* and *A Connecticut Yankee in King Arthur's Court* might be involved in these murders?"

"No, don't be ridiculous, Bal. The league is a peaceful organization, it petitions the government, attempts to educate the public on the evils of empire, and so on. But they are at the forefront of the global anti-imperialist movement. There may be some overlap between those who attend the league's meetings and those who belong to the shadowy network of these dangerous killers. There may be something to be learnt by talking to them. Know thy enemy, and all that sort of thing. Though, of course, the league isn't our enemy. Truth be told, I've been thinking of joining it."

I found myself somewhat confused by this speech—and was about to interrogate it further when, for the second time that day, there was an unexpected knocking on my door. It was insistent, loud to the point of belligerence, and put a pause on Maud's and my conversation. Indicating that she should stay in the study, I headed downstairs.

My assumption was that Raffles, having got bored of inaction, had decided to come help with the research after all, and by the time I had reached the door, I was already formulating a plan to bar him access to my quarters. Under no circumstances could he be allowed admittance whilst Maud was on the premises. I ran through alternative ruses—I would suggest we adjourn to the local pub and share in a simple supper together; or I could fabricate that I was still miffed with him, or unwell . . .

None of these lies proved necessary, as my visitor was not Raffles but a young "street Arab" (an expression I have never fully understood, as these boys are seldom if ever of Arabian descent), no more than fifteen years of age, more than a child but not yet a man, whose dishevelled appearance was topped with greasy hair and a cheeky grin. I was about to send him packing, assuming him to be up to some mischief, when to my surprise, he extended his hand in a formal introduction.

"Wiggins, sir. At your service, Wiggins of the Baker Street Irregulars. You'll be Mr. Balvin-*daa*, I take it?" He put an incorrect emphasis on my unfamiliar name, but otherwise his manner was so proper and so at odds with his appearance that I could not help but smile, and shook the proffered hand with enthusiasm.

"Wiggins, of course. I know of you from Dr. Watson's accounts."

"Never read 'em myself. Does he do me justice?"

I considered the matter. Watson had described the Irregulars, Holmes' rag-tag troupe of child spies and errand boys as "unsavoury," "dirty," and "ragged," and whilst the latter two adjectives were factually accurate, there was nothing unsavoury about young Wiggins, who radiated a good-natured intelligence and a robust capability in every fibre of his wiry frame.

The lad had doubtless been born in a dungery and raised in the gutter, but even on our brief acquaintance, it was clear that he had more wit and good sense about him than many high-born youths who spent their time flitting fecklessly from debutante ball to hunting party.

"I would say you do yourself justice, Wiggins. And that you should keep doing it. Do you bring me a message from Mr. Holmes?"

"From the good doctor, actually. Wants to meet you for drinks, 'e said. Long Bar at the Criterion at six, if you please, and I'm to take your reply."

"The invitation is for me alone? Not for my friend Raffles?" I inquired.

"Dr. Watson was very specific, sir. You and you alone."

Remembering that Watson and I had been deputized as liaisons between our principals, I was reaching into my pocket to find tuppence for the boy when, to my great consternation, a voice rang out from above:

"Bal? Is everything all right?"

Behind me, at the top of the narrow staircase, emerged Maud Adler, still clad only in my dressing gown and stretching delightfully. Wiggins' omnipresent grin grew still wider.

"Top of the evening to you, missus. Just delivering a message to your fella," he shouted cheerfully past me, and then, lowering his tone to what he doubtless considered a conspiratorial whisper, added: "Ooooh, sharp work there, Mr. Bal, she's lovely. I'll tell the doctor you'll be along presently, but if you want my advice, don't hurry out till you fully see to your business!"

And with that impudent slur, he doffed his cap, accepted the tuppence I had been mutely holding out, and was gone.

For the second time that day, I looked out at the street to see if I had been observed, and satisfied that there were no prying eyes, I shut the door and headed up the stairs to Maud. I started the ascent determined to issue a reprimand and urge her to behave with more discretion, but by the time I reached her, she had unfastened the sash of my dressing gown, and as it fell open, all such thoughts fled my mind, entirely superseded by the imperative, in Wiggin's loutish phrase, to see, for the second time that afternoon, to my business.

The glistening gold of the neo-Byzantine Long Bar greeted me as I sidled in from the cold and wet evening. The red velvet banquettes were filled with the great and good of London. In the far corner, seat carefully angled to limit one's view, was the science fiction writer Herbert Wells, he who was set to be master of parlour games at Stanway House later that season, engaged in a deep conversation with a young lady who I knew to be neither his wife nor his mistress, but my attention was quickly drawn to the bar itself, where, seated at the far end, I spied Dr. John Watson.

I approached him and offered my hand in greeting, which he shook firmly without getting out of his seat. Now that we were alone and my attention was not distracted by the penumbra of fame and genius that radiated from Holmes, I was able to give Watson my full attention.

Always a well-built man, he had grown heavy with age, and his gut had grown broader even than his considerable chest, and both strained against his waistcoat, threatening at any moment to expel its buttons across the room.

Watson's walking stick was propped on the bar-stool next to him, and with something of a grunt, he leant over to move it aside and indicated I should take its place.

"Scotch?"

"Thank you."

He nodded to the bartender, who clearly knew him well, and who efficiently provided me with a dram of aged whiskey whilst refilling Watson's glass. "To a swift resolution of this nasty matter" was the toast he offered, and I was pleased to drink to that, the honeyed, smoky essence of the fluid heating me up from within.

We sat in silence for a moment, each savouring our drinks and organizing our thoughts. For my part, I was anxious to discover what further information or assignment Holmes had for us, but the doctor seemed in no hurry to get to the business at hand and, when he spoke, instead turned the conversation to more general subjects. He asked about my time in Africa, and we compared notes between his experience in the Afghan conflict with mine in the Boer Wars. He told me tales of close escapes and of the Jezail bullet which, long moons ago, ended his military service.

Slapping his left thigh with his hand, he described how, to that day, it still ached at every change of weather. Indeed, the good doctor seemed in the mood for reminiscing, as he, on accepting his third drink and encouraging me into my second, remarked apropos of nothing that it had been at this very bar, nearly twenty-five years ago, that he had first heard the name "Sherlock Holmes."

"I know the lore, of course," I confessed, and he looked surprised for a moment and then reached the obvious conclusion:

"Oh, you have read my little stories?"

"Each and every one of them. Several times, in fact. You are most popular in India."

"Really?" The doctor blushed a most surprising shade of red, his natural modesty reacting with pride and the whiskey. "You know, I never knew that. My publishers don't seem to account for Indian sales.

Still, that is most gratifying, my dear fellow. Most gratifying indeed. One puts these things out into the world, and then who knows . . . Certainly, Holmes himself sets little store by them, but I have always believed that there are those in the reading public who find them of interest, and to learn they stretch as far as India . . . well, well. That is most"—he sought for the word, and failing to find a new one, returned to an old favourite—"gratifying."

I smiled, amused by the fellow's clumsy charm, and seized upon the opportunity to resolve a puzzle that had long concerned me. "I had a question, actually, about *The Sign of the Four*, your wonderful account of the mystery pertaining to the lost treasure of Agra. Would you mind if I asked you about it?"

"Of course, dear boy, of course—I should be delighted to shed any light I could upon the matter. What can I tell you of Jonathan Small and his compatriots?"

"It is the compatriots' names that confuse me. You list them as Abdullah Khan, Mahomet Singh, and Dost Akbar."

"Dost Akbar! My word, it's been a long time since I thought of that fearful name, but yes, that's right. Akbar, Small, Khan, and Singh, the terrible Sign of the Four. What of them?"

"Well, here's the thing. Abdullah Khan and Dost Akbar are both Muslim names, though Dost Akbar is more Arab than Indian."

Watson made a gesture waving away the distinction. "They were Mohammedans, more I do not know."

"Perhaps, but that does not explain Mahomet Singh," I persisted.

"I don't take your meaning."

"The last name 'Singh' makes clear that he is a Sikh, a member of my religion. Yet 'Mahomet,' or 'Muhammad,' tells us that he is also named for Islam's high prophet. That would be inconceivable for any Sikh. So which was he? Muslim or Sikh? He cannot have been both."

Watson's brow furrowed, and I immediately regretted my questioning. I was motivated only by curiosity, but even as I raised the matter, I realized that the old man before me simply lacked the sophistication to understand how his careless account, with its almost certainly erroneous naming of the Indian participants, flattened and erased distinctions that were definitional to my people. He meant nothing by it; he could no more see the gradations between Sikh or Muslim than he could deduce a man's profession from his gait or his home address from the mud on his boot. All this was unseeable and unknowable to him, in his well-intentioned but limited perspective. Hindoos, Sikhs, Mohammedans, we all merged into one category to his English mind: that of "foreign," and of any more nuance than that, he was not only ignorant but also ignorant of his ignorance.

Watson was stuttering through a defensive and incomprehensible justification of his long-ago error when, out of mercy towards him and as much to spare my own feelings of discomfort, I changed the subject. "Doctor, why have you summoned me here tonight? Does Holmes have fresh instructions? Have there been any developments in the case?"

He spluttered to a stop and, patting his pockets till he located what he sought, produced a small envelope which he placed on the bar before us. He nodded at it, indicating that I should pick it up, so I did so, and opened it. Inside was a single sheet of paper, writ on which was an address in Penrith, Cumbria.

"What is this? A potential target?"

"No. The opposite."

It took me a moment to figure out what the opposite of a target was, and I could tell that Watson was pleased that, this time, at least, he was a step ahead of me.

"Their headquarters. Or at least their headquarters here in England. It will be from this place that they will be preparing to launch whatever fearful atrocity they have conceived."

I looked at the paper again. The house it described was not known to me; I had seldom ventured as far north as Cumbria.

"How did you find it?"

"Oh, we have our methods, you know . . ." said he, trailing off in a way doubtless meant to express a mysterious, near-mystical process but, in fact, revealed to me the more prosaic and sadder truth, that

Holmes had not seen fit to reveal his methods to his companion, but was treating him here as little more than a carrier pigeon.

"What would you have us do?" I asked, hoping that in this, at least, Holmes would have confided in his lackey.

Watson looked around the bar and lowered his voice to a whisper. I was reminded of young Wiggins, and his leering look at Maud. That look felt different on Watson's lined and greying face, but it was still indisputably the look of someone who believes they have an advantage on you. The look of someone who knows your secret. "You and Raffles pride yourselves on being the finest burglars in the land, do you not? Well, here's your chance to prove it. Go to Penrith, gain access to this house by any means possible. Discover their target. Probe their weaknesses. Then we'll have the buggers!"

A rush of purpose and pride filled my body. At last, we had a clear objective, a concrete assignment. I had a mission, and in the action of the same, perhaps all these crippling thoughts of doubt and confusion could be silenced. Certainly, the task was one that played into our skill set. Rather more so than my futile efforts at deduction with the society pages this morning. I put the paper in my breast pocket and rose to leave, but to my surprise, Watson placed his hard on my arm and gestured with his head to the barman for another round of drinks.

I settled back into my seat. "Is there something else, Doctor? Surely time is of the essence in this matter; I must go to Raffles and we must begin our preparations . . . ?"

"Well, that's actually what I wanted to talk to you about. This Raffles fellow of yours. Is he a good man?"

The question was not one I had been expecting and put me back on my heels. I found myself stammering and flailing around, much as the doctor had been a moment earlier. Perhaps this had even been his intent.

"He . . . he . . . well . . . Raffles is a singular man. A man of talent and integrity."

"A thief with integrity? Is that not somewhat paradoxical?"

"It is perhaps unusual. But then Raffles is most unusual. As is your friend, of course."

"My friend? You seek to compare Sherlock Holmes with AJ Raffles?"

"They are both men of rare abilities and singular focus, are they not? The best there is at what they do?"

"Perhaps, but what they do is very different. Holmes has placed his gifts, his focus, as you put it, in the service of justice, of king and country. He has proved himself time and time again to be the indispensable man of our time who acts on the side of justice and the law. Your friend is a common crook—as, if you'll forgive me for pointing out, are you. And a crook, by definition, serves only himself."

I took a deep sip of my drink, though, in truth, its effects were fast evaporating under the heat of our conversation. "I make no defence of myself, but you must concede that Raffles is, at the very least, a most *uncommon* crook. And one whose talents his king and country now calls upon, who you call upon this very moment, to do what you and your aged detective cannot or dare not do."

There was still a stern temper in the old dog, and I had roused it now; his wide jaw worked itself, and even against the noise of the bar, I could hear the grind of teeth as he chewed out his emotions. I sought to defuse the situation, for whatever my loyalties to Raffles, I could not deny the reasonableness of Watson's concerns. Raffles was as likely to join the assassins as he was to foil them, such a creature of endless variety was he.

Yet, he was my friend, and so defend him I must, and in so doing, I had driven the gentle doctor to fury. His face moved rapidly from red to purple to white, like some exotic chameleon, and I expected at any moment a racist slur to pass from his lips, but I found I had misjudged the man. As quickly as it had flared, he quieted his passion, and turned to me and with eyes filled more with sorrow than with anger, opening his palms in gentle surrender.

"You mistake my intention, Mr. Singh. I spoke carelessly and I apologize. In a matter of this nature, a man has to trust his compatriots, and you and Raffles are new to me, and my purpose in inviting you here tonight was to get your measure."

I nodded. "I understand. I am sorry if I came up wanting."

"Far from it. You have loyalty. You have intelligence, integrity, and fire. And you can handle your drink. All those count for the good. But you also have youth, and youth, I have learned, is a double-edged sword."

"You were a young man yourself when you and Holmes first embarked on your mutual adventures," I observed.

"We both were, in years. Though in Sherlock's case, his mind has always been mature beyond age." He paused, reflecting. "Mutual adventures, you say. Mutual. That is an interesting word, is it not?"

"From the Latin *mutuus*—shared," I said, almost automatically, for I had been well drilled at school. Apparently, not as well drilled as the doctor, who shook his head and corrected me.

"Not merely shared, but also reciprocal. *Mutatis mutandis*: those things that must be changed, have been changed. Holmes and I have shared many a caper, and he has certainly changed me, but have I changed him? Has transmutation taken place in his fine orb of a head? I do not know. Perhaps he came into this world so fully formed, so completely and utterly and uniquely himself, that no change was possible or necessary."

"You are friends. Companions. Brothers-in-arms!" I found myself speaking a little loudly. Made uncomfortable by Watson's discomfort, seeking to reassure him—or perhaps myself—that the storybook version of his and Sherlock's friendship was, in fact, the truth.

"Friends perhaps, but never equals. We each have our role to play, and mine is the supporting one." He looked for the bartender, a child seeking his mother.

"Is that a matter of resentment between you?"

"Never. I wrote of him long ago that 'mediocrity knows nothing higher than itself, but talent instantly recognizes genius.' What a piffling mediocrity I would be if I did not recognize that the greatest contribution I could ever make in this life is to serve at the feet of my friend's genius. If not for

Holmes, my life might have been happier, easier perhaps, but it would have been ordinary. An ordinary life. Alongside him, I have been part of legend. A small part, but that is enough for me."

I realized in this exchange the answer to the puzzle that had been plaguing me. Watson was neither as slow as the version he presented to the world, but neither, of course, was he a mind to rival his illustrious companion. How could he be? What was remarkable is that he chose, volunteered, to play the role of dunce, knowing that his friend's genius would shine all the brighter in relief. He had willingly played down his own abilities all these long years, both to satisfy the ego and burnish the mythology of the great Holmes, and he had done so without being asked and without thanks and for the greater good.

He turned to me. "And you, Balvinder, is it enough for you?"

The question hit me with unexpected force. Had I cast myself in the same role as Watson, but with Raffles as my North Star? Was this to be my role for all time?

I saw that Watson was studying me closely, waiting for my answer, but I had none, not for him, nor even for myself, so instead I ordered another round of drinks and plagued him with more questions about his past cases and traded war stories and reminiscences.

It was past midnight by the time we parted ways that evening, and, deep in our cups, we embraced each other like old lovers. With his mouth pressed against my ear, he whispered something that surprised me and left me reeling, even more than the whiskey:

"Break with him before he breaks you."

With that, the old warrior slapped me heartily on the back and turned, leaning heavily on his stick, and wandered away into the foggy London night.

CHAPTER 9

We've Gone on Holiday by Mistake

The next morning, I woke early, shaved carefully, and feeling only slightly the worse for the previous evening, set off immediately to see Raffles. I arrived at his apartment building, The Albany in Piccadilly, at a little past eight o' the clock, and was admitted by the night porter, Seth, who was just completing his shift.

I had come to know Seth well; he was a recent émigré from Poland, of Hebrew stock, with a wife and three young boys. We greeted each other with warmth, and I asked after his family. The correct protocol was for guests to wait in the lobby whilst being announced, but Seth knew that Raffles and I were intimates who stood not on such ceremony, and after we had completed our pleasantries, he waved me up with a good-natured grin.

As I ascended the gilded staircase to Raffles' set on the second floor, I found myself remembering my first visit to these rooms, three years prior, on the occasion of our first "job" together, and marvelling at all that had changed in my life since that time.

Since that fateful evening when I had agreed to follow Raffles in his life of crime, our route had taken us down many well-paved roads to dark places and into many capers that had proved both exciting and remunerative. From the White Elephant Job to the Levy Affair to the matter of The Jubilee Present, we had discreetly relieved the wealthiest houses up and down the country of their most treasured possessions, enriching and amusing ourselves in equal measure as we did so.

Applying the earnings from these ventures, I moved out of my lodgings in Bethnal Green and into my current set of rooms in Bayswater, and was able to apply myself to the study of the law without the stress or distraction of worrying where my dues would come from.

At Raffles side, I had infiltrated the great homes of England, not as a thief—or not only as a thief—but as a guest; I had rubbed shoulders and broken bread with some of the most illustrious and even the most famous men and women of the land, attended premières of new plays and operas, debated politics with leading politicians, and discussed the finer points of poetry with the most celebrated writers in the land.

In all this, my life now vastly outstripped the ambitions I had held for myself when I first arrived at London Docks, and I had journeyed such a distance away from my beginnings in the Punjab, and from the bloody fields of Transvaal, that I felt it likely that my family would not even recognize me when we met again.

In all this, though, I had been living a false life. I had been true neither to myself nor to those whose hospitality and approval I so craved. I had allowed envy and ambition to disrupt the true working of my compass, and I knew that the issue was not that my family would not recognize me but that I scarce recognized myself.

So now, my course was clear. It was time to make recompense by carrying out the task ahead of us, and then to quit this life all together. First, Raffles and I would infiltrate this house, discover the plans of the unknown assailants, and bring them to justice.

Then . . . then . . . The "then" was unclear. I could not see exactly what my future would bring, but it would include Maud Adler, and it would see me being called to the bar, becoming one who upheld the law, not one who broke it. Where Raffles fitted into all this was uncertain, but that was a dilemma for another day.

All this was in my mind when I explained with urgency to Raffles our new direction from Holmes and showed him the paper that Dr.

Watson had given me, with the address of our target. He heard me out, with full attention, and then, studying the address closely, considered the matter.

I felt time stop, knowing that on the fulcrum of this moment the future of our friendship was balanced. As it had three years ago, pathways of possibility opened up before us in Raffles' drawing room. Should he choose to fulfil the mission, we could be our old selves again, a team on a job, but this time on the side of the angels. Should he refuse me, then I would have no choice but to break with him forever, and attempt to carry out the job alone.

He looked up at me, and his mouth broke into a broad smile. "The fellow is too long in the tooth, too weak in the leg, eh? He needs us young bucks to do his dirty work. Well, we'll show him! This will be a lark, eh, Bunny? Our greatest adventure yet!"

"Oh, Raffles! I am so glad you see it as I do." The paths resolved before us, into the one true road.

"See it? Of course, I see it. This address belongs to one of the richest families in the north. Think of the baubles we might find there. This will be a profitable expedition!"

I was horrified. "But, Raffles! Our job is not to steal valuables but extract information."

"Two birds, my dear Bunny, with one singular stone. We can help the Crown and we can help ourselves. What could be finer!"

I took a deep breath and considered. Perhaps this was as good as it was going to get, a compromise acceptable. If Raffles helped himself to a few trinkets while we saved lives, who was I to stand in his way?

"Very well," I said, then realized I had missed a detail. "Wait, you know this place, then? The house is familiar to you?"

"Of course," said Raffles, waving the scrap of paper like a herald's flag, "it is the ancestral seat of the Clayton family. Lord John Clayton and his young bride were lost at sea, oh, perhaps fifteen years or so ago, in tragic circumstances, and I believe the estate is held by a trust. What a trust it must be, as the Claytons' wealth was well documented!

"Come, there will be plenty of time to talk on the train. I must pack a bag, and you doubtless will do the same. I will meet you at Paddington for the, let me see"—he pulled a timetable from the shelf and consulted it—"yes, for the two-thirty-two train, that should get us into Penrith in time for an early supper, and we may even have time to walk up and see the house for ourselves. I'm sure it's worth seeing. People talk of Greystoke Castle as quite the Gothic nightmare!"

~

So it was that later that evening, Raffles and I found ourselves enjoying a hot supper at the Boot and Shoe Inn, Greystoke Village. The inn was a handsome building, dating back to the fifteenth century but recently remade in the modern style, with white rendered sandstone and a green slate roof.

We had procured a set of rooms, modest but comfortable enough and Raffles had persuaded the innkeeper to dig deep into his cellar and procure a quaffable bottle of claret to go with our steak and kidney pies.

My friend's enthusiasm had only grown through the course of the journey, and all through the meal, he regaled me with anecdotes. From old war stories to tales of his finest moments on the cricketing green, Raffles was in rare form, funny, charming, and full of good humour. Anyone listening to our conversation would conclude that we were no more nor less than that which we purported to be, a couple of city gentlemen, come to the north country for a few days of fishing and relaxation.

When our plates were clear, however, his mood changed, and an air of focussed professionalism came over him. "Get yourself into a warm coat and gloves, old chap, don't forget the torches, we have reconnaissance to do."

Properly attired, we strolled through the cool evening air and in less than ten minutes found ourselves in sight of the house. Or rather, the castle, the name was no exaggeration. Skirted by a nine-foot-high wall, Greystoke Castle sat at the heart of a substantial estate. Deer parks, farmland, woodland at the outskirts, and in the areas more proximate to the house, exquisite landscaping, including carefully clumped trees and discreet Ha-Has designed to focus the eye on the house itself.

Raffles had called it a "Gothic nightmare," and whilst I found the latter descriptor somewhat unfair, Gothic it certainly was—four corner towers and stone battlements advertising its medieval origins—though it was a thing of majesty and beauty. For all this show of fortification, however, to Raffles' and my experienced eyes, the building offered little resistance. The wall, though tall for the most part, was not continuous; there were several side gates designed for livestock which were located out of the line of sight of the main house, and once on the inside of the wall, as long as we approached under cover of darkness, we would be able to get to the main building unimpeded.

"And how to enter the house itself?" I asked Raffles.

"Oh, one of our usual tricks. The locks in a place like this, even if the owners use them, are seldom sophisticated. The cunning of a sixteenth-century locksmith is unlikely to prove proof to my modern pick for more than a minute, and failing that, I am sure we might wrap an elbow in a scarf and make quiet work of some kitchen window. The real question is: Who's at home? Absent the family, who lives here now? And what is their degree of paranoia against intruders? To know that we will make some gentle inquiries in the village tomorrow and then make our approach tomorrow night."

With this plan so clearly formulated, we returned to the good Boot and Shoe, and after ordering a whiskey and water to take to my room, I bade Raffles goodnight. He said he wished to stay a little longer by the fire, and so I left him in deep conversation with the bar-boy, a sleek-haired lad, who seemed very charmed by Raffles' cosmopolitan airs.

~

The next morning, Raffles was nowhere to be found at breakfast, and so after two eggs and chai, I took onto myself the research assignment he had postulated the previous night and made my way to the local post office.

The postmaster was a grizzled veteran of the Afghan Wars, who had spent time in India, and even after all this time, his enthusiasm for my homeland was undiminished, and he asked with fondness after places I had never been, and foods that neither of us had eaten for years.

"That *dal*! I still wake up dreaming of it. And for a good piece of *roti* to dip in. I try rubbing cumin on my toast and adding lashings of pepper to the soup, but it's ne'er the same. You can't get the spices out here, you know?"

I was happy to furnish him with intelligence as to the best places to procure authentic Indian spice and then turned the conversation to Greystoke Castle. He took little prodding, he remembered the "lost lord and lady" only too well, and had nothing but praise for *his* manners and *her* beauty. Their murder at the hands of mutineers of the good ship *Fuwalda* was a great tragedy, no question about it.

As for who lived in the house now, he said it had sat vacant for many a long year, but that of late, there had been a sudden spate of activity. The rumour was that the trustees had identified a distant heir who had a legitimate claim to the estate and were readying the castle for his arrival. I asked if there were any specific personages who had been staying there, and he leant towards me with a knowing look and said, "Aye, there is one fella in particular. One of your kind."

I was surprised. "Indian?"

"No, but a darkie for sure. African maybe? A proper colonial gentleman, you know? All suits and boots and airs and graces. That's what I mean when I say he is like you, no offence."

"None taken," said I, bemused to realize that, to this son of Penrith, the commonality that bonded me to an African was that we both were dark of complexion, acquainted with a competent tailor and spoke English properly.

I decided to walk a little around the village, puzzling through all I had learnt. The presence of an African of aristocratic bearing, who had somehow got access to Greystoke Castle, was clearly a salient point. Given Sherlock's belief that Greystoke was the headquarters of the assassins, this man must clearly be their leader. As to how he had succeeded in getting the trustees of the estate of one of the richest families in England to grant him access to their ancestral home, well, that was yet another little enigma nestled into the folds of our larger mystery.

Suddenly, I realized that I had within my reach a means to investigate this question. I returned to the post office and requested a telegraph form and quickly dispatched a missive to my Trinidadian colleague at the bar, Sylvester Williams, sketching out a research assignment I needed him to carry out with the utmost urgency.

Then, on an impulse, I sent a second telegram, this one to Maud, again with a specific assignment that she was well placed to execute, indeed one that she had previously suggested.

That done, and feeling gratified with the productive nature of my morning, I decided to fill the time before lunch with a stroll. I thought best whilst ambulatory, and so I set myself on a long route, with no particular destination in mind. My thoughts alternated between the puzzle before us and happy recent memories of Maud.

Strolling thus, my mind distracted, I was nearly run off my feet by a carriage drawn by two fine black mares, moving at pace. I had been so deep in thought that I had not registered its approach, and if not for a quick natural reflex, I would have been badly injured under the hooves of the charging horses.

As it was, I leapt aside at the last moment, and the carriage thundered past me—I shouted in anger, waving at the carriage. It did not slow, but out of the back window, I caught a glimpse of the passenger. To my surprise, it was the very man about whom I had been lost in speculation.

A dark blue-black face, pockmarked at the cheeks, but otherwise handsome and regal in bearing with wide, expressive eyes and a strong mouth. I could not see his dress, but if the coach and the caparison of the horses were any guide, it would be expensive and fashionably cut.

We locked eyes for a moment, this mysterious man and I, and to my great surprise, he nodded to me, a nod of recognition and fellow feeling that somehow communicated much. It was as if, at that very moment, I heard in my mind the phrase "I see you, Balvinder Singh. I see you, and we will meet again."

I shook my head to clear it of such fanciful imaginings and, as the carriage disappeared into the distance, took myself back to the more prosaic setting of the post office, hoping to discover a response from my legal colleague.

I was not disappointed. Not one but two telegram envelopes awaited my review. The first was from Sylvester. At my request, he had made a visit to the Chancery Division and, paying the requisite shilling, consulted the Cause Book, there he had found the following entry:

15 MARCH 1905—CAUSE NO. 2014 IN RE:
CLAYTON FAMILY TRUST—ORDER TO
RECOGNIZE BENEFICIARY

Sylvester further reported that, not content with the limited information contained in the Cause Book, he had sought out the court reporter on the day in question and persuaded him to describe in detail those who had been present at the hearing.

REPORTER NOTED THAT ACCOMPANYING
PETITIONER WAS ONE MICHAEL MADUKA
LATE OF LAGOS COLONY

As I was contemplating this, I opened the second telegraph, this one from Maud. It was fulsome and long, sent with no regard for expense or decorum, including as it did several long and distracted digressions on how she was missing my strong hands, which, whilst my complexion does not readily disclose evidence of blushing, certainly brought heat to my face. Past all that, though, she had carried out the task I had requested, and made a visit to the newly opened London branch of the Anti-Imperialist League, and there, having established a warm friendship with the organization's secretary under guise of joining, had made inquiry as to their recent benefactors. In that list was the final proof of our suspicions. In the last three months, one entity had made three separate sizeable donations to the Anti-Imperialist League: the Greystoke Family Trust.

The face I had seen framed in the back window of the carriage reappeared in my mind's eye, and I saw him nod at me once again. This time, I nodded back: "I see you, Michael Maduka. I see you, and I am coming for you."

~

It was a little past noon when I returned back at the inn, and not finding Raffles in the public areas, I headed up to his room to impart my findings. As I rounded a turn on the stairs, I bumped into the young bar lad from the previous night, who seemed in a terrible hurry and scarcely met my eye as he pushed past.

I knocked on Raffles' door. "Enter" came his imperious tone, and I pushed the door open to see my friend fresh from the bath, wrapped only in towels. Given it was early afternoon at this time, one who knew him less well might have found it strange that Raffles was only now getting dressed, but I knew that my friend alternated his days of high energy with those of utter indolence, so was unsurprised that he had given himself the luxury of a long sleep and a late rise.

"Ah, Bunny, you choose your moment well. I am damned hungry, and you know I hate to eat alone. Shall we see what the innkeeper's wife has ready for us?"

~

Over a simple ploughman's lunch—a block of tangy local cheese, fresh-baked bread, a limited selection of pickled vegetation, and a pint of local ale, I shared my information with Raffles, and he listened intently and asked questions in his usual penetrating manner. At the end of it, he sat back in his chair and gazed at the ceiling reflectively, commenting, "I must say, Bunny. You have done rather well here. Better, I would hazard, than that ageing charlatan Sherlock and his lackey would have managed."

I brushed aside the compliment, partly out of embarrassment, but more because I had no desire to get into a defence of Sherlock and Watson, my esteem for whom had only risen in the course of our acquaintance. "Do you think this Maduka fellow is the ringleader, then? And how has he persuaded the courts to give him possession of Greystoke? He cannot really have found an heir, can he?"

Raffles considered. "As to if he is the ringleader, or merely a lieutenant of some absent and shadowy superior, who is to say? I am inclined towards the latter view, as it seems to me that this is a very elaborate and sophisticated operation, and I struggle to see it as the handiwork of a native African."

Something in Raffles' statement landed poorly with me, and my face must have shown it, as he quickly clarified, "Now, if it had been an Indian, a fellow Sikh whom you had seen in that carriage, then I would have little doubt that we had found the master criminal. You Indians are a wily race, in cunning and determination every bit the equal of an Englishman, but an African . . . as I say, I struggle to see it."

Some part of me wished to debate Raffles on his crass assertions. To tell him he had neither the experience nor the insight to make such generalizations about either my people or the inhabitants of such a large and varied continent as Africa, but I decided that, for the moment, it was best not to provoke him, as I would have need for his unique skills that evening.

Not seeming to notice my internal discomfort, Raffles languidly continued his evaluation. "As for the matter of the heir, it is likely to be a complete deception. They may have produced some imposter and coached him in some particulars of the family sufficient to satisfy an overworked judge. Absent any opposition from other family members who also fancy themselves as claimants, it might go through on the nod. There was a famous case much like this in the last century, perhaps you studied it for your bar exams, the Tichborne matter?"

I knew the case, of course; no law student would not. The greatest cause célèbre of the past century and comprising a body of jurisprudence in perjury, probate, and fraud. Over the span of nearly a decade, and through multiple extensive litigations, a corpulent butcher named Thomas Castro had laid claim to one of the great fortunes of England by purporting to be the true heir, one Sir Roger Tichborne, who had been lost to sea years before.

Despite bearing scant resemblance to the lost baronet, Castro, by playing on the susceptible emotions of Sir Roger's elderly mother, and the credibility of an uneducated public, had amassed considerable support for his absurd claims. In age, weight, general appearance, speech, and demeanour, the man was as different to Sir Roger as two members of the same species could be, and yet he had come extraordinarily close to inheriting a great fortune in no way his own.

I had not only studied the court reports, but also became so intrigued by the strangeness and baroque nature of the events that I had sought out other accounts, and in particular had taken great pleasure from Mark Twain's essay in *Following the Equator*, which cannot be bettered and so from which I will quote here:

> *It was, out of the midst of his [Castro's] humble collection of sausages and tripe that he soared up into the zenith of notoriety and hung there in the wastes of space a time, with the telescopes of all nations levelled at him in unappeasable curiosity—curiosity as to which of the two long-missing persons he was: Arthur Orton, the mislaid roustabout of Wapping, or Sir Roger Tichborne, the lost heir . . .*

> *It cost the Tichborne estates $400,000 to unmask the Claimant and drive him out; and even after the exposure multitudes of Englishmen still believed in him. It cost the British government another $400,000 to convict him of*

perjury; and after the conviction the same old multitudes still believed in him . . . The Claimant was sentenced to fourteen years' imprisonment . . .

The fiction-artist could achieve no success with the materials of this splendid Tichborne romance. He would have to drop out the chief characters; the public would say such people are impossible. He would have to drop out a number of the most picturesque incidents; the public would say such things could never happen.

The idea that our group of anti-imperialist assassins might have constructed a ploy of similar scale and scope to gain control of Greystoke Castle and its attendant fortune seemed to me incredible. If it were true, it was evidence that their strength was greater than Churchill, or any of us, had hitherto imagined. Their scope of operation must be formidable, indeed, if they could not only strike down agents of empire across the globe, seemingly at their whim, plan a major terror attack, and simultaneously perpetuate an elaborate fraud against the British legal system.

Holmes and Watson had, of course, triumphed over many powerful opponents in their long careers, yet Holmes and Watson were not here with us now. At this moment, the heavy responsibility of the matter was laid squarely upon our shoulders, and the near-omnipotent nature of our adversaries seemed to me most daunting. I said as much to Raffles.

"Really? You sell us short, dear chap. A house is a house is a house, regardless of how complicated the legal niceties of its underlying title may be. We have broken into many great houses, and we will break into this one tonight. As for the violence these blighters are capable of, well, there we must step careful. You have brought your firearm, I trust? Good, so have I. We will go in forewarned and, therefore, judiciously forearmed."

With that, the die was cast.

CHAPTER 10

The Lord of the Manor

For the rest of the day, we made our preparations. We had brought our equipment with us, carefully packed in an innocuous leather physician's bag. Instead of a stethoscope, thermometer, scalpel, and the like, our Gladstone contained lock picks, chisel, picture wire, cooking oil, matches, a torch, a claw hammer, twenty feet of climbing rope, and many other tools of our specialized trade.

Raffles had me unpack, check, and repack the bag three times, on each occasion watching me and inspecting each item as it was packed and unpacked. That done to his satisfaction, we moved to an inspection of the weapons.

My sidearm was a Webley Mk IV, which I had acquired on the field from a dead British soldier who had no further use of it, and which I always kept in working order, oiled and clean. Raffles, for his part, favoured the Mauser C96, the so-called Broomhandle—a semi-automatic weapon capable in theory of firing up to 120 rounds per minute, a muzzle velocity which put my little pistol to shame.

I would never tell Raffles this, but in my heart, I felt that no true marksman required a gun as powerful as the Mauser. After all, it did not take 120 rounds to kill a man, only one if you placed it correctly. I suspected, with Raffles, it was the style of the thing, rather than its excessive power that appealed, but in any case, we cleaned and loaded our weapons and then changed out of our day clothes into the costumes of our profession. In my case, I had chosen my service dress uniform, khaki wool serge: a snug-fitting tunic over loose pyjama-style pants and ankle boots. Perfectly designed for fieldwork and camouflage, the uniform had served me well in the veldt and would serve me well tonight. Raffles' choice of work apparel was as eccentric as you might expect; he wore a set of silk and velvet tails, dress trousers, both in matt black, with a pair of soft black ballet shoes which allowed him to step silently on the hardest of wood floors. Instead of a white dress shirt, he favoured a black merino wool sweater, the combination of which rather suggested he was the lord of the manor, rather than the crook robbing it.

A little after ten o'clock, when the inky night had fully blotted out the moon, Raffles and I slipped from our rooms and made our silent way on foot towards Greystoke. The evening was cold, and the chill country air hung heavy around us. We moved in silence and, avoiding the main streets, travelled by the side paths and byways of the country.

After fifteen minutes of double pace, we arrived at the high stone wall, and following it round for a few minutes, we came to the cattle-gate we had identified on the previous evening as an ideal access point. Raffles leapt it gracefully, and I followed in more prosaic style; once on the other side, it was the work of a moment for us to proceed, under the shadowy cover of a well-shaped hedge, to the side entrance of the looming house.

Raffles worked his picks dextrously at the side door, and the lock quickly yielded to his ministrations, as a hard-boiled egg caved before the onslaught of a teaspoon. As easily as that, we were in.

Until this moment, so consumed by the task in hand, by the detailed application of our craft, was I that I had not stopped to fully reflect on the nature of the danger that we were launching ourselves into. Putting aside my growing and increasingly informed speculation as to the vast, pan-national nature of the movement we found ourselves pitted against, there was the simple and inescapable fact that our adversaries were cold-blooded, brutal killers. At least one of them possessed superhuman strength and agility, capable of tearing apart a human body as easily as a hunting beagle might rip a rabbit—or a Bunny—to pieces.

"Forewarned and forearmed," Raffles had quipped, quoting the old proverb, yet Rutledge and his sons had been well-armed, and it had done them little good. I am no coward, and I knew that I could rely upon Raffles to discharge himself well in a fight, but all our previous encounters had been against mortal men, fought in the realm of the ordinary world. This was something different.

As the night sky crept unremittingly overhead, my mind was suddenly full of the grotesque horror of the Rutledge family being forced into cannibalistic postures, and of Raffle's description of Fitzwilliam's head, dangling from a thread fashioned of his own throat.

Assailed by such images, my rational self retreated, and the wilder parts of my mind began to allow for the possibility we were against something extraordinary which hailed from the realm not merely of the politically disaffected but of the supernatural, and that somewhere within this house lurked a creature of pure evil, capable of killing us in a moment, guns or no guns.

I spoke not to Raffles of these concerns, knowing he would dismiss them as the weak and whirling speculations of an unquiet mind and mock me for my credulity, but I gripped my little Webley pistol tightly as we navigated our way through the large kitchen, and up into the main house.

We moved cautiously, in silence and in darkness, aware that there might be inhabitants asleep within, and whilst we had seen no sign of dogs on our reconnaissance the previous night, it seemed likely that a house of this size would have some animals present, but as we entered into the main entrance hall, with its soaring triple-height ceiling, bisected by a thrust of a grand staircase, it became clear to us that the house remained uninhabited.

The furniture was covered by sheets so as to protect it from dust and light, giving the impression of a room populated by lumpen ghosts, and the place had the slightly dank smell that infests unused spaces in the winter months.

This was a disappointment. Our mission here was premised on the presence of Michael Maduka and his compatriots; if they had not, in fact, taken up residence in Greystoke Castle, then there was unlikely to be evidence of their plans within, and we had gone to some considerable trouble for no reason.

Raffles gestured to the staircase, and I nodded, and we went up it together, each of us carefully stepping on opposite sides of the treads, in well-practiced choreography designed to avoid the possibility of squeaking from the boards. Like so many of our habits, this was a routine so long established as to be second nature to us now. As we reached the first-floor landing—less a landing, more of a long, thin balcony that ran three sides of the space—we hesitated, trying to decide which of the many rooms would prove most fruitful to our investigation.

I listened at the first door and, hearing nothing, cracked it open. It was a children's nursery. Or rather, it was intended to be a nursery: only partly furnished, and with a few mouldy and abandoned dolls, as if it had been created in expectation for a child who had never come. I found myself speculating as to what tragic untold story informed its abandoned and desolate condition. In my heightened emotional state, I found the sight of this deserted room most unexpectedly saddening and was glad when we continued on to the next door.

This time it was Raffles who laid his ear to the wood, and I saw his eyes open wider—I joined him, and for a moment, we crouched there together, faces almost touching, my right ear and his left pressed to the wood. Hearing nothing, I frowned, and shrugged my shoulders at Raffles to indicate my confusion. He mouthed his response to me, "Warm. The. Door. Is. *Warm.*"

I realized he was right. Unlike the adjacent door to the abandoned nursery, unlike the rest of this cold, unheated house, this room must have recently had a fire lit within, because its door was pleasantly warm to the touch. I got down to my hands and knees and attempted to peer through the crack beneath the door. No light was visible, no flicker of flame, so if there had been a fire, it was now extinguished, but the difference in temperature made clear that it had been alight recently enough.

Raffles and I looked at each other, stepped back, and in unison drew our weapons. Did our enemy sleep within? Raffles nodded, and I opened the door and went in, with his steady gun hand providing me with cover. The room was unlit, but the curtains on the back window were open, and by the moonlight, I could see that we were in a study. Shelves filled to overflowing with books and periodicals, a central desk and adjacent table—all piled high with paperwork.

There were no covering sheets here; this room had clearly been in recent use, with notebooks open, sharpened pencils and inkpots left out, and in the corner, as we had deduced, smouldering embers in a deep fireplace.

Raffles shut the door silently behind us, and moving to a side lamp, lit it, even as I carefully drew the curtain shut to ensure that the light was not witnessed from without. We did not exchange a word, but both quickly went to work—he on the desk, I on the side table, each of us quickly parsing through the documents in search of . . . well, of what, we knew not exactly, but of something useful—something that might betray the intentions of our enemies, and would enable us to effectively frustrate them.

After several minutes of silent review—flicking through bills, invoices, correspondence that all appeared to pertain mainly to the proposed refurbishment and restoration of the house, and not to a global criminal enterprise—I came across something that seemed to warrant further attention. It was a detailed schematic of a construction project of some scope and scale. Plans for tunnels and tracks, engineering specifications, and bills of work. I was not well enough versed in these matters to read the diagrams themselves, so I scanned the periphery of the papers to see if they identified themselves. Before I could find anything of use, however, my focus was distracted by the unsettling sound of footsteps from outside, the unmistakable sound of feet on gravel. Someone was on the front drive, approaching the house!

I turned to Raffles; he had heard the approach also, and we moved swiftly in tandem. I secreted the plans upon my person, he extinguished the lit lamp, and in two short steps, we left the study and shut its door behind us.

In the corridor, we hesitated for the moment, considering our best course of action. Here on the landing, we were exposed, but to go back downstairs made us vulnerable to the possibility of encountering this new player as they entered the building. We came to the same conclusion simultaneously, and moving as silently as we might, we re-entered the abandoned nursery.

There was no reason for anyone to come into this room; we could conceal ourselves within and wait for an opportune moment to escape.

The sound of footsteps on the gravel driveway came closer. Whoever it was seemed in no hurry, but there was a strange irregularity in their pace. A few slow steps followed by a few quick ones, and then the pattern repeated. Almost like they were . . . skipping? That thought arrived in my mind, but made so little sense, I put it away at once. Inching carefully to the edge of the window, finding an angle which would allow me to look outside without being visible to the intruder—for as such I considered him, though, in truth, we were the intruders, and he, most likely, through nefarious schemes, the legally sanctioned resident of Greystoke—I took my position and peered intently out of the window to see . . .

Nothing.

There was no one there. Raffles raised his eyebrows in my direction, hungry for information, but I had none to give him. One moment, the fellow had been audibly present on the gravel, and the next, he was gone. Abandoning caution, I stepped squarely in front of the windows and scanned the entire façade of the house. The moonlight coldly illuminated the expanse before me, and I could clearly see the manicured hedges, the wild oaks, the periphery wall, the long, snaking gravel driveway, and the lake in the distance.

What I could not see was the intruder, who seemed to have vanished as rapidly as he had appeared. Raffles was at my side now, and softly, he whispered, "He must have entered the house."

I nodded, and we quickly took up positions on either side of the door, ready to respond in the unlikely circumstance that the man chose to inspect the nursery at this late hour. We listened closely for any sound of his approach. For a moment, there was nothing, but then, we did hear an unexpected sound, not from within the house, or from the gravel outside, but instead . . . from above!

There was the sound of footsteps coming from the *roof* of the castle. Faint but unmistakable and in the same strange rhythm—slow, fast, slow, fast—that we had heard from below. Our adversary was . . . skipping . . . on the roof?

"This must be the same . . . thing that you saw at Fitzwilliam's," I hissed at Raffles. "The creature who climbs like an ape!" Raffles nodded, his attention fixated on the sounds from above us.

Could it actually be an ape? A trained animal that did its master's murderous work? I remembered a detective story I had once read by the American Edgar Allan Poe that featured a murderous ape. I struggled to remember the details precisely. Was the murderer in the story a trained creature or a wild one? Was it a gorilla or some other varietal? How did it kill? I had a memory of a cut throat, which seemed to militate against an ape, which surely would have no use for a blade as a weapon? Damn it, why could I not remember the story more clearly?

Such are the strange ways that fear can affect the human mind! I was in a heightened state of alertness, preparing myself for battle against a mysterious and deadly adversary, but even so, I was unable to arrest these ridiculous literary speculations going through my mind.

So it was thus that I was somewhat distracted when the windows behind us exploded.

Glass shards met us like an angry rain, and a veil of blood descended from my forehead. I instinctively went to wipe my face clean but immediately realized the danger that, by so doing, I would further embed the shards into my eyes, and in that confusion, the creature was upon me, lifting me like a toy and flinging me across the breadth of the room, into the far wall, where I lay dazed.

Up close, it smelt of animal, covered in a thick pelt, yellow like that of a lion, but spotted—a leopard's skin?—but its face was that of a great ape, a gorilla, I thought, though there was something strange about its expression. What monstrous chimera was this?

Raffles was first to get a bead on it, his remarkable nerve and steady hand meaning that he got a shot off before I had even made sense of what had happened, but the creature was fast, faster than any man, and even at this close range, it leapt and skipped around the room, bouncing 'twixt floor and wall and ceiling such that Raffles' rapid shots blazed a snaking path into the plaster but left the beast unharmed.

Then, as Raffles reloaded his clip, the monster sensed its moment and descended upon him with a blood-chilling growl of fury and, wrapping him in its long limbs, bundled him into the door, which shattered on impact like so much kindling, and they stumbled out onto the landing.

I scrambled to my feet, checked my pistol, and followed in pursuit, weapon at my waist, held tight for accuracy as I had been taught, ready to fire. It took me mere seconds to get onto the landing, but by the time I arrived, the situation was already dire. The creature had forced Raffles over the edge of the balcony railing; he was balanced precariously, held in place only by the creature's grip, twenty feet above the floor of the great hall below. The creature held him by his coat, casually, like a child might dangle a toy, and Raffles' feet scrambled for purchase on the ledge.

My gun was ready, but I knew not what to do. If I shot, the creature would attempt to attack or evade and, by so doing, release its grip on Raffles, and my friend would surely fall to his injury or death, but if I did nothing . . . Raffles caught my eye but remained silent, wishing to keep the creature focussed on him to allow me the element of surprise.

Almost by instinct, I came to a decision. I pursed my lips and made a smacking sound with my tongue, as one might to a wild dog. "Tsch

tsch tsch!" The creature turned slowly, its great monkey head facing me, even as its long arms continued to dangle Raffles over the edge of the banister. I saw now why its face had seemed so strange; it was no face at all, but a mask—a carved wooden mask of a gorilla, with exaggerated features and a wide, laughing mouth, open in perpetual mockery of the world.

Hard upon that realization came a more shocking one. The creature was no creature at all, but a *man*, clad in a mask and leopard skin. A hugely tall, muscular brute of a man, but a man nonetheless, as for even in this moment, the mask came partially loose and revealed his face. A dirty white face . . . with wide eyes, a wild shock of dirty-blond hair, and the jutting, strong chin of a man of action. No, less than a man, this was a boy, scarcely older than young Wiggins, a youth of ten and six at the most, with no stubble on that chin, yet with the musculature of an athlete and the agility and strength of the wild animals in whose skins and visage he was dressed.

I found myself immediately speculating on what this meant, on where this boy had come from and why he killed so wantonly, but before I could process this thought any further, I was interrupted by a direction from my precariously placed compatriot:

"Shoot. The. Bugger." Raffles had found his voice, and speaking softly and evenly, even as he struggled for breath, he urged me to action, but I knew this to be a false course, so I focussed instead on trying to reason with this wild child.

"We don't want to hurt you," I said, which was not true, but seemed at least a thing to say. "Please let my friend go . . ."

"Let go?" repeated the boy in a voice so tentative that it was as if he had spoken but rarely, or perhaps that he was accustomed not to English but to some language of his own. He took my meaning well enough, though, because his face then broke into an unexpected smile of unmalicious joy. "But if let go, fall down!" And he started to giggle, like a mad imp. "Fall down! Bang! Break head!"

"The creature reasons. How remarkable," said Raffles, somehow finding it in him to pass sardonic commentary even as his feet scrambled above the abyss.

"No bang. No break. Give me my friend." I spoke as patiently and calmly as I could, somehow sensing that this approach would yield more than threatening the boy with my gun. "Please?"

"Why you go my room? My room!" The boy's tone shifted; he was petulant now, upset, offended even.

His room? The nursery was the creature's room? But that would make him . . . My mind boggled. Was this filthy creature, naked in skins and rags, this murderous monster of bizarre agility and limited vocabulary, was this demonic youth somehow the heir to the lords of Greystoke?

Such speculations would have to wait. "Your room," I repeated. "We no go your room. We go home . . . Give me friend and we go home."

The boy considered, and for a moment, it seemed as if my campaign of persuasion had been successful. Keeping his eyes fixed on mine, he began, almost absent-mindedly, to pull Raffles back from the precipice; but then, for no reason I could discern, the boy changed his mind. His face hardened, and he pulled his lips wide into an exaggerated grimace that I can only describe as apelike. "You bad men. No bad men come to Greystoke. Greystoke my house." Then he turned and in a single casual movement shoved Raffles hard in the chest, so hard that he went flying off the balcony—I lurched forward, futilely hoping to catch Raffles, but fast though I moved, the boy was faster, and leaping towards me, grabbed me by the shoulders and, using both my momentum and his own, spun me off the ground like a twirling top, flinging me down the staircase with such force that I heard the banister shatter even as my own ribs cracked.

That feeling of wood and bone splintering together was the last thing I knew as consciousness deserted me and I was taken by the dark.

CHAPTER 11

They Called Me Black Michael

Anyone who has been unconscious can tell you that it is an experience entirely different to normal sleep. Sleep is a balm, a replenishment of the soul. Being unconscious is the opposite: a trial, an ordeal. One does not arise from unconsciousness refreshed, but rather ragged. Nevertheless, it is possible to dream whilst unconscious, though the dreams of the insensate are inevitably nightmares.

On this occasion, my battered mind was consumed by the sensation that I was falling, endlessly descending down a vertical tunnel into the deepest recesses of the earth. I was like Carroll's Alice falling to Wonderland, except beneath me waited neither cake nor caterpillars but rather an endless hell of disappointed expectations and the dead eyes of those I had failed to save, those killed by Maduka and his bizarre ape-child.

When I came to, my head and chest aching, I found myself in a large armchair in the castle's library. This was another room that had clearly seen recent use. A fire blazed even as the cold sun shone through large bay windows. Every wall was filled with shelves, and every shelf was filled with books. Still woozy and disoriented (*"dis-oriented"* to have lost the orient, to have lost the east, was that what had befallen me?), I scanned the titles of the handsome volumes, my addled mind taking a giddy pleasure in their leather spines.

Whoever had assembled this library was well read, indeed, and with most particular interests. The collection was rich with histories and political treatise—Macaulay's *History of England*, James Mill's *History of British India*, texts that celebrated and justified British rule were arrayed next to titles such as Dadabhai Naoroji's *Poverty and Un-British Rule in India* and *The Arctic Home in the Vedas* which argued against it.

Kipling's *Kim* sat incongruously alongside Tagore's *Chokher Bali*, whilst *Through the Dark Continent*, that sensationalised account of African exploration, rubbed shoulders with Edward Wilmot Blyden's *Christianity, Islam and the Negro Race* which critiqued Western presumption, and Darwin's *Descent of Man* shared a corner of a shelf with a slim volume entitled *The Souls of Black Folk*, the author of which I did not know.

Dozens of other volumes by Rhodes, Carlyle, Haggard, Conrad, and an entire shelf of Kipling sprawled around me as far as the eye could see. If any doubt remained that we were in the right place, it was removed by the presence of an edition of *Decline and Fall* which matched my own, propped next to the slim volume of *Paradise Lost*.

In different circumstances, I reflected, this was a room I could be happy to be in.

Those circumstances, however, were far from my current reality, and I was far from happy. My ribs hurt, my head hurt, and when I tried to ascertain the extent of my injuries, I found I could not—because my arms were tied to the armchair with my own coil of climbing rope. The bite of the hemp around my wrists roused me properly from my dazed dreamings, and I began to struggle to free myself—at which point, a deep voice made apparent that I was not alone.

"Lieutenant Balvinder dev Singh, late of the 2nd Patiala Infantry, loyal subject to the maharaja of Patiala, stretcher-carrier in the Second Boer War, and now a pupil barrister at 9, Stone Buildings, Lincoln's Inn."

The voice reciting my meagre credentials came from behind me. I strained my head to see who my captor was, but the chair had been positioned such that I was prevented from doing so. In truth, I needed not to see the speaker to know his identity, for I knew that such a voice, so arrogant and so heavily accented, could belong to only one man, the man I had seen in the carriage yesterday.

"And you are Michael Maduka. Late of Lagos, recently the petitioner in the matter of Clayton Family Trust, the false claimant to this great house, an imposter, and a murderer."

I put a confidence in my voice I did not feel, but I was determined to show my captor no fear. He had me in his grasp and at his mercy, and I expected precious little of the latter. Raffles was almost certainly dead, and I would be joining him soon enough, but till that moment came, I would resist this villain.

"Very impressive. The detective has chosen a worthy agent; you have done your work well. So we know who each other are, good, that will save time. I loathe introductions. They are so . . . preliminary." As he spoke this absurdity, he stepped into my line of sight, and I was able to gaze upon him.

His face was as I remembered it, strong featured, handsome in its way, save for the pockmarks on his cheeks, the remnants of some childhood illness, no doubt. It was his frame, however, that took one's attention. He was a huge man, perhaps six and three-quarters feet in height, and I would guess weighing twenty stone or more, with a broad chest, hands like cricket bats, and each thigh as wide and as curved as the torso of an adult woman.

He was dressed in a finely cut suit, but no tailor's subtlety could conceal that the body within was that of a giant and a warrior. Indeed, it was possible the tailor's instructions had been to extenuate this effect because the suit fitted tightly, and despite that the man was in his advanced middle age—his tight curls were flecked with silver—his musculature and strength were apparent in every casual motion he made.

I found myself reflecting on the dissonance of a body that seemed built for combat being clad in the finest fabrics of Savile Row, and a mouth that looked like it had been designed to shout commands indulging in playful wordplay, but my chain of thought was arrested by the memory of the village postmaster general drawing comparison between myself and Maduka as both "colonial types" in suits. I realized now that the comment was a racialized one. The simple postmaster, despite all his affection for *lassi* and *dal*, found it somehow incorrect or unbecoming, in his scheme of the world, that an African or an Indian should be dressed in the costume of an English gentleman or spoke his language better than he spoke it himself, and here I was, perpetuating the same condescension, regarding Maduka in the same way that the English regarded me.

It is an indication of how addled my senses still were from my injuries that I was about to apologize out loud for this sin committed only in my mind, when Maduka spoke again: "You are wrong in one regard. My claim to this house is quite bona fide. As the courts have agreed."

"So you are the lord of Greystoke?" I spat it out contemptuously, his arrogance causing the apology on my lips to twist into a fresh insult. "Your suit is not well cut enough for that!"

He looked surprised at first, and then, considering my words, his face split open, showing a mouth full of gold dentures and an alarmingly red gullet, and he laughed at this, genuinely laughed at my poor gibe, a rolling bell of laughter that spread from his face through his entire body, and each guffaw travelled across the room and hit me with force.

"That's very good, though my tailor will be sad to hear it! No, no, friend Balvinder, I make no claim to the title of this noble family. I am a humbly born man, but a proud one, and my simple name is good enough for me. Nevertheless, my claim to the house and to the Greystoke fortune is legitimate, not as principal but as steward, you understand. In my role as legal guardian to the legitimate—and only—heir."

"Heir? What heir? What fiction have you constructed to aid your dark purpose?" I asked, even as I began to suspect the horrible truth.

"No fiction, Balvinder. My concern is politics, not myth. Young Clayton is quite real. Why, you've met the boy! You made quite the impression, as a matter of fact. Not as big as the impression you and your friend made upon the walls, though. I am sorry about that. The boy became convinced you were trying to steal his dolls, or so he told me. He can be a little impetuous when it comes to such things. But one mustn't blame him; he was raised in the jungle, you know."

This history prompted so many questions, but a different line of inquiry had become paramount in my mind: "Raffles—my friend—is he . . . ?"

I trailed off, not wanting to show Maduka the extent of my fear.

"Oh, your friend is quite alive. A little banged up, shall we say, but the coffee table broke his fall. Not, however, before he broke the coffee table; I shall have to send him the bill when he recovers. But neither he nor the table are my primary concern just for the minute. You are."

Overcome with relief at the news of Raffles' survival, I found myself, for the moment, speechless. Some part of me wanted to rail and abuse my captor, to cry defiance. The greater part, however, was . . . curious. Whatever I had expected, this elegant villain was a surprise to me: his dress, his speech, his extraordinary claims regarding the young savage who had attacked us . . . I had been sent here by Holmes and Watson to discover the truth. So I would not shout, I would listen. I kept my silence.

"You have nothing to say? Nothing to ask me?" inquired Maduka, his voice as deep as the roots of an ancient tree and as smooth as palm oil, though inflected with the hard consonants of his native tribe.

I twisted my head against my restraints to meet his eye. "I will hear anything you care to tell me. I am, after all, a captive audience."

He laughed again at my weak attempt at bravado, long and loud as before. "You really are a delight, young Balvinder. I wish we had met before; you would have helped pass many a long night on board the *Fuwalda.*"

The *Fuwalda?* That name rang familiar, and I focussed my throbbing head to identify it. Of course! *Fuwalda* was the name of the ship the postmaster had mentioned. The one that had carried the lost lord and lady of Greystoke from England to Africa, all those years ago. It had been the subject of a mutiny, and all passengers, including Lord and Lady Greystoke, had been lost. My captor read the recognition on my face as plainly as if I had spoken—

"Look at you, busy little mind joining together the loops of the chain." He smacked his lips in what I took as a gesture of exaggerated approval. "I ask you, has the world ever seen anything so charming? The detective has indeed chosen well. Would you like my assistance in fleshing out this narrative, or perhaps you would like to use your skills of induction to tell me my own story?"

In truth, I had only the slightest glimmers, a mere outline of possibility, but I feigned more surety than I felt and represented my manner as rising to the bait, hoping to learn more than he might otherwise choose to reveal by making statements that would provoke him. "You were a member of the crew of the ship *Fuwalda*, chartered to transport Lord and Lady Greystoke to his colonial posting."

He nodded approvingly. "Very good. Correct in all details. Though you should perhaps add that the captain of the *Fuwalda* took it upon himself to whip his crew when they failed to meet his expectations, but that was nothing new to me. Do you know what I was before I joined the *Fuwalda*?"

I sensed a trick in the question, but I had little choice but to ask it: "What?"

"I was a slave." And whilst I could see nothing funny in this, he then laughed again.

I frowned, struggling to process this new information. To most Londoners, slavery was a practice consigned to history. After all, slavery had been outlawed some sixty years ago, first on Britain's shores and then across the empire. To meet someone who claimed to have been a slave must seem rather like meeting a dinosaur strolling down Pall Mall.

To me, though, one who came of age in India, where slavery was technically banned but, in truth, was still widely practiced in the form of indentured servitude, the concept was less alien. Indeed, going back further in time, Indian history is full of slave-kings, African warriors brought to India in captivity, who, through martial prowess, advanced to positions of power. Was it to this tradition that Maduka aspired?

My captor saw the confusion in my face and misinterpreted it. "Ah, Balvinder, you have disappointed me for the first time. You imagine because your precious British have outlawed slavery that it has simply disappeared from the face of the earth? No, alas, there were slaves in Africa long before the British, and there will be slaves there long after."

I agreed with him on that, of course, but saw no reason to correct his misapprehension but instead used the opportunity to gather more information. "You were enslaved by your own people?" I asked.

"My people? Who are my people? Are all who live on the subcontinent of India one people, or are you better understood as a loose confederation of warring tribes, divided by caste, language, tradition, and ritual? As it is with you, so it is with us. I was taken as a boy by a rival tribe, and then sold to a Portuguese merchant."

I did not know how to respond to this. In different circumstances, I might have pitied Maduka for the horrors he had endured, but since I was currently his prisoner, tied to a chair much as he had once been chained, I found my softer feelings towards him somewhat muted. Not noticing or caring for my inner conflict, he continued his narrative:

"The *Fuwalda* was meant to be my salvation. I escaped from the Portuguese slavers, and I took a job on board a British ship. A *British* ship, because Britain no longer permitted slavery. I was a free man. I had a job, and wages. I was so proud. Till a new captain took over the *Fuwalda*. He was a brutal bully, loud of voice and profane of speech. He ruled his ship with an iron hand, cursing and striking the sailors for the least provocation. His great bulk, short neck, and beetling brows gave him the appearance of an enraged bull, and his manner was no less savage. The crew hated him, and the passengers feared him. I was no longer a slave in name, but, in practice, I was treated as badly as I had been before. Perhaps worse, because before my owners knew my value and would not destroy an asset they had paid good funds for, but this fool of a captain took all his crew as replaceable and would kill a man in a drunken rage without calculation or regret."

Maduka paused here, lost in contemplation of his ancient nemesis.

"He gave me a new name, you know. Can you guess it?"

I shook my head, and he continued, in an almost kindly voice. "He called me Black Michael. That has always struck me as singularly redundant, but there was already a Michael on board the ship, the cook, in fact, and so it was necessary to differentiate me from him. These days, I am just Michael again, and the happier for it, though I bore the cook—White Michael—no ill will. No particular ill will at all. The captain, though, well, the captain I could not abide."

"So what happened?" I asked, hoping to keep him talking for as long as possible, in the hope that the more time I was given, the more likely it was that an opportunity to act would emerge.

"For the second time in my life, I engendered my own emancipation from bondage." His face took on a broad smile, terrifying in that it was prompted by the recollection of historical violence.

Throughout this conversation, I had been systematically straining against the ropes, and now for the first time, I felt some slight give in the binding around my wrists. I resolved to keep Maduka talking for as long as possible to give me time to make my escape.

"You staged a mutiny and took control of the ship. You murdered the captain and took control of the ship?"

He nodded his confirmation.

"But what did you do to the Claytons? And this boy, that you claim . . . The Claytons were but recently married . . . There is no record of a son, so that part of your story must be a fabrication . . . unless . . ."

"Unless . . . ?" Maduka smiled, an indulgent parent taking pleasure from an offspring's display of cleverness, and at the moment, the truth hit me.

"Alice Clayton was with child?" I had got three fingers loose on my left hand now, and if only I could follow them with a thumb, I believed I could get myself free.

"Indeed. She only realized herself midway through their journey and confided in her husband, who, once the mutiny had been successfully accomplished, brought the matter to me, and pleaded with me to spare his wife and unborn heir. 'Kill me,' he said, 'but only set them free!' He was a decent man, of his type, John Clayton and not without courage. Earlier in the journey, he had intervened on behalf of one of my men who the captain had beaten senseless, and had gone so far as to demand better treatment for the crew. For that reason, and out of compassion for the lady who shared her husband's sweetness of disposition, I consented to spare their lives, even as every other white crewman and passenger, including, I should say, the cook, White Michael, was given a long walk off a short plank, or a bullet in the brain."

"I thought you said you bore the cook no ill will?"

"No *particular* ill will. He was still the enemy. Besides, I wanted my name back, and he was using it."

"What did you do with Lord and Lady Clayton?"

"We could not take them with us, the life of a pirate is not suited to a pregnant woman, so we settled them on a small, deserted island, leaving them sufficient food and medical supplies such as to ensure their survival—at least for long enough for the authorities to mount a rescue mission."

"You abandoned them to die, at the mercy of the jungle and the elements."

"That was not my intention. I even left them a pair of pistols with which to defend themselves from the local wildlife. But perhaps it is fair to say I had . . . different priorities. My responsibilities were to my men, not to these agents of the very empire that had enslaved us, however pretty or charming they may have been.

"Still, I did my part and even sent word to the provincial author-ities of the protectorate that should they see fit to mount a search party at a particular longitude and latitude, they might find the Claytons. Apparently, they did not believe us, or perhaps they were distracted by their own problems, or perhaps they were simply not that keen to welcome an incoming commissioner, preferring to muddle on without."

"I see how the responsibility lies entirely on their shoulders," I said, laying on bitter irony as thickly as I knew. My left hand was loose now, but the right remained tautly tied to the chair, and try as I might, I could not free it. I would have to make such mischief as I could with one hand tied behind my back.

"A dozen years passed, I rose up in the world, from pirate to privateer, and that work made me rich. I had all but forgotten the name 'Clayton,' but then, one hot summer day, we found ourselves sailing past that same deserted island, and on a whim, I ordered the men to cast anchor and we rowed ashore. I had no expectation that the Claytons would still be there, but imagine my amazement when I discovered that their son had somehow not only been born and survived but had grown into . . . well, you have seen how splendidly the lad has turned out!"

I considered the extraordinary tale I was being told. Given both its provenance and its patent absurdity, I should have dismissed it out of hand, but the detail of Maduka's narrative fitted so well into the facts as I had discovered them, served as so complete an explanation to all the grotesque murders and our own assault by the boy-creature, that extraordinary though the story was, I found myself minded to believe it. Which was not to say I would not interrogate it.

"How? How could a child survive when his parents had perished?"

"He appears to have been raised by the local troop of great apes. Gorillas of a most unusual species. Larger, more intelligent, and more savage than any other I have seen. He had been taken in by a mother as one of her own, nursed and fed, and taught their ways. This is unusual but not unheard of, either in my home continent or in your own country. Did not Mr. Kipling make quite a little industry out of that *Jungle Book* of his?"

"You are saying he is like Mowgli? Mowgli is a character of fiction, and bad fiction at that! It conjures an India that has never existed." My disbelief was obvious.

"I assure you, I saw it with my own eyes. When we arrived at the island, the boy was swinging from the trees, naked and filthy but with such agility as to be a thing of grace. Indeed, the apes were loath to give him up. His mother fought for him so fiercely, I was forced to shoot her and several of his . . . well, his siblings, I suppose, to get him, but get him, I did. From where I stood, I was rescuing the lad, but, at first, he saw it differently. He put several of my men out of commission, biting and clawing. Took poor Edgar's eye right out of his head. He was a wild thing. It's been quite the effort civilizing him, I tell you. Well, perhaps I haven't succeeded in that completely. Perhaps it is not in my interests to do so."

"Not whilst you can use him as your weapon. In his confused and damaged state, he has utility to you." As I spoke, I felt discreetly about with my free hand, looking for something to use as a weapon, because even unbound, I had little doubt that Maduka would best me in an even fight, and so I would require some advantage.

He nodded acknowledgement at the truth of this, as if to say that we were beyond deception, he and I. Indeed, he seemed to take some pleasure in the conversation. Not in a boastful manner, but simply grateful to have someone with whom he could discuss these matters. I wondered if he had been working alone, just he and the wild-boy, who, from our brief acquaintance and whatever his other virtues, was not a great conversationist, whilst Mr. Maduka clearly enjoyed the sound of his own resonant voice.

"Darwin would find him a bewilderment," he continued, proving my point with a digression, "as Clayton's state refutes his theory that evolution is a long, slow affair needing many generations to do its work. In little over a dozen years, the boy has grown from a mewing, shitting, helpless human baby, no different from any other, into a creature of sublime power. Every characteristic of his adopted ape family—agility and endurance, savagery and strength—he has acquired a hundredfold. Though, as he is the heir to a long imperial line, perhaps the savagery was there already? Who can say?" At his own joke, he began laughing again, and I shut my eyes to better endure the waves of his humour.

"What will you do with me? With Raffles?" My hand had found a hard oblong object that by touch I knew must be a pen. I carefully unscrewed the cap, and felt the nib with my thumb. It was no broadsword, but it was sharp, and hard, and the best weapon available to me, and applied with force to the neck or eyes, it could do real damage.

Maduka stepped close to me, lowered his immense bulk onto his haunches so that we were eye to eye. I braced myself to attack, but then he said the most unexpected thing: "This mission you have been set, this task force that the young pup Churchill has established . . . you are . . . devoted to it?"

I sought to contain my surprise that he knew of our mission, and of Churchill's involvement. I had hoped that he would have taken me and Raffles for the thieves that we so often were, but it appeared that Black Michael was, not for the first or last time, several steps ahead of me. He stepped back, and out of my reach; my moment had been lost. Maduka continued with his soliloquy.

"Of course I know of your little conspiracy, Balvinder. How could I not? Who is it that keeps the empire running? Who delivers their telegraphs, who types their letters, cares for their babies, who are the drivers, the *ayahs*, the house boys and the *chai wallahs*?"

I realized his meaning. The servants of the empire, people with access to every secret, every message, those who were present to observe every unguarded moment of the imperial lords and to note them for Mudaka's benefit—they were, in overwhelming numbers, of the African and Asiatic races. They were the subjugated subjects of the imperial project, those compelled by force or necessity to serve the empire, to administer it even, but they had no love for it, no loyalty or protectiveness. What if these people were offered an opportunity to fight back, to weaken their oppressor?

"You have spies."

He inclined his head in a show of modesty that sat ill with the arrogance of his tone. "In every corner of the empire, at every level of the imperial engine. Quiet, patient, knowing that they might not live to see the destruction of the leviathan that has been crushing them their whole lives, but willing to use their own labours, their own bodies, if need be, as the grist to break it."

I contemplated what Maduka had built. An empire-wide network of informants and saboteurs, feeding him information and ready to act on his command. To the irresistible force of empire, he had attempted to build a karmic counter. A brotherhood of secret soldiers and spies, willing to risk their lives on his order, and for the cause. It was impressive if also, ultimately, inadequate: neither an equal nor opposite force to that which it opposed.

I sat back, hoping to draw him close again, to afford me a second opportunity to stab him with his own pen and then to effect an escape.

"What do you hope to achieve with all this? What can you realistically seek to do? You kill a few aristocrats in London, a few regional governors in Africa. A tragedy for those men and their families, but a mere pinprick for the empire as a whole. You are a gnat, buzzing around the body of a great rhinoceros. You may annoy it, but you cannot kill it."

My captor smiled condescendingly, happy to indulge my critique, confident in his own strength and remaining frustratingly out of reach. "Your metaphor is amusing but inaccurate. We are not a singular gnat but a great cloud; we are legion, and we hover above all the lands of the globe, working in unison, ready to swarm, ready to bite. Against such overwhelming odds, even the mighty rhinoceros might be forced to retreat."

"That is what your note, your poem foretold? You plan some great attack—what is it?"

For the first time, Maduka grew coy, and he answered me not. I knew then for certain that those plans we had found in the study did augur some terrible ill. I adjusted my seat and felt them still upon my body, tucked betwixt my trousers and my vest. Suddenly I knew that I *must* escape, for I now had a purpose beyond simple self-preservation. I had to escape now, had to decipher those plans and inform Churchill of the specifics of the threatened atrocity so that it might be prevented.

To achieve any of that, I knew I would have to provoke the man further, and so, borrowing a trick from his own arsenal, I began to laugh. Softly at first, scarcely a smirk or a giggle, but then, I grew it from deep inside my body, channelling every past amusement I could remember until it burst out from me in gasping guffaws, barks of laughter, and such uncontrollable exuberance as I had rarely, if ever, felt. I had not Maduka's steel drum of a diaphragm, but I laughed so loud and so long that he grew unsettled, which had been my intent.

"What is so funny?" Like many men of his nature, who used laughter as a weapon, Maduka had little sense of actual humour. I kept laughing, but between the laughs, I gave him his answer:

"You are a fool. For all your sophistication, for all your show of strength and your very impressive network of helpers and accomplices, for all that and your fine suits and legal stratagems and your monkey-boy assassin, you are a *fool*. You are not an irresistible swarm, you are a cloud of smoke. You will blow away when the empire exhales."

"You are so sure of this? You, a traitor to your own kind?"

"I am no traitor!" The insult arrested my laughter, and I found myself deviating from my plan, improvising to this new script. But my adversary was capable of taking the conversation wheresoever it went:

"Really? You are an agent of the very empire that subjugates your homeland and your family. Since the moment you served under the British you chose a side, and you chose the wrong one. You fought, never asking if the Boer was truly your enemy also, or if perhaps the people of the southern cape, on whose ancestral lands you were fighting, caught in your crossfire, might have some view on the matter."

"You know nothing of me or of my allegiances." I was no longer play-acting, my anger and indignation real. "You talk of the evils of imperialism, but you are a murderer."

"I am an agent of freedom. I stand for the emancipation of the oppressed. What, Balvinder, will you stand for?"

I whispered my response, hoping he would lean in to whisper in return and give me an opportunity to strike the pen clenched tight between my fingers: "You do not know your enemy. You tilt at windmills, whilst the true giants sit comfortably in their palaces."

"Then who is? Tell me my enemy's true name, so I may carve it in blood on the streets of London."

The threat reminded me, though no reminder was needed, of the stakes for which I was playing, but my answer was simple: "Empire itself is your enemy, and your actions declare that for all your books, for all your talk, you know nothing of the true nature of Empire."

Maduka glowered. I had succeeded in angering him, but somehow I had also interested him, and he stood silent, waiting for me to continue. To my surprise, I found I had more to say, that our argument had sharpened my thoughts, focussed arguments that had been raging in my head for years and which recent events had forced me to consider anew.

"Empire is a machine, an engine of extraction built by history and fuelled by economics. It sits above motivations of race or class or manners. It is a mighty mechanism that, once it has been set into motion, cannot be stopped; its purpose is to shift the centre of the world. To rebalance the globe around a new axis. The engine churns and whirls, extracting wealth and power from one place and funnelling it to another, from the old order to the new. It cares nothing for the people it crushes in its path, for Empire is not a person or a philosophy but a system of gears and pulleys, and a system has no place for fear, no use of values. Empire works not by rules of morality; it writes its own rules, laws designed not by Lady Justice nor by her sister Pax, but instead by their bastard offspring, Avarice and Plenty.

"The engine of Empire will suck our homelands dry and leave them divided and broken. There is nothing you can do to stop it, because even if you despoil its workings and throw sand in its gears, you have nothing to replace it with, and so even a damaged engine it will churn on, malfunctioning and less efficient, perhaps, sparking and spitting, but more brutal and relentless than ever before.

"If you persist in your mad plan, you will provoke not only the agents of imperialism but the system itself. The machine will react to safeguard itself, and if it has to, it will kill us, not in handfuls but in the millions; not just with guns but with famine and division. It will put into motion processes that will damn us for all time, and then it will grind on its predestined path. You will look at the destruction of all you love, and you will know you were complicit in its destruction."

To my surprise, I found my face wet; first I thought my head wound had reopened and I was bleeding, but then the liquid reached my mouth, and I found it to be salty tears. I had nothing left to say, and so I sat, quietly drinking my own tears and contemplating not just my current predicament but the bondage of the world.

Maduka stood there, watching me. His great fists clenching and unclenching in frustration, his powerful brow furrowed, as he considered his next course of action. When he spoke, there was a softness in his voice I had not heard before, even as the actual words he said were damning.

"You see the truth so clearly, yet still you serve them? You betray your own kind, your own cause? You bow and scrape and aspire to play in this system that despoils and destroys your home? You belong on our side, not on theirs, Balvinder. Join us. Build a better machine."

He leant in for this final moment, and finally giving me my opportunity, I swung my left hand with all the force and speed I had, aiming for his jugular vein, throbbing visibly in his neck.

Quick though I was, he was faster still, and sensing rather than seeing my movement, he turned and instead of making contact with his neck, the pen pierced instead his cheek, provoking a mighty roar of pain—but doing far less serious damage than I had hoped. I stumbled to my feet and rushed forward, hoping to capitalize on the meagre advantage that surprise had granted me, and knock Maduka off-balance.

I launched at him with all I had in me, but he moved with unexpected speed and grace, and danced out of my path; my own momentum worked against me, and I stumbled to the ground, my right hand still awkwardly attached to the chair. I turned and braced myself to attack—but once again, Maduka's speed gave him the advantage.

I felt his fist smash into my face before I even saw his arm swing, and then he kicked me, his huge boot propelled by his cow-like calves with such force that I, and the chair I was tied to, were lifted clean off the ground and went flying across the room, landing in a great crash against a bookshelf, which overbalanced and fell upon me. I had just enough time to note the irony of my being crushed to death under books about the empire when, for the second time that day, darkness descended and I was no longer conscious of irony, or of anything else.

CHAPTER 12

On Trains

I was still unconscious when Raffles found me. Through my sleep, I dimly heard his voice and smelt his familiar scent. With swift, efficient motions, I felt him use a knife to cut me loose, and his strong, capable hands quickly investigated my injuries. He said little beyond repeating my name and asking me if I could walk, but I could sense the concern in his voice as he worked to free me and get me on my feet. I tried to open my eyes, but they didn't seem to want to open; I tried to speak, but my mouth failed to form words, so I just made a faint groan, and leant into my friend's strong shoulder and let him frog-march me out of the ancestral home of the lords of Greystoke.

~

I would find out later that Raffles' own injuries had been equally extensive; his left ankle had broken when the boy had dropped him off the banister. He had splinted it himself with a plank from the very table that had broken his fall, but to walk on it, still less to have to support my weight as well as his own for the nearly mile march back to the Boot and Shoe, must have induced incredible agony. Yet Raffles made no sound of complaint, and when we arrived at the inn, and when the local doctor arrived, fetched by the barboy at Raffles' direction, he insisted he attend to me first, and only when that rustic medic had given me the all clear would Raffles submit himself, reluctantly, for treatment.

Once the doctor was done with us, we were quite the exhibition. My three broken ribs well bound, my battered head once again wrapped in a turban, this time one made of medical bandages; Raffles equipped with splint and a crutch, we sat at a corner table of the quiet bar looking like two refugees from a convalescence home for injured veterans. Still, now we finally had the opportunity to compare notes. I told Raffles of my conversation with Michael Maduka, and its singular conclusion, whilst he relayed to me his experience of being kept in a cage for several hours under the supervision of the Clayton boy, who seemed to exult in the inversion of normality, that he, the savage creature was free and in charge of a gentleman in a cage.

After some length of time, Raffles explained, the boy had been summoned by a low whistle—from Maduka, we deduced—and abandoned his charge, leaving Raffles to utilize the skeleton keys he always kept sewn into his trouser lining to pick the lock, and after carefully establishing that the house was empty, that the boy and his master had gone, he came looking for me. As to why they had left us alive, we could only speculate; certainly there seemed little mercy in either of them.

"Perhaps they did not regard us as worth the killing—" I hazarded. "They seem to restrict their worst atrocities to those who, by their lights, deserve the worst. Perhaps they simply didn't take us seriously as either threat or enemy?"

"If so, that will be their final mistake," responded my friend grimly, and I could see by the set of his features that this was no longer a jape or a jolly for him, no longer simply a distraction or an excuse to enrich himself. Somewhere over the last twelve hours in Greystoke Castle, this had become personal for AJ Raffles, and for that I was grateful, as, once sufficiently motivated, Raffles is a formidable opponent.

What had previously been vague and macabre was now precisely known. Our adversaries were no longer shadowy figures but concrete men. In this respect, our mission had been a success. We had information to impart to Lestrade and Churchill, the identity of the ringleader, a sense of his objectives and methodology and . . .

. . . I remembered the plans. The plans we had found in the study and which I had secreted in my trouser pockets. I checked them—they were still there. Looking carefully around the pub to make sure we were not being observed, I pulled the papers out and placed them on the rough table between Raffles and myself.

Raffles glanced at them but with only mild interest. "You picked these up in the study. I remember. You think they hold significance?"

"I do, but I cannot decipher them. They are engineering plans, that much is clear, but of what and where . . ."

Raffles took the papers, and traced the designs with his elegant fingers.

"Do you recognize it?" I asked. "It's a building of some sort, but with either a tunnel or a tower perhaps. There are a lot of steps . . ."

Something clicked in Raffles' mind, and, drawing a pen from his pocket, he wrote three words on a beer mat, and pushed it across the table to me. Then, with some little effort, he pulled himself to his feet.

I stared at the note in horror, as the full scope of what Maduka was planning became clear. I looked up at Raffles, my mouth opening to speak, but he shook his head tightly: "Not now. Not here."

"Come, Bunny, I think we are rather needed back in London. As quick as you can. Time, I suspect, is rapidly becoming of the essence."

On the way to the train station, we stopped at the little post office, where my new acquaintance the postmaster once again did service to our cause by dispensing telegrams for each of us. Raffles' missive was to Lestrade, giving him our train details and instructing him to meet us at the station and to inform Churchill that we would require an immediate audience. My telegram was of a more personal nature. I sent word to Maud, telling her that I was returning to London that night, reassuring her of my safety, and urging her in as forceful terms as I could conjure without disclosing secrets to the postmaster's eyes to avoid central London for the next few days. I did not disclose the recipient or contents of my message to Raffles, and if he was curious, he made no sign of it.

On the train journey back to London, Raffles advised that we both get as much rest as we could. I saw the logic in his suggestion. If his reading of the plans was correct, there was no sleep for either of us in the nights to come, so it made good sense to replenish ourselves whilst we could. Raffles stretched himself out in the first-class compartment, elevated his broken leg, in the way the doctor had advised, and was swiftly snoring with the angels.

I took the little coaster from the pub out of my pocket. On one side was a charming line drawing of Greystoke Castle, heavily marked and distorted from having had a thousand wet mugs of beer placed upon it. On the other, in Raffles' elegant hand, were three words: *Trafalgar Square Station.*

For the contemporary reader, it must seem like the London Underground railway system is in a state of perpetual expansion and renewal. Nearly every year, a new station, a new extension of an existing line, or even a new line is born. Today, we take it for granted and groan with fond intolerance when a delay is announced or a station closed for refurbishment.

Back in 1905, though, when the system was still young and only encompassed a limited section of London, its very existence seemed a miraculous glimpse into the future. The underground trains transformed London from a vast, unnavigable megapolis to a modern, traversable city. Whilst the wealthy had always been able to move freely in their carriages and hansom cabs, the working population of the city had been constrained by geography, compelled to live in close proximity to their places of work, that concentration of community giving each of the many villages and boroughs that comprised London their unique character.

With the advent of the Underground, a window cleaner could live in Bethnal Green and work in Buckingham Palace without spending three hours of his day journeying between the one and the other, and with that change, London changed. The city's dynamism was redoubled, and the character of its streets became immediately more varied and egalitarian.

In this transformation, the construction of the Trafalgar Square station was a major landmark. The new station would be the southernmost stop on the Underground system located in the very heart of London. What a station it was to be; the plans that Raffles had recognized called for two three-hundred-foot platforms, an underground ticket hall, four Otis lifts, and a spiral staircase, all invisibly enclosed in the space beneath the Trafalgar Square itself, the mighty pavilion no longer on solid ground but floating above the marble and tile cavern of the station beneath. As a feat of engineering, the new station pushed the limits of what was possible, being one of the largest underground facilities in London, and the train line that reached it was a pioneering example of the deep-level electric trains, the very cutting edge of technological progress.

The station was due to open in the early months of next year, but construction was now virtually complete. The timetable that had inspired in us a sense of urgency, however, was not the date of the station's operation but rather a different event that was scheduled to take place the very next day—an event that had, in fact, appeared on my list of potential targets:

> *21 October—Centenary anniversary of the Battle of Trafalgar.* Lavish celebrations in Trafalgar Square, including the decoration of Nelson's Column, to be attended by the king, and all his ministers, and a crowd of thousands is expected.

A crowd of thousands, at an event commemorating Britain's greatest military victory, where the king himself, the Emperor of the Empire, would preside, with all his ministers and courtiers present. The First Lord of the Admiralty, the Chief of the General Staff, Under-Secretary Churchill, and his boss, Lord Curzon—every leader of the empire would be present, with thousands of ordinary Londoners cheering them on—and beneath them, a vast underground chamber, empty except for a group of determined assassins, with a taste for the dramatic and access to every detail of the plans of the station and of the celebrations, and who had spent months planning this attack and were hell-bent on bringing the empire to its knees.

This was their plan. A decapitation attack. Everything they had done up to this point was mere prelude, or perhaps, more ominously, a feint—designed to distract and confuse as this, Black Michael's masterstroke, was being executed. If successful, this operation would cripple the empire . . . deal it a blow from which he thought it would never recover.

I knew, however, that he was mistaken. Because even if he was successful in this audacious decapitation, in this terrible atrocity, all he would achieve would be to set the world on fire. Churchill would rally the government to retaliate on a massive scale, and they would do so indiscriminately. My brief acquaintance with the man made clear to me that he was not one given to proportional retaliation, and he would unquestionably regard an act of this nature as a declaration of war. Across the globe, in every corner of the empire, Churchill would turn the full power of the British state towards retribution, and he would regard as enemy not only Maduka and his organization but anyone who sympathized with them, or even looked like them, which is to say, he would regard every colonial subject as a suspect.

So enraged and humiliated, the only possible response would be for the British to respond disproportionately in kind, and Churchill would be the implementer of their destruction. He would burn Delhi and Nairobi to the ground, arrest and brutalize thousands. I saw then with a terrible certainty the future that would come to pass if we did not prevent this attack. A future of occupation and suppression, of asymmetric warfare and institutionalized brutality and endless cycle of strike and counter-strike from which there would be no turning back. The world would become a theatre of war, and the sides would not be nations but ideologies. The imperial powers and the colonized, the East and the West, would be locked into a never-ending conflict that would consume the globe. The murder and famines and oppression of the past hundred years would seem like a child's story compared to what would come—millions yet unborn would pay the price for Maduka's grand design.

I glanced at the newspaper that Raffles had folded neatly over his face, to block out the light. The masthead proclaimed today's date: 20 October 1905. The event was taking place tomorrow.

I looked out the window. This train could not travel fast enough.

CHAPTER 13

The Battle of Trafalgar

We were greeted at Paddington station by an agitated Lestrade with a police carriage waiting, one with a duty guard of two earnest bobbies, all tall, hard hats and flat, stolid faces. We drove fast and directly to Churchill's private residence at 12 Bolton Street, Mayfair, where he was awaiting our report. I had wanted to confer first with Holmes and Watson, but Raffles had overruled me, pointing out that we could ill afford the delay.

Throughout the drive, Lestrade repeatedly demanded explanation and information from us, but Raffles demurred, saying only that it would be more efficient to discuss the matter when we were all together. I could not help but smile at my friend's obvious delight at exercising authority over the pompous superintendent.

A maid greeted us at the front door, and ushered us through to a small but well-appointed dining room. Sitting at the centre of the table, arrayed in a voluminous silk dressing gown that I would not have thought to see him in, was Winston Churchill.

Without the garments and trappings of state, the boyish nature of his features was more apparent: his soft, hairless face, his weak chin. It seemed strange to me indeed that this young man, a half dozen years my junior, had in his charge not only this matter but, in effect, the oversight of the empire's vast colonies and dominions. The fate of much of the populace of the great globe was dependent on the whims and fancies of this one precocious personage.

If the weight of his responsibilities depressed his spirits, Churchill gave no indication of it. He listened intently to Raffles' account of our adventures, asking a few focussed questions where he needed more detail and making a note in illegible longhand in a thin leather notebook. He got ink on the sleeve of his dressing gown, but he didn't seem to notice, or care if he did.

When Raffles had finished, Churchill sat back in his chair, lit one of his omnipresent cigars, and took a few contemplative puffs. I reflected on what an odd company we made: a silk-clad minister, a besuited and agitated police officer, and a pair of bandaged burglars. Could it really be so that the fate of the empire rested in our hands?

"Superintendent. What is your counsel?" barked Churchill, still contemplating the cloud of smoke he had exhaled.

"You believe all these men have told you?"

"Do I have a reason not to?" inquired Churchill casually, without apparent concern.

"It is fantastical. Implausible. Boys raised by apes? African criminal masterminds? A global network of spies? Surely this is a fever dream!"

"Is it? What say you, Mr. Singh? Do you and your friend Raffles' brains run too hot? Are they overcooked? Like a good curry, what?" And he laughed his strange barking laugh.

I considered him. This titan in training, this man-child of empire; for a second, he seemed to me like a strange inversion of the ape-boy, young Greystoke, two youthful scions of noble lines, repurposed by fate for savage ends.

"Everything we have told you is the truth, and will happen," I said. "It is improbable, of course, but as Mr. Holmes says, when you eliminate . . ."

"Yes, yes, very good. There's no need for cliché," said Churchill; apparently, like Raffles, he was not fond of the detective's most famous maxim. "Well, then, Lestrade, let us say I do believe it. Let us even say it is true. What is your advice, then?"

The rodent-faced policeman looked at Churchill, then at me, and then back at Churchill, formulating his thoughts carefully. By the time he spoke, he had a full plan ready.

"If we are to take it seriously, then the evidence described points to a substantial and potentially devastating attack in Trafalgar Square. Perhaps these men have explosives and other munitions. Their examination of engineering plans suggests they are looking for structural weakness. They may plan to collapse the station at the height of the celebrations, which would cause great carnage and panic. Thousands might die. We must cancel the ceremony," responded Lestrade, and then, quick as silver, he continued:

"His Majesty and the cabinet must not be exposed to this risk. We call off the procession and keep the streets clear; that way, no one will be at risk and there will be nothing for this"—Lestrade consulted his notes—"this Mr. *Ma-doo-Koo* to attack."

Churchill nodded, but even as he was inclining his head in affirmation, he spoke to the opposite effect. "No. That we must never do. We are British, and we are celebrating our greatest naval victory. We will not be cowed by a pack of degraded savages, led by a blackamoor waving his arms! Besides, if we cancel, we'll never catch them . . . they'll disappear like mist on the moor. On the black-a-moor! Ha!"

"But, Under-Secretary! Think of the safety of the king."

"I am thinking of him, you imbecile. The king is a symbol of empire, and our symbol isn't going to declare himself a coward. Kings don't hide. No! The commemoration ceremony continues . . . But perhaps . . . perhaps some other way may be found . . ." He smiled to himself for a moment, and then his smile blossomed into a laugh, not the booming laugh of Maduka but an escalating sniggle, more than a sneer, less than a giggle.

"I have it! The *entente cordiale*!"

"I'm sorry, I don't quite follow?"

"Oh, do keep up, Lestrade. I'd have thought in your elevated position, you would at least make a pretence of staying abreast with matters of state. Britain and France signed the *entente cordiale* last year, a diplomatic landmark between the Frenchies and ourselves. Lansdowne has been working on it with the French ambassador—what's his name, Monsieur Cambon—for years. People believe they've brought ten centuries of war to an end, and ushered in a new age of Anglo-Franco cooperation . . ."

"I fail to see—" began Lestrade.

"The French are unlikely to be pleased if the king and all his ministers attend a celebration of our greatest victory over them, just as we seek a new age of cooperation and fraternity," I said, explicating Churchill's point. "They would regard it as an affront."

"Precisely so, sir!" shouted Churchill, getting quite excited at his own cleverness. "A *faux pas*! There has been much head shaking about it in Whitehall, but caught between conflicting demands, politicians have done what politicians always do: nothing. Hah!

"Until now. This offers us the perfect opportunity. The ceremony will go ahead. The crowds will gather. But the king and the cabinet will be obligated to stay at home, not out of fear but out of tactfulness. We will make an announcement at the last moment, and say it is a diplomatic decision, so as not to offend *nos amis et alliés français*. And in the place of the royal court and the cabinet, Lestrade, you shall send the largest force of police officers ever assembled on London's soil, and you shall have them ready, spoiling for a fight. We shall want them in uniforms in plain sight, and we shall want them in plain clothes. Black Michael will come looking for big game, but he will instead find himself in a trap of our design! This is how the game is played, and the braggard will find himself outclassed."

~

I stood on the highest step, my back to the National Gallery, seeking the best possible vantage point from which to survey the square. To my left was Raffles, to my right Lestrade, each, like me, scanning the crowd in a state of high alertness.

In front of us, the expanse teemed with the full spectrum of humanity. From street urchins and beggars to various minor dignitaries, Trafalgar Square was crowded with bodies, and the bodies were loud and excited. Men and women with little to no knowledge of the history they were commemorating were pleasantly drunk, toasting a dead hero who they remembered only because of the impressive column erected in his memory and the vague idea that he had "beat the Frenchies!"

None of this was our concern. My concern was not the decisive naval battle one hundred years ago, but one that might be taking place here, on land, today.

I had not slept much the night before; between my injuries and my intense anticipation of the events of the next day, restfulness eluded me. I had considered calling on Maud, but decided that it was best that I stay focussed on the task at hand, so I spent the night reviewing all we had learnt on this strange affair, and playing over in my mind my conversation with Michael Maduka, his words and taunts echoing in my battered head. Was I really a traitor to my race, my home? I had believed that my time in London and my study of English law were of a piece with my patriotism, that I would return to India more ready to serve it, an instrument of justice.

To hear Maduka, though, my efforts served no higher goal than my own vanity. I was betraying myself and my people in pursuit of a pipe dream of acceptance. That I had subscribed, subconsciously genuflected, to the underlying philosophy of empire.

Was I lying to myself?

I was tempted many times through the long, dark hours to go to Maud. Not only for the comforts of her body but so that I could unburden myself of these questions and seek her counsel and her perspective. I vowed that when this business was resolved the next day to seek her out and pledge my love to her anew, and, with her, get to the work of untangling the mess of contradictions and confusions that Maduka had unleashed in my mind.

Then it occurred to me that even my love for Maud might not be free from the contaminations of empire. Did I love her because she, like me, was a victim of colonialism? Or was she also simply a symbol of my ambition and aspiration, an elegant white wife the better to ingratiate myself into British society? Down every turn, time and time again, the road travelled was revealed to be a maze, and there was no exit for my indoctrinated psyche from the trap of imperialism.

I pulled my consciousness away from these metaphysical considerations. The here and now was what mattered. Lestrade's men had worked through the night to search every crevice and cupboard in the train station below the square. It was in such pristine shape, and still so empty of the trappings of operation—rooms unfurnished, platforms vast and vacant—that the search had proved a simple enough affair. They had found nothing. No explosives, no weaponry, no evidence at all of a dastardly plot. We should have perhaps been relieved, but, in fact, both Raffles and I were disappointed, in part perhaps because we could feel our credibility with Lestrade evaporating with each moment our seemingly extraordinary claims remained unsubstantiated.

So now the vigil began. Would Maduka stage some brazen daytime assault on the square from locations unknown? Or had he decided that in the king's absence, the game was not worth the candle, and abandoned his plans?

I turned to Raffles. "I'm going to go down into the crowd," I said. "Walk the perimeter." He nodded his acknowledgement but, gesturing to his ankle, now fully encased in a plaster of Paris cast, indicated his inability to follow. "I will keep vigil from the high ground," he said, with a tone of light ruefulness.

I set forth on my perambulation. We had established four police checkpoints, one on each corner of the square, from which all ingress and egress could be carefully monitored. It was my intention to visit each in turn and check in with the presiding officer at each station and get their update. Lestrade, whatever his personal misgivings, had accepted Churchill's directive that Raffles and I be given some field authority, and so the men would report to me, however much it pained their sensibilities to treat an Indian as their superior.

The officers on the northwest and southwest corners had little information to impart. They were in a stage of high alert; the seriousness of their mission had been imparted to them in no uncertain terms from Lestrade and through the chain of command. To a man, they were on edge, primed to explode into action at the slightest provocation. In this moment, however, they seemed a massive overreaction to a non-existent problem. Good-natured drunkenness and some attempts at vandalism were the worst of the crimes they had had to contend with thus far, and you could tell that the rank and file were growing sceptical of the apocalyptic warnings received from their superiors.

All this changed as I approached the southeast corner, limping slightly and adjusting my waistcoat, which fitted less well than usual, bulked out by the bandages holding my ribs in place, I became aware of shouting and chanting from behind me, of a quite different character to the joyous and raucous hubbub of the rest of the crowd.

I spun around, seeking the source of the disturbance. I saw approaching the square, a tightly formed phalanx of several dozen individuals marching in unison. They were men and women, white and coloured, several of them holding large bells which they were clanging vigorously even as they shouted slogans. The majority of them wore large advertising boards around their bodies, the words on which I could clearly discern:

END THE EMPIRE

OVERTHROW IMPERIALISM!

MIGHT IS NOT RIGHT

These phrases also formed the basis of their chanting, which had a percussive, rhythmic quality. A flag was unfurled and waved, and on it I could discern the group's name, or rather the name of the organization they represented: THE ANTI-IMPERIALIST LEAGUE.

The league's members moved with determination, positioning themselves centrally in the square, at the foot of Nelson's Column, and then, never ceasing in their chanting, began producing chains and locks and proceeding to secure themselves in a human barrier around the column. This action immediately provoked the police to engage.

Accustomed to dealing roughly with suffragette protestors, and already on their guard, they chose to interpret this protest as a threat, and moved at once to deal with the newcomers.

I stood stationary for a moment. Uncertain what to make of this latest development. Was this protest an innocent peaceful one, or was it cover for Maduka's assault? Was its presence here coincidence or carefully planned distraction?

The police constables suffered from no similar indecision, and the call went round: "Break it up! Break it up!" Drawing their nightsticks, they quickly surrounded the column and set upon the protestors with the efficient, workmanlike brutality that is the hallmark of British law enforcement. Chanting gave way to screaming as the dull sound of wood against flesh built in intensity. Some of the protestors sought to engage the police directly, and one tall, elegant African in a fitted jacket and pin-striped pants, in particular, seemed to be giving as good as he got, repurposing the length of chain that had been intended to affix him to the monument into a flail. He spun it with increasing speed and succeeded in taking down two bobbies in short order. Others were less lucky, and I saw a woman protestor grabbed by the neck by a block-faced policeman, shaken like a rat, and thrown roughly to the ground, where she lay, whimpering in pain.

The mood in the square quickly changed as revellers realized that a fight was underway. Some ran in fear of getting caught up in the escalation, others seemed more than eager to get involved in the fray, and with the essential fairness of a British mob, the majority seemed minded to side with the protestors against the police. Within minutes, a dozen or so smaller fights and altercations were breaking out between different groups of revellers and the police, between the police and the protestors, and between the Anti-Imperialist League protestors and pro-imperial celebrants. Things were tending rapidly towards out and out chaos, and I decided there was little to be gained by remaining in the thick of it—I should return to Raffles on the steps and remain on guard for the real threat. If this protest was Maduka's feint, designed to distract us from his true intent, then I would not be drawn by it.

I had turned my back on the fracas and made to leave when, to my horror and surprise, I heard a familiar voice, raised in anger and defiance—

"Unhand me, you lout! This is a peaceful political protest! We have every right to be here!"

I spun round to see Maud, dressed from head to heel in suffragette white, her face aflame with anger, waving a sign bearing the slogan EMPIRE IS EVIL, being roughly handled by a pair of policemen. They were trying to pry the sign from her grip, and she was resisting for all she was worth.

"Maud!" I shouted, and hearing me, her head swung round, at which precise moment, I saw one of the police officers raise his nightstick and make as if to strike her.

I broke into a run, disregarding the protests of my broken, bound ribs, hurling myself with every ounce of energy, every drop of speed, into the space between Maud and the men who would harm her.

Maud heard me roar, and, turning, she recognized me and shouted my name—"Bal?"—in surprise. I had hoped that she would take seriously my warning to avoid the central parts of London. Obviously she had not, and now here I was, charging upon her assailants with all the power my body had left in it.

My surprise at seeing Maud was matched by the shock felt by the two officers who suddenly found themselves not dealing solely with a diminutive Irish woman who, whatever her skill with invective, was unlikely to present them with a physical threat, but also with six foot two inches and fourteen stone of muscled, bearded, and furious Indian, head wrapped in bandages, like Mary Shelley's monster, hurtling amok towards them. They were young police who had most likely never been in a situation such as this.

"Bloody hell, he's a savage!" exclaimed one—and for once, I did not reject the racial slur, as their fearful prejudice worked in my favour. I was able to close the distance between us before they had decided on a course of action and, without slowing my approach, made a battering ram of my shoulder and slammed full force into the first officer. With a satisfying "OOOOF!," he flew fully five feet back, his flight arrested by the hard plinth of Nelson's Column, which his head cracked against in a sickening *crunk*, and he was down.

Later, perhaps, I would feel regret, but now there was no time for anything but the fight. The second police officer was upon me, swinging his nightstick and hitting me hard across the shoulders. Maud leapt on his back, like a wild cat, her nails seeking out his eyes. My heart swelled with admiration for her even as I slammed my extended fingers hard into the man's throat, a simple but effective move that her distraction had left him vulnerable to. He choked as his larynx collapsed, and, struggling for air even as he coughed up blood, the man fell to his knees.

I reached for Maud's hand, keen to move her to safer ground, but when we turned, we found ourselves surrounded by a half dozen more policemen. Reinforcements had arrived, and these were cut of a different cloth. Large men in the prime of their lives, rough specimens, hardened by years on the beat, and from the expressions on their faces, hungry for a fight. Their sergeant was a grim-looking fellow, with a scar across his left eye and a hard look that left no doubt as to his intentions.

Knowing there was no way to win, I sought to calm the situation. "Officers, we will submit to your custody. I am here on the authority of Superintendent Lestrade . . ."

The sergeant raised his hand to stop me. Attempting conciliation, I obligingly fell silent. What he said next made clear that no reconciliation was possible. "Friends with the super, are you, lad? Of course you are. Come on, lads. Let's show this coolie and his Irish whore what happens when you mess with the Metropolitan Police."

I knew then there was no circumstance in which I could save myself from violence, but I hoped to buy Maud enough time to escape harm. I put myself in front of her, and under my breath hissed, "As soon as you can, run," and launched myself with everything I had at the sergeant.

Everything I had wasn't nearly enough.

CHAPTER 14

The Case of the Other Raffles

It will add little to this narrative to detail the beating I endured at the hands of the police, and since I have still the scars to remind me of each blow, I shall skip briefly forward to the moment, some hours later, when I found myself nursing my injuries in a dank, dark little cell in the bowels of Scotland Yard, my trousers soiled with my own waste and my mouth caked with a mixture of blood and vomit.

I felt agonizing pain in almost every part of my body, but in a way, I took that as reassurance, for the pain served at least as evidence of function. It was the parts of me I could not feel that I was more concerned about. I performed a gradual inventory. First, I coaxed slow movement out of each limb and extremity, noting that several of my fingers were broken; then, using my tongue, I identified one missing tooth and several loosened. I moved to an account of my ribs and discovered two newly broken to add to the three fractured by Maduka. Eventually, I dared to push myself up from the floor, into a sort of crouching position, now clear-minded enough to focus on the important question: Maud.

What had the *bhenchod* done with Maud? That thought was enough to get me to my feet, though my entire body screamed in protest at the effort. Using the bars as leverage, I hauled myself up and began to shout for the guard.

I shouted for some time till I was hoarse and spent, but answer came there none. I had been abandoned in some holding cell, disregarded and forgotten.

I sat down again to contemplate my options. I listened closely, seeking to determine if there was activity above. I pressed my ear to the bars of my cell, hoping to discern through the conductive vibrations of the metal some clue as to my situation. All was disconcertingly silent. This worried me. A police station is seldom a quiet place, and after the events at the square, I would have expected intense activity as protestors were processed, complaints lodged, solicitors attended to their clients, and so on.

Further, where were my colleagues in this matter—where was Raffles? I gave myself no illusions about my importance in the scheme of things, but Raffles was loyal, and when I had failed to return to his side, he would surely have investigated and quickly learnt of my run-in with the rogue and brutish police. Unless . . .

My brain began to scan the possibilities, but quickly returned to the prime question: Where was Maud? If she was at liberty, she would have, knowing of my imprisonment, used every resource at her disposal to have me freed. Her family was of substance, she knew members of high society, she was apprised of our brief from Churchill, so I knew she would have found some route to Whitehall, some way to plead my case. Her absence made me fear the worst for her, remembering the other female protestor being so cruelly manhandled by the police, thrown whimpering to the ground, discarded like so much refuse. I would kill them if they had hurt her, I would kill them all. I would find that sergeant and tear his head from its very shoulders, I would feed his heart to him . . .

I ceased my raging. The truth was, whilst the proximate cause of any injury that had befallen Maud might have been the brutish policeman, the true cause was none other than myself. I had brought Maud into this dark and dangerous business, confided in her, sought her advice, and even sent her on the errand to make inquiries of the

Anti-Imperialist League. Doubtless this last was what had led to her joining them in their protest; her kind and gentle sensibilities were always aligned with the plight of the oppressed, and it was inevitable that they would enlist her to their cause and, in so doing, put her in the path of danger.

Danger from which I had been unable to protect her.

It was I, and not the officer, who was to blame for Maud's plight. This awful thought consumed me, and I collapsed in a self-pitying pile onto the soiled floor of my foul cell.

Having lost the capacity for physical action, I could at least exercise my mental facilities. Crunching systematically through all I knew, I came eventually to a hypothesis that would explain why I was in a police station empty of policemen and why my friends had not come for me: Maduka had attacked after all.

Whatever his grand plan had been, he had somehow been able to activate it, despite all our precautions. Sometime after I had been removed from the board in the back of a police wagon, Maduka had played his master move. He had unleashed whatever hell of violence and chaos he had engendered, and it was in dealing with this horror that Raffles and the police alike were currently engaged. The blood and foul on my clothes was caked and dry. I must have, at some point, lost consciousness—possibly for much of the night. So we were no longer dealing with the attack itself but with its aftermath.

What was the nature of the attack? Again, I worked through the options. We had searched the empty underground station and found nothing, no explosives, no poison gas nor chemical agents. We had prevented the king and his ministers from attending, so there was no chance of them coming to harm. Whatever the strength of his spy network, Maduka did not have access to a conventional army, and whatever the murderous prowess of the ape-reared Greystoke, he would be little match for a hundred armed policemen in the full light of day. What did that leave? What nature of attack would have done such damage as to still require the joint efforts of all the city's police the next morning?

I remembered Maduka's taste for the grotesque and the dramatic. How his killings were not simply brutal but also carefully designed provocations; symbols, written in blood.

So what would Maduka's message have been here? It would have to be a dramatic escalation, the pinnacle of all his efforts—something so horrific in scale and scope as to, by his lights, hold up the mirror to empire, show it its own evil face, and shame it into submission.

He was a fool, of course; empire felt no shame, but that would have been his thinking.

I considered the worst excesses of colonial history, the most horrific instances of the abuse of imperial power that Maduka might have sought to duplicate, to refract back at the British. It was not a short list. The massacre of Delhi in 1857, where British soldiers laid siege to the great city to end the first war of independence and slaughtered not only sepoys but more than fourteen hundred civilians, women and children; the siege of Ajnala of the same year, in my native Punjab, where the British summarily executed more than 280 soldiers, throwing their bodies into a well in the centre of the town, to rot and contaminate the water supply, as a reminder to the rest of the population to not get too brave again. This very year, not six months ago, in British East Africa, Major Richard Pope-Henessey had used a local tribal conflict as an excuse to unleash a hail of machine-gun fire on a village armed with clubs and spears, killing nearly two thousand, including untold numbers of children and non-combatants.

With a growing sense of horror, I realized how easy it would have been to replicate this last atrocity. Maduka would have no need of an army, simply a pair of rapid-fire Maxim guns set up on the roofs of the buildings surrounding the square. Perhaps of the National Gallery itself, directly above where Raffles and I had set up station. We had been so focussed on threats from below that we had not considered that the danger could come from above.

With the mass public squashed in close proximity, drunken revelry would quickly transform into panic as the rooftop-mounted guns opened indiscriminate fire on the crowd. Hundreds would have been killed in minutes, both from the hail of bullets and also by being trampled underfoot in the resulting panic.

Even if the police responded quickly and succeeded in killing or apprehending Maduka—and having come up against him myself, I knew this would not be easy—it would matter not, the damage would have been done. Hundreds or thousands would have been killed in the very centre of the empire, in the square that had been built as the ultimate emblem of British imperial power, their bodies floating in its marble fountains, their blood staining its stones. Their deaths leaving a perpetual scar on Britain's pride and its confidence.

The image loomed up before me in such specific vividness that I was convinced it had happened. No more imagining, but certainty. Maduka had done it. He had won.

Even if they killed or arrested him, by his lights, Maduka would have seen his work as done. He was not a man who struck me as being overly concerned with self-preservation. The cause was all for him, and he was ready to spend his life, as long as it fetched him a high enough price. This humiliation of Britain would serve his cause; the soft belly of the empire would have been exposed, its weakness manifest.

Across the globe, populations cowed into submission by a belief in the power of their oppressor would question the absolute nature of that power. Revolution long repressed would once again show its head. The guns would have sparked a flame that burnt the globe and birthed a new order.

I recoiled from this conclusion and the carnage it pointed to, but could see no other explanation. In that moment, I coined my own principle of inductive reasoning, a dark companion to Holmes' dictum: *When the evidence leads you to a horrific conclusion, the horror alone is not a reason to discount it.*

Once again, I shouted and railed, hoping to arouse some junior functionary left to man the station, and this time, after what felt like hours, my calls were answered. There was the sound of a key in the lock, and a young officer was in my cell. Still wary from my recent beating, I instinctively recoiled from him, but he looked horrified and threw up his hands in supplication. "Easy, sir. Let me help you."

With surprising gentleness, he supported me to my feet and then out of the cell, and into an adjoining washroom, where clean clothes and towels had been laid out.

"You should have everything you need here, sir. I'll be waiting outside if you require any further assistance."

Being called "sir" by someone wearing the same uniform sported by those who had very recently been engaged in beating me nearly to death was a cognitively disconcerting experience, but I was under no circumstances going to let this boy bathe me, so, despite the pain, I dismissed him and set about the agonizing business of cleaning and dressing both my wounds and myself, the overlap between the two being fairly extensive at this point.

This done, I called for the lad, who returned, bearing a crutch, and with its assistance, I made my way up a staircase and out a side exit of the Yard, into an alleyway, where, to my considerable relief, Raffles was waiting for me, smoking a cigarette and leaning nonchalantly on a hansom cab.

His manner was, well, it was quintessential Raffles—laid-back and relaxed, with an air of faint amusement, which led me to believe that the circumstances of the night had been awful indeed, given my friend's perverse relationship to the stimuli which, in normal men, would induce great tension and anxiety.

"Thank you, lad, I'll take it from here," he drawled in the manner of one acknowledging a hotel bell-hop who has provided assistance with a heavy bag. Offering me his shoulder, Raffles bundled me into the cab. He shut the door, and banged twice on the wall with his open palm, indicating to the driver that we were ready to proceed.

The cab quickly picked up speed, and I gathered my energies and turned to my friend—

"Tell me what has happened, what was the attack, what did we miss—how many are dead?"

Raffles looked at me quizzically. "My dear fellow, I think you perhaps are misunderstanding—"

"Please, AJ, do not patronize me. I am aware I must appear in poor condition, but I am quite myself, tell me the worst so we can go to work."

"There was an attack, Bunny. We were right about that. But it was not the one we anticipated."

"I feared as much. Maduka outsmarted us. Did he use Maxim guns? How many dead?"

"Maxim guns?! Bunny . . . Listen, dear boy, why don't you lean back for a moment and get some rest. We will be at the scene of the crime soon enough, and then you can put your poor battered noggin to work, figuring out all there is to figure, but till then, I'm not sure you are quite running at full steam."

I looked at my friend, annoyed to be so condescended to, but instead of going directly at the thing, I decided that I would pursue a different tact.

"Raffles. There is something else. A matter of some delicacy."

My friend's eyebrows were reassuring in their predictability.

"There was a young lady with me when the police took me. Did any harm come to her?"

Raffles smiled. "Ms. Adler is quite well, Bunny. Why, who do you imagine told me you were in the custody of the authorities?"

So prepared was I for the worst that this news caught me unaware, and I found myself involuntarily gasping for breath, with unexpected tears bursting forth. I could see Raffles was taken aback by my reaction, and not wishing to discuss it, I took his earlier counsel and sat back in my seat and gathered my energies for whatever was to come.

The cab made its way northward, passing Trafalgar Square and shooting rapidly up Park Lane. This was confusing to me, but I kept my peace, determined to figure out the solution myself rather than submit to more of Raffles' superior tone.

As we traversed Marylebone, I began to suspect that our destination was Baker Street, where in a set of rooms located at number 221b, Holmes lived and worked. Had Maduka unleashed his assassin against the detective? But we instead headed farther north on Great Portland Street, presently arriving at Regent's Park, and continued farther still.

I was increasingly confused; we were now out of central London, far from Trafalgar Square and from the densely inhabited thoroughfares that I had imagined were necessary prerequisites for an attack yielding mass casualties. Yet Raffles had told me we were going to the scene of the crime. The cab reached the Outer Circle of Regent's Park, where it came to a stop, and Raffles assisted me in disembarking.

"AJ, what has happened here?" I asked, baffled enough now to give up on my attempts to figure things out for myself. It was hard to imagine the bucolic splendour of the park being the site of a terrorist attack, yet we were parked amongst more than a dozen police carriages, and even as we disembarked, a garrison of cavalry on horseback arrived. "Bunny, trust me, this is something you want to see with your own eyes."

So, leaning on my friend Raffles' arm, I staggered into the park entrance to see what he wished to show me.

Raffles' sense for the dramatic had not been diminished by the crisis; he was correct, this was something it was necessary for me to see for myself. Not least because I would not have believed it had it been merely recounted to me.

The sports pitches of the park, flat and well manicured, had been transformed into savannah, inhabited by wild antelopes and a herd of wildebeest, grazing languidly. As I watched, a young lioness, a symphony of muscle and fang, emerged from the long grass and gave chase to the wildebeest, which scattered in panic. The lioness skulked away dejectedly. She was not yet a trained huntress, and had mistimed her approach.

I turned to Raffles in abject confusion and utter amazement, but he merely directed my attention to the duck pond which I saw was populated not merely with the usual flocks of *Anas platyrhynchos* but also by toucans, flamingos, and, most wondrously, by a family of hippopotamus, lounging magnificently in the shallow mud.

Taking my arm, Raffles indicated that I should follow him up onto the bridge, where we would have a clear view of the rose gardens. There, I observed a family of giraffes, elegant and absurd in equal measure, grazing peacefully and ignoring the collection of policemen attempting to corral them.

This was chaos, certainly. Just not the chaos I had expected.

"Come on, Bunny," said Raffles, "time to go to the zoo. If you're lucky, I'll get you a Hokey Pokey."

～

On the short final leg of our journey, Raffles confirmed that no attack at Trafalgar Square had taken place. The only injuries at the square had been those resulting from the fracas between the police and the Anti-Imperial League protestors. That is to say, the fight I had found myself in the middle of. Instead, it appeared, Maduka had turned his attention to the thirty-six acres of Regent's Park that housed the nation's store of exotic animals: the zoo.

We reached the leafy main entrance to the Zoological Society of London, at the northeast corner of Regent's Park, and with a positive spring in his step, Raffles led the way in. He had, in this moment, apparently confused his role for that of a docent, and embarked cheerfully on a brief lecture reminding me that the zoo had been founded, some eighty years ago, by his great-grand-uncle Sir Stamford Raffles, who, amongst his many other exploits, had embarked on an unauthorized invasion of Java at the age of thirty and went on to found the colony of Singapore. That Sir Stamford, a man quite prepared to pilfer entire nations from their inhabitants, was the ancestor of the gentleman thief, AJ Raffles served, to my mind, as compelling evidence of Darwin's theory of inheritable traits.

As we passed the inner gates, it became clear that the zoo had been closed to the general public, and a group of police was present, working in strange collaboration with the resident zoologists and animal keepers.

"Here's the very fellow to tell us all about it, unless I am very much mistaken," commented Raffles, and I looked to where he was indicating, to see Lestrade deep in conversation with an elderly man, skinny and tall, in a three-piece tweed suit, with a wild mop of white hair, and glasses perched uncertainly at the end of a long, beak-like nose. The overall impression was of an individual who, whilst technically human, seemed to be, for the most part, some variety of great bird, an ostrich such as I had encountered in the Transvaal, or perhaps the famed emu of Australia, which I had only seen in illustrations.

"Ah, Raffles, you found your . . . friend. Mr. Singh, I trust you will accept my apologies for the . . . overenthusiasm of some of my men. Trust me when I say those responsible for your . . . accidental incarceration have been given firm reprimands. Most firm."

I waved away Lestrade's empty protestations, and turned my attention to his ornithological companion—

"This is Dr. Peter Straker," said Lestrade, making introductions. "He is the secretary of the Zoological Society of London. Dr. Straker, may I introduce Mr. Raffles and Mr. Singh. You may speak freely before them, they are, um, assisting me in this matter."

Dr. Straker inspected us through his glasses with the air of a scientist examining specimens for dissection. I had no time for this—so bluntly put the question to him.

"Straker, what has happened to your zoo?"

"Ah, well, it is most distressing, gentlemen. Most distressing indeed. Last night, late in the after-hours, when the zoo was closed to the public and all but the nocturnal animals were asleep, a group of criminals broke into the zoo compound, overpowered the solitary nightwatchman, and obtained access to the animal enclosures, and proceeded with speed and thoroughness to release all the animals into the park."

"All of them?"

"Mr. . . . ah . . . Singh, is it? Mr. Singh, we house here within our walls the most lethal, vicious predators, the most poisonous snakes, the most unpredictable, dangerous, and powerful of wild creatures. Each of them is housed in an enclosure specially designed to keep them contained and keep our visitors safe from them. It is on these animals, principally, that the saboteurs first focussed their attention. But over the course of the night, yes, they succeeded in releasing very nearly all our specimens."

Dr. Straker proceeded to take us on a walking tour of the zoo, pointing out one empty enclosure after another; there was a vast variety in their design and size. Some were small glass boxes, designed for spiders or snakes; others were large, naturalistic enclosures designed to replicate, for example, a watering hole in the Indian jungle. They all had two things in common— their locks had been forced, and they were entirely empty.

The tour culminated in the childishly named "Monkey House," a large space with tall trees and climbing frames that, until recently, had housed the zoo's collections of primates, including, the zookeeper informed us, a family of mountain gorillas from the Congo Basin. The enclosure now was empty; the lock had been forced, and the animals had escaped. As the erudite naturalist launched into a monologue about the social habits of the missing apes, I turned my focus on an examination of their erstwhile cell.

My attention was drawn to something small, hard, and metallic, and singularly out of place, on the floor. I bent to retrieve it—no one noticed me do so—and I slipped the item into my pocket to inspect more closely later.

That done, I was able to turn my attention back to Dr. Straker, who had gestured for us to come into a secondary chamber, this one a viewing atrium of sorts, enclosed in glass to allow visitors to congregate and see the animals up close. On the wall of this space, positioned for maximum visibility, had been scrawled, in large letters of red paint, a distinctively human slogan that would the next day be cited on the front page of every newspaper and periodical across the globe:

UNTIL WE ARE ALL FREE, WE ARE NONE OF US FREE.

CHAPTER 15

A Study in Perspective

Under-Secretary Churchill was in an ebullient, expansive mood, sitting back behind his huge desk and placing his legs up on its polished surface. "A job well done, lads! We saw the blighter off—this Maduka fellow was left with nothing to do, no one to strike, so he contented himself with this rather mawkish practical jape!"

It was three days after the events at Trafalgar Square and the London Zoo, and we had been summoned once again to the Colonial Office to give an account of our failures, or so I thought. As it happened, Churchill had decided to take the outcome as a success and was celebrating. He had simultaneous glasses of whiskey and champagne on the go and seemed to think he was presiding over a celebration rather than a council of war.

I looked round the room, hoping that one of the others would present an alternative point of view, but Raffles was smiling widely and helping himself to a tumbler of Churchill's whiskey, whilst Lestrade was lighting a cigar. Only Dr. Watson sat here alone, as Holmes had been unable to attend the meeting, looking uncomfortable and inspecting his shoes.

Clearing my throat, I spoke my piece, or tried: "Under-Secretary, I think it is perhaps rather more complicated than that—"

"Complicated? Nonsense! Your terrible villain was made to feel like a school bully left with no one to hit! Hah! A few displaced orangutans, hardly a fatal blow to our way of life! He's nothing but a busted flush now. We'll find him eventually, his likeness has been circulated to all of Lestrade's men, they will hunt him down, him and the poor Greystoke lad he's brainwashed to his cause, but they present no threat anymore. They are yesterday's problem. Accept the gratitude of His Majesty's government, Mr. Singh, for your part in this matter. After all, you wouldn't want to be an Indian giver, would you? Hah! Hah!"

I suppressed both my annoyance and the need to point out to this infuriating man-child that the phrase "Indian giver" derived not from any behaviour of my people, but rather from the misunderstandings that arose around property rights and ownership between Europeans and the indigenous tribes of the Americas, but I correctly surmised that such an anthropological and etymological lesson would not have been welcomed.

I turned to Watson for support. "Dr. Watson, what have you and Mr. Holmes to say on this matter? Is it his opinion, having reviewed all the evidence presented, that the danger has passed? Is that why he is not in attendance?"

Watson adjusted his glasses and spoke in careful and measured tones. "Holmes regrets that he could not be here in person today. He is currently engaged in a delicate matter involving one of the foremost families of Liechtenstein, but he did send a telegram this morning in which he said it was just as well to regard the matter as closed."

"Hah! There you have it!" exclaimed Churchill, exhaling a skyscape worth of blue smoke. "The Great Detective agrees with me, we are vindicated!"

~

Later, when we were in the street, waiting for cabs to arrive, I asked Watson if that was really Sherlock's final word on the matter. He reached into his pocket and pulled out a telegram—he handed it to me. It read in full as follows:

> CHURCHILL WISHES FOR THE MATTER TO BE CONCLUDED *STOP* LITTLE POINT IN ARGUMENT *STOP* THE DOWNSIDE OF GOVERNMENT WORK IS THE NATURE OF THE CLIENT *STOP* TELL BALVINDER TO *STOP*

I handed the missive to Raffles, who glanced at it and laughed his agreement. "The trouble with these problems of national security, Bunny, is people tend to take them so frightfully seriously. There's much more fun in a spot of everyday jewel theft than there is the hunt for a terrorist, no matter which way you look at the thing!"

This all seemed terribly wrong to me, but at that moment, Raffles' cab arrived and he offered to drop Dr. Watson off, and I was left alone with my misgivings.

I decided to do as I always do when my mind is overburdened with worries. I would walk. So, leaning heavily on my stick, for my injuries were still healing, and moving a little more slowly than was my usual habit, I set out into the streets of the capital.

I walked for perhaps fifteen minutes, but the process did not provide me with its usual solace. The pain in my side and general fatigue proved distracting, and my mind remained frustratingly clouded. I decided to take a break at a street bench, to catch my breath and gather my thoughts. As I sat, I felt something hard in my back pocket, and reaching in, I discovered the metallic object that I had picked up from the floor of the gorilla enclosure. It had sat in my pants, quite forgotten and uninspected, these past few days, and I looked at it carefully now.

It was a single bullet. Not a casing, this bullet had not been fired, it was not spent. It was a round of live ammunition that had been somehow dropped on the floor of the monkey house. I looked at it, my tired brain determined to unpick this clue.

The bullet was large, this was not ammunition for a handgun, it was both of greater calibre and more than twice the length. I had seen such rounds before, but it took me a moment to identify it. It was a .303—of the nature used in Maxim guns. The rapid-fire, self-acting, belt-fed machine guns that the British Army deployed when they wished to dominate a battleground—or massacre protestors. The very gun that I had deduced that Maduka might unleash on the revellers at Trafalgar Square . . .

I looked at the bullet, willing it to tell me its story, and slowly, painfully, it became clear to me that it was not a clue but a communiqué. A message left for me by Maduka. He was telling me that he *could* have struck in fire and horror. That my deductions had been correct, that he had the armaments at the ready, that his Maxim guns had been poised and aimed. That he had intended to strike British civilians in the same way that British troops routinely massacred Indian and African innocents. That he could have killed thousands . . . and that he had . . . what?

Been deterred by the police presence?

Shown mercy?

Chosen.

He had chosen not to open fire. Not out of mercy but as a tactical decision. He had decided at the final hurdle to do things differently. The bullet had been left to send me the message that Maduka was evolving his methodology from direct warfare to a more subtle and insidious approach. More, it was telling me that he was—horror of horrors—*taking my advice*. I had told him that to unleash fire would only result in him damning those for whom he claimed to act to eternal flames. What had he said to me—that we should "build a better machine." Was London Zoo the first step in this new endeavour?

A friendly and familiar voice interrupted my train of thought: "That's a pretty trinket, Mr. Balvin-*daa!*" I looked up into the beaming face of young Wiggins, chief of Holmes' Irregulars, who had somehow found me here in my moment of deductive reasoning and was grinning at me. I put the bullet away hurriedly, and rearranged my features into something I hoped resembled an urbane demeanour.

In truth, I was delighted to see him. Wiggins' appearance surely meant that Holmes had reconsidered and that we were to be called back into action, and this feeling filled me with immediate relief; I was not to be alone in this matter.

"Ah, Wiggins! Good to see you, lad. What message do you have for me from Watson, or are you sent perhaps from Holmes himself? Does the detective require a meeting?"

The lad sat himself down next to me, and I noticed that he was rather better dressed than the last time we had met. You would not call him a street Arab now, though his accent remained resolutely working class, he wore a well-cut suit, albeit in rather a garish pattern.

"Mr. Holmes ain't the only game in town, Mr. Bal," he whispered to me confidentially. "Truth is, he scarcely uses us Irregulars anymore. Much of his business is overseas these days. But that's alright. You see, we have somewhat *diversified*. It doesn't pay to rely too heavily on a solitary client, you see."

I didn't take his meaning at first. But then, reaching into his newly purchased waistcoat, he pulled out between his dirty fingers, a bullet to match my own, another solitary .303, long and elegant and terrible.

He placed it on the bench between us.

"Black Michael says he's ready to talk whenever you are, sir. Ready and willing. Please do pass on my compliments to your good lady."

~

In the days and weeks that followed, I was left with the uncomfortable question of what to do with myself.

I saw less and less of Raffles. There had been no specific break or incident to diminish the closeness of our bond, I had not acted in any way on Dr. Watson's warning, but Raffles' way of life, previously so glamorous and appealing to me, was no longer of interest. I no longer felt the draw of the chase, and was no longer willing to participate in his "adventures." I did not tell him of my visit from Wiggins, or what I feared it might portend. Somehow I no longer trusted him to do the right thing with such confidences.

Indeed, I had shared the story with no one, not even Maud. Quite the opposite, I did everything I could to put the encounter from my own mind, so unwilling and unprepared was I to engage with the implications of it.

I focussed my attention instead on planning the next stages of my own professional career. I passed my bar exams and became a pupil barrister, called to the Inns of Court and entitled to argue, whilst decked out in wig and gown, cases before even more impressively wigged and gowned judges, and generally bring my abilities to the service of law and justice.

The question facing me was a simple but confounding one: Where should I do so, and who should I seek as my clients?

My previous plan, as promised to my father, had been to return home to Punjab and take the local legal exams and set up a practice there. That still seemed a noble ambition, but I could not ignore that there was much about London that remained appealing to me, and that returning so soon to India was not a course that generated excitement in me.

The alternative was to set up a practice here, in partnership with Sylvester and a few of our other classmates of colonial persuasion. We thought that perhaps the fast-growing immigrant population of the city, striving to navigate building new lives and new businesses in an unfamiliar context, would benefit from the services of a law chamber intrinsically sympathetic to the challenges of being a foreigner living under Britain's laws.

The advantages of this second course of action were many, but high amongst them was . . . Maud.

～

"Bal, Bal! Quick—come!"

I was in my little nook of a library, reading the latest pamphlet from the Anti-Imperialist League of America when Maud's cry roused me from my contemplations, and I made it up the stairs quickly, two at a time, fearing some danger had come into our home.

I reached the bedroom to find Maud perched precariously on a three-legged stool taken from our little galley kitchen, attempting to hang an oversized oil painting above the bed. My relief at the absence of any external threat was short-lived, because as I entered, she lost her battle with gravity and came tumbling down. I ran to arrest her fall, but only succeeded in knocking into her in midair, and we found ourselves falling in a tangle atop the sheets of the bed.

"Oof—you great lump, that hurt," she complained, rather unfairly, I felt.

"I was saving you!" I objected.

"I don't need saving, Bal. I just needed help with the picture."

I turned to her, our faces only inches apart on the cool sheets, and in a tone most serious that I hoped befitted my status as the head of a modern London household, spoke as follows: "Decoration is not my domain. As master of the house, I have high concerns, and I defer to you on such matters."

She nodded sagely. "Of course, my lord and master, I apologize for disturbing your terribly important work." And so fetching was her expression as she said it, so meek and submissive, that I failed to notice the pillow she had gathered in her hands which she proceeded to place over my face as, with lightning moves much like a cat's, she straddled me with her knees around my neck, pinning the pillow in place and depriving me of both oxygen and movement.

"Apologize, Balvinder Singh, or I'll sit here till you are quite dead."

Unable to speak and with my face covered, I could only signal my surrender with my arms, but eventually she took my meaning, and removed the pillow, though she remained seated atop me, her dress having risen above her knees from our struggles, the weight of her firm derrière on my chest making me thankful that my ribs had healed.

"You have learnt your lesson?" she inquired.

"I believe you have made your point," I said, a little sulkily. "Will you release me now?"

"Do you want me to?" she asked, her tone changing slightly, and I saw that her cheeks were red and her chest swelling.

"This is not the most comfortable of positions for me," I hazarded, sensing that the mood was shifting, but not yet certain of its direction of travel.

"Perhaps not for you. But from my perspective, it is not without its convenient applications," she commented and inched herself forward slowly till my head was covered by the hem of her dress and I was given access to all the wonders within.

~

So Maud and I had begun to build a life together and to settle into a pattern, one both domestic and routine, and yet none the less delightful for that. Indeed, the wonder and joy that my association with her brought to my everyday life seemed to me almost magical. We each spent our days absorbed in our respective practices, her of music, me of the law, then in the evenings, we came together in my rooms, and recounted to each other the toils and triumphs of our days, each individual failure salved, each triumph made sweeter, by the simple process of being shared.

Looking back, it was this joy, so unexpected and so richly treasured, that I was fighting to preserve. That allowed me to put the past events, the message of the bullet and Wiggin's visit, far from my mind. I willed the world of politics and empire and imperialism and terrorism away from our little safe harbour, determined to convince myself that it was over, that it no longer concerned Maud and I, that we had done our duty and could now retreat and live normal and good lives.

Beyond the narrow confines of our home, however, ripples were spreading. I received letters from friends and family in India, asking me what I made of "the zoo matter." Maud's cousin Irene reported that American society was talking of little else, some wits comparing the incident with that of the Boston Tea Party, a symbolic declaration of defiance that foreshadowed a future conflict.

The Anti-Imperialist League, for its part, was delighted and wasted no time in publishing a pamphlet, which many suspected to be written by Mark Twain himself, satirizing the ineptitude of the British establishment in allowing the "Grand Animal Escape" to take place:

> *If the greatest empire the world has ever seen cannot even keep*
> *its apes and lions safe in their menagerie, constrained with a*
> *solid padlock, then I for one begin to doubt its housekeeping.*
> *If the crocodiles swim free, surely the colonies cannot be far*
> *behind? For shame—for shame! Ye mighty lords and ladies,*
> *mind your knitting else you lose the yarn.*

We received these pamphlets because Maud was now not only a supporter but a card-carrying member and, with a seat on the leadership committee of the London branch of the league, in charge of "political outreach," which meant that far from being an innocent bystander, she had, in fact, masterminded the protest at the Trafalgar Square celebrations which had ultimately resulted in her being placed in such danger.

I had attempted to chastise her for her recklessness, but when she pointed out that all she had done was engage in a little peaceful protest, whilst I had broken into the headquarters of our foes, been strapped to a chair, and beaten almost to death by a giant pirate and his vicious subhuman pet, I was forced to concede that recklessness was a relative concept and that I was ill placed to advise her on this matter without opening myself up for accusations of hypocrisy.

Hypocrisy, I was fast discovering, was the sin that Maud loathed above all others. "It is the sin of the enemy," she said. "It is the most English of all sins, and we will not have it rear its ugly head between us."

So, life progressed, the thrill of high adventure being gradually replaced by the smaller but no less meaningful drama of quotidian existence, and gradually enough time had passed that entire days would go by when I thought not once of Michael Maduka and entire nights when my dreams were free from the looming spectre of the cursed youth in his borrowed skins. On an intellectual level, I knew they were still out there somewhere, and I feared their next move, but I had also come to believe that my role in that grand drama had come to an end. I had played my small part, done what I could, and now the world would turn on without me. Whatever Maduka was planning, it was no longer my business, no longer my problem.

Which, in the predictable arc of hubris and nemesis, by the unavoidable rules of Karma, was when he, frustrated by waiting, came for me.

CHAPTER 16

The Difference Engine

Whilst I am schooled in the traditions of my people, and my father and mother are people of abiding faith, I confess that I had by this point in my life grown increasingly lapsed in my practice of religion.

In part, this was of necessity—London had no *gurdwaras* in which I could worship—but if I am to speak honestly, the truth is that my understandings of the workings of the world had so been impacted by my recent experiences that I now struggled to find space in my conception of the cosmos to accommodate Onkaar, the singular Sikh god, still less the ineffable Christian trinity.

On the whole, this absence was not a source of disquiet to me. My nature has always been practical, and whatever the metaphysical benefits of religion to the masses, God himself has never been of much use to me, and so I was content to bumble along without him.

Until, that is, approximately six months after the Trafalgar centenary, in the spring of 1906, when Maud and I began to discuss the specifics of formalizing our union, that is to say, when we began to consider entering into the state of holy matrimony.

It was I who first brought the matter up; knowing that Maud had been raised in the Catholic faith, I feared that our current bohemian arrangements would be upsetting to her family. Whilst she spoke little of her parents, who I understood lived still in Dublin, it seemed to me impossible that we could continue as we were indefinitely, and I had little desire to be responsible for any rift between her and her God-fearing kin.

Accordingly, I set about making inquiries as to what it would take for us to be married in the Catholic Church, and these inquiries led me on that fateful Thursday afternoon, to the newly constructed edifice of Westminster Cathedral.

The building—which rejoices in the formal name The Cathedral of the Most Precious Blood—had only recently been completed a few years prior. It is a looming edifice in the Byzantine tradition, constructed largely of red brick. To my eye, it lacks the elegance and sweeping grandeur of, say, St. Paul's, and there is something about the repeating pattern of brickwork that recalls a municipal building, an academy or barracks, rather than a house of worship.

These were not my primary concerns, however, as I ascended the steps and entered the church, seeking a priest with whom to discuss my predicament. I knew Catholic doctrine to be exacting, and I was apprehensive that they would refuse to even discuss the marriage of a non-practicing Sikh man and a lapsed Catholic woman, currently living in delicious sin. I had constructed an alternative version of the facts to supply to the priest, but no matter how much gloss I placed on events, that I was a Sikh was as undeniable as the, archetypically Punjabi, nose on my face. I would have to decide if I was ready to undergo a baptism in order to give Maud the wedding ceremony she deserved. On the face of it, trading one imaginary god for another should not have been an issue for me, but something deeper than rationality held me back, the strange sense that by swearing allegiance to the blood of Christ, I would be betraying my own blood.

A choir was singing as I entered, and the soothing lilt of their voices combined with the cool interior air was both welcoming and refreshing. I decided to sit in a pew for a moment, to gather my thoughts and calm my spirit.

They finished the hymn they had been working on, and some discussion took place between the choristers and the choirmaster. I could not hear the details, but they appeared to be debating what to practice next. Eventually a consensus was reached, and the organist struck up a tune. One that I, unschooled as I am in Christian liturgy and music, was surprised to immediately recognize, the tempo slow but regular, like the beat of a marching drum.

> *When Britain first, at Heaven's command,*
> *Arose from out the azure main;*
> *This was the charter of the land,*
> *And guardian angels sang this strain:*

The choir taking the place of the guardian angels, their voices soared into the triumphalist, militaristic chorus:

> *Rule, Britannia! Britannia, rule the waves!*
> *Britons never, never, never ever will be slaves.*

I was confused. "Rule, Britannia!" is not a religious song, and certainly not part of any Catholic liturgy. I did not understand how this nationalistic, imperialistic anthem was being sung in a house of worship. Unheeding of my unspoken objections, the choir thundered cheerfully into the second verse:

> *The nations, not so blest as thee,*
> *Must in their turns to tyrants fall;*
> *While thou shalt flourish great and free,*
> *The dread and envy of them all.*

I stood up, suddenly angry. I wished to confront the choirmaster for permitting this atrocity, for sullying the sacred space with this paean to persecution and oppression, for enlisting these beautiful children with their soaring voices as a tool of imperial propaganda. The lyrics were rank, full of lies, each rhyme a hypocritical offence. Britons would never be slaves? But the empire had been built on the slave trade, on the broken backs of those the British enslaved and sold. The "tyrants" to which so many nations had fallen were the British monarch and their agents. Men like Lord Randolph Churchill and his damned son.

I felt most keenly the final line: *The dread and envy of them all.* This spoke to my soul. I hated the British for their arrogance, their cruelty, their race-based prejudice, and most of all for their incuriosity about the world they had conquered. At the same time, I was envious of all they had and all they were. I loved their language, their literature, their laws—their theatre, their clubs, their cricket—I loved it all. I wished to live here, in London, and love Maud and be a man . . . but I could never be an Englishman.

The song taunted me, taunted my very sense of myself. All that I had endured in recent months: the horror of Maduka's crimes but also the cool confidence of his justification, all this and all the events of my life, now swirled around within me like some bitter concoction. I felt sick and stood, my boots echoing against the hard wood of the pew. The sound drew the attention of some in the choir, who turned towards me, singing still, giving the impression that they were singing this cursed tune directly *at* me:

Rule, Britannia! Britannia rules the waves!

I wished to scream. Or at least to march up to the choir and demand an explanation.

I hesitated. I was here as a supplicant. A heathen, seeking blessing for my union with a Catholic daughter of Christ. Any sympathy which I might hope to elicit from the priest would be surely squandered if I made a scene now. So I stood, frozen in the aisle, locked in indecision. To go forward, or to go back? Neither seemed a viable option.

Which is when a voice deep and smooth and familiar spoke from behind: "It is true what they say, then, the Devil does have all the best tunes."

I spun around, tensing my body for battle, knowing that the assault I had feared all these long months was now upon me. Maduka had returned, and he had come for me . . .

The only inhabitant of the pews behind me was an elderly pauper woman who appeared to have entered the cathedral mainly to get some sleep, and was currently snoring, roughly in time to the music.

Surely, I had not imagined it?

I slipped out of the aisle, and, ignoring the choirmaster's call of "Excuse me—is everything all right?" I rushed to the main door and looked out. The sounds and smell of the spring day hit me; any trace of the cathedral's cool calm was expunged. I looked around wildly, and saw the door to the adjacent bell-tower, the spiraling campanile, swing shut. There!

I ran to it, slamming the door open—the chamber was small, housing only a spiral staircase that ascended steeply—I could hear foot treads above me. Maduka! At last, my second chance had arrived. I was unarmed, and so I cast around in vain for something to use as a weapon, but short of a thick hymnal, nothing afforded itself. Empty-handed, I ascended the stairs as quietly as I could, keeping alert to the slightest sound from above.

The staircase wound upwards with the relentlessness of a corkscrew. It was narrow and precarious. I marvelled that a man of Maduka's bulk had even fitted through it, but then I remembered his lightness on his feet. There must have been more than three hundred steps, and I was out of breath by the time I reached the top. The great bell loomed before me, occupying nearly all the room, but there was a narrow corridor circling it and leading to a viewing gallery: an even narrower walkway that encircled the bell dome.

Knowing I was putting myself in precarious danger, I stepped out onto the gallery. The wind and the view hit me like two simultaneous slaps to the face. The air, cool, sharp, but so strong as to be nearly violent. There had been no such wind on the ground below, but here, high above, it had the force of a gale. I instinctively reached for the railing to steady myself, but it was the view that startled even more. I had never been this high above London, and in a different context, I would have stopped and stared, so exhilarating was it to see the city laid out before me in all its teeming glory.

"It is magnificent, isn't it? This cruel, terrible, beautiful city?"

Maduka stood perhaps ten feet to my left. His manner was casual, his dress, as ever, immaculate, a cross-hatched suit in deep burgundy and a fine felt hat, kid-skin brown gloves, and highly polished shoes. He acknowledged me with a sideways nod, but kept his eyes fixed on the horizon.

"Why are you here?" I demanded, aware that it was an inadequate opener, but suddenly unclear of my role in this encounter.

"Is the view not reason enough?" He laughed, his deep, rolling laugh carrying on the wind. "I am here to see you, of course, Balvinder. You would not come to me, so like Mohamet before me, if I may be permitted an Islamist metaphor within this Christian structure, I have come to you. Our last conversation ended so abruptly, I apologize for that. I have a terrible temper, it is a flaw which I seek to remedy, but you gave me much to think upon."

I had no response to that, so putting my hand in my waistcoat pocket, I pulled out the little metal canister I had been carrying around with me these last few months. The bullet I had found on the floor of the monkey cage. I held it before him, between finger and thumb.

"You could have killed hundreds. Why didn't you?"

"You had removed the only ones worth killing from the equation. A decapitation strike was a worthy endeavour, to take out the king and the cabinet, that was the plan. But you and your Churchill, you took that move off the board; well played, I say. Perhaps there was a time when I would have gone ahead, unleashed indiscriminate hell in the manner of the British, killed all those drunken, ignorant innocents, let London weep at their loss. Yet . . . to win the long game, it is necessary not to move intemperately. As I say, I am learning to control my temper."

I spat my reply at him with a disgust I did not truly feel: "And the bullet left behind to inform us of your magnanimity. Perhaps they'll give you a medal before they hang you." He laughed at this. I seemed to have lost none of my ability to amuse him, for what good that might do me.

Throughout this exchange, I had been edging closer to Maduka, hoping to find some advantage, some position from which I could overpower him, take him captive. I was not hopeful of this approach, knowing the raw power of the man, and the perilous perch we both occupied. The most likely outcome of any sudden struggle was that we would both fall off the tower, to our certain death on the stones far below. So certain was I of the threat this man posed to the world, however, that in that moment, I was prepared to regard such an outcome as a qualified success; if I was to die, at least I might take him with me. I spoke again, seeking to keep him distracted, raising my voice over the screaming wind.

"And the liberation of the animals, what function did that serve?"

"Why don't you tell me, Balvinder? I know you've been thinking about it."

He was right, of course; indeed, for weeks, I had thought about little else.

"The symbolism is clear enough. You described yourself as a freedom fighter, so you dispense freedom to all, even to dumb animals. But it was more than that, the nature of the crime was carefully chosen. Policemen in helmets chasing down giraffes in a royal park, animals from every continent unleashed on the capital. Chaos and confusion and comedy in equal measure. You made authority a laughing stock. You caused the empire itself to look ridiculous, laughable, a circus sideshow. We prevented you from damaging the apparatus of empire, so instead you damaged the idea of it."

I was close enough to spring now. I tensed myself. He was larger than I, heavier by far, but if I could exploit the element of surprise, then perhaps . . .

"Before you attempt anything heroically stupid, Balvinder, perhaps look around you?"

So much for surprise. I followed where he indicated, looking up at the dome of the tower looming above us. At first, I saw nothing, but then, at its very apex, sitting cross-legged, completely relaxed as if he were sitting on a Persian rug in his own living room, was the young Lord Greystoke, dressed in his customary rags and skins. He waved at me, smiling cheekily, and indicated with a nod of his head that I should look at the rooftops behind me; turning, I did so, only to be confronted with the incongruous vision of three large gorillas, lolling, relaxed, on the opposite side of the roof. I gawped at them for a minute as they regarded me, supremely indifferent to my quandary.

"The boy and his cousins would be on you long before you would be on me. Besides—I didn't come here to fight you, Balvinder."

I backed a few steps away from him and held my palms up in surrender. I felt an unexpected surge of relief that I would not be required to make the ultimate sacrifice this day. That I would possibly still return to Maud that evening with another tale to tell, another day to share. Some part of my brain was already relishing the surprise on her face when I told her of the gorillas on the roofs. But to see that look, I would have to navigate this moment. "Why are you here, Maduka?"

"Bal—you told me once that empire was a machine. An engine, do you remember?"

I nodded, uncertain where this was going.

"I have thought about that statement deeply and have come to believe that you are correct, but that you were insufficiently precise."

"How so?"

"You know of Professor Babbage and his genius strumpet Ada Lovelace?"

I was aware, of course, of Charles Babbage, the Cambridge mathematician and eccentric inventor, who had left behind some dozen or more unfinished calculating machines about which he had made great but unsubstantiated claims, and I was dimly aware that Lord Byron's daughter, the Countess Lovelace, had some association with the man—but I struggled to see their relevance to this conversation, and said as much.

"You should read the lady's paper on the Analytical Engine and the Difference Engine," he said, his tone turning professorial. At this point, receiving a lecture on theoretical mathematics from a terrorist, at the top of a bell-tower with an audience of great apes, was beginning to feel like an ordinary way to spend an afternoon.

"She claims that Babbage succeeded in the design of two computational machines capable of great feats. The simpler one, the Difference Engine, came first, designed to perform mathematical calculations. Addition, subtraction, multiplication, and the like. This is a brute of a machine; it can perform these functions with greater power and precision than the human mind, but it can *only* do those things. It runs on fixed tracks, unalterable in its direction and function, it repeats itself over and over and over again.

"But the Analytical Engine! This was Babbage's true breakthrough. The good countess claims it to be a machine capable of general application, of solving different categories of problems, subject only to the ingenuity of its operator. She sets forth an elaborate series of equations whereby she is giving the machine a set of instructions, and by so instructing it, she alters its purpose. The more subtle and sophisticated the instructions, the more sophisticated the functioning of the machine. Such a machine does not need to be destroyed; it can instead be re . . . repurposed. Reprogrammed, if you will. The more sophisticated the instructor, the more one can bend the machine to one's design."

I began to dimly perceive what Maduka's meaning was. My head spun with the implications, and I grasped the guide-rail tightly, for to be dizzy at this height was a dangerous matter.

"Do you think the engine of empire susceptible to such . . . reprogramming? Your assault on the zoo was a first attempt in this endeavour?"

"A crude beginning. But a beginning nonetheless. It was you who suggested we needed to build a better machine. Perhaps we can simply . . . remake the one we have to behave differently?"

I considered this; the metaphor was an elegant one and accorded with my own speculations as to the true import of the zoo attack, but I needed to fully understand what was being proposed.

"And you are committing to this as your new course of action? Instead of murder and terror, you are proposing, what, a programme of propaganda? A campaign of trickery?"

Michael shook his head sadly, and stared out across the London skyline.

"We are engaged in war, Balvinder, and there is no war without death. If I am required to be a monster, I will not hesitate. We fight against a brutal, implacable enemy, and we will need every tool at our disposal. My campaign of violence will continue when it is needed, but I see now that if we fight only on that singular front, we will not win.

"In soldiers and muskets, we are outnumbered and outarmed. But we are also losing in the battle of sentiment. You have seen yourself, the enemy has all the best songs, the best poets, the best stories. From 'Rule, Britannia!' to that propagandist Kipling, empire is clad in mythology that makes it inevitable and heaven-sent. We need to create a change in . . . context. A change in the way both the oppressed and the oppressor perceive themselves, and each other.

"To achieve that end, I will need a new operative. I have no illusions about myself, Balvinder; I am a crude object. I am someone who destroys, not a creator of what is to come next. What is needed is someone capable of the act of invention, a subtle pen, a weaver of words and ideas. Our cause requires a hero who can tell a different story of the empire to counter the ones it tells. Someone who can replumb the imperial engine so that it will eat itself."

He paused, and I found myself, in equal parts, anticipating and fearing his next words, like a lover of the Marquis de Sade, wishing to be beaten to find pleasure in it.

"I told you, Balvinder. You are not my enemy. You are my secret weapon."

I wished to protest, but I stood there, silent.

"You have studied their laws, their stories, their customs. You have moved amongst them, from the high to the low. You have access to their most trusted institutions and their finest families. You know how they think, how they love, how they hate. You have stolen from them before, used their trust against them, but now you will do so for a far greater cause, not for the petty trinkets that so delight your erstwhile friend Raffles, but for real stakes. For the great game, the only one worth playing. We will defeat the empire not with brutality but with true power. The power to shape the story. I asked you once before, and you rejected me. I will only ask this one more time. Are you with me?"

I looked at the man they used to call Black Michael, his face strong and passionate, his words clear and articulate. He waited for me to react. Only moments earlier, I had been willing to sacrifice my life to end his, I considered him a lunatic murderer, a monster to be captured or destroyed . . .

"What is it you ask of me?"

"Everything. You would risk everything. Forsake everything, sacrifice everything—and everyone. Your life, your regular life, would become a façade, a performance to distract from your true work. Beneath it all, your purpose must remain hidden, a life in service of the cause. What we must do will take time. Years, perhaps even decades. The leviathan will not alter course quickly, but alter it will, under the sustained efforts of men such as ourselves. If you dedicate your life to this great calling, your children may be born into a better world. A world free of hegemonic power, and the brutality that comes when a petty island people believe themselves to be the inheritors of the earth."

I turned away from him, focussed my eyes on the vastness of London spread out before us, this extraordinary vibrant, cruel, wondrous, teeming city from which so much of the world was ruled, and to which so much of the world's riches accrued.

I looked at the city as a whole, and I let my imagination fly over it. I saw pathways of possibility, branching and looping in a mad dance. I saw Maud, rehearsing a raga in a room in the Royal Albert Hall, perhaps some part of her looking forward to the dinner we would share together. I saw Winston Churchill, in his chambers at Whitehall, dreaming of the greatness of England and his own greatness, making decisions that would affect the lives of untold millions. I saw Sylvester and my colleagues in our little chambers at Lincoln's Inn, sitting in an empty, client-free office, awaiting white clients who would never come and brown clients who could never pay.

I saw Sherlock in his rooms, injecting himself with his 7 percent solution of cocaine, despairing at the stupidity and mundanity of evil and good alike.

I let my mind's eye travel even further afield: I thought of my grandmother playing the sitar and of my parents in the Punjab, of their early pride in me and their disappointment in the life I had chosen. I thought of the children massacred by British soldiers for no reason other than they stood in the way of the machine.

I thought of my foolishness in thinking Maud and I might be married, my stupidity in imagining that we might have children of our own—ignoring that they would be half-breeds, creatures caught between culture and nations, accepted by none, cursing their parents for bringing them into being. I felt the weight of the sergeant's nightstick against my skull, and the coldness of Raffles' condescension.

I heard the song rise from below:

The dread and envy of them all.

I turned away from the view. I turned to the monster who was extending his hand to me in anticipation. I calculated that if I moved quickly, there was a chance I could have us both over the edge of the balcony before the apes or the boy could reach us. I imagined our flight to the bottom and the finality of the sound we would make as we met the ground below.

I took the monster's hand . . .

And I shook it.

Smiling widely, Michael Maduka pulled me to him, and we embraced like a pair of long-lost brothers, reunited at the end of a difficult journey.

Timeline

1810	Hindoostane Coffee House, London's first Indian restaurant, opened by Sheikh Din Mohammed at 34 George Street, just off Portman Square
1826	Zoological Society of London established by Sir Stamford Raffles, imperialist, adventurer, and founder of colonial Singapore
1857–1859	First War of Indian Independence ("Sepoy Mutiny"), brutally put down by British military force, ends the rule of the East India Company and transfers India to direct British rule; the start of the Raj
1874	Winston Leonard Spencer Churchill born at Blenheim Palace
1880	Dr. John Watson wounded at the Battle of Maiwand, Second Anglo-Afghan War
1881	Sherlock Holmes and Dr. John Watson meet and take rooms together at 221b Baker Street
1885	Lord Randolph Henry Spencer-Churchill, as Secretary of State for India, directs the viceroy to invade Upper Burma, presents the Burmese kingdom as a "New Year's present" for Queen Victoria
1888	Lord John and Lady Alice Greystoke set sail for Africa on the ship Fuwalda and are lost at sea
1892	Dadabhai Naoroji elected as Britain's first ethnic-Indian member of parliament

| 1896–97 | Famines in India, worsened by imperial policy, cause millions of deaths |

1896–97   Famines in India, worsened by imperial policy, cause millions of deaths

1895   *The Importance of Being Earnest* premiers on 14 February in the West End to universal acclaim, and Oscar Wilde is sentenced to two years' hard labour on 25 May for "gross indecency"

1898   American Anti-Imperialist League formed in Boston in response to US annexation of the Philippines

1898   Marriage of Prince Victor Albert Jay Duleep Singh to Lady Anne Coventry, with the support of the Prince of Wales and Queen Victoria

1899–1902   Second Boer War; Harry "Bunny" Manders KIA; Winston Churchill, serving as a war correspondent in his late twenties, is taken prisoner, escapes, and publishes an account of his adventures, becoming internationally famous as a result

1900   Oscar Wilde dies in Paris. His last words: "My wallpaper and I are fighting a duel to the death. One of us has got to go."

1904   *Peter Pan; or, the Boy Who Wouldn't Grow Up* first performed in London

1905   Winston Churchill appointed under-secretary of state for the colonies, his first ministerial position; centenary celebrations of the Battle of Trafalgar at Trafalgar Square; Sotik Massacre of 1,850 Kipsigis men, women, and children carried out by Major-General Richard Pope-Hennessy in the British East African Protectorate (now Kenya)

"Trying to unpick our history is not the right way forward, and it's not something that we will focus our energies on."

—Rishi Sunak, Britain's first prime minister of Indian descent, on being asked if he would apologize for Britain's past involvement in the slave trade, 26 April 2023

BIBLIOGRAPHY

It feels rather redundant to list the works of fiction which inspired this volume, as I have worn my influences so blatantly; instead I will simply express the hope that the long-dead authors who created the worlds in which I have played would have appreciated my resurrection and interrogation of their creations. They are geniuses and gentlemen, all.

In the non-fiction, real world, I am indebted to Sathnam Sanghera's *Empireland* and *Empireworld* and to Caroline Elkins' *Legacy of Violence: A History of the British Empire*, which between them served to both ground and stoke Balvinder's (and my) anger not only at empire itself, but at the lies we have been told about it.

Arup K. Chatterjee's *Indians in London* provided valuable historical context and detail, as well as the timely and potent reminder that we have always been here. The National Trust's brave self-examination *Interim Report on the Connections between Colonialism and Properties in the Care of the National Trust, Including Links with Historic Slavery* was a valuable guide to the foundational sins that England's great houses were built upon. I have been a reader of William Dalrymple's work for almost as long as he has been writing it, and the *Empire* podcast which he hosts with Anita Anand also pointed me towards some interesting investigations.

The two historical figures whose shadows fall on every page of this book have both been long obsessions of mine, and they exist in many ways in direct opposition to each other: Winston Leonard Spencer Churchill and Oscar Fingal O'Flahertie Wills Wilde.

My love for Churchill is perhaps best characterized as sadomasochistic. I admire his greatness and historical indispensability even as I recognize that it grew almost directly out of his deeply held racism. Of particular use in constructing my version of the young Churchill were his own *My Early Life*, William Manchester's definitive *The Last Lion Volume 1: Visions of Glory 1874–1932*, Andrew Roberts' *Churchill: Walking with Destiny*, and *Becoming Winston Churchill: The Untold Story of Young Winston and His American Mentor* by Michael McMenamin and Curt Zoller. Also instructive and enormously fun is Anne Sebba's *American Jennie: The Remarkable Life of Lady Randolph Churchill*.

Whilst Oscar Wilde is not a character in this book, having inconveniently died five years before the events described within, his essence infuses it. Wilde and Bosie were as much an inspiration for E. W. Hornung when he created Raffles and Bunny, as were his brother-in-law's creations, Holmes and Watson. The literature on Wilde is voluminous, and I have read too much of it, but, for me, Richard Ellmann's magisterial and beautiful *Oscar Wilde* remains the work that best captures the spirit of the flawed titan, though I also am informed by Matthew Sturgis' immaculately researched and utterly devastating *Oscar Wilde: A Life*.

Indebted as I am to all the preceding historical scholarship, my main focus has been the creation of a work of fiction, and it should be understood that when forced to choose between facts and a good story, my inclination has always been towards the latter. I am confident that Wilde and Churchill would approve of this approach, and can only hope that historians and other readers will prove similarly forgiving.

ACKNOWLEDGEMENTS

It is perhaps dangerously close to obsequiousness to have one's publisher as the first acknowledgement, but it is a simple fact that if Kjersti Egerdahl, editorial director at Amazon Publishing, had not read a two-page pitch for a short story and, seeing something in it that I had not yet seen myself, decreed that it should become a novel, Balvinder would not have been born. She has my (and his) collective gratitude forever.

Celia Johnson has been an exemplary editor, challenging and cheering in equal measure, our shared love for Sherlock Holmes never preventing her from pulling me up when I got too self-indulgent. Michelle Hope, Nicole Thomas, and Steve Schul copyedited, proofread, and cold read this novice novelist with kindness and an eye for detail that was both much needed and much appreciated. Nicole Burns-Ascue wrangled production and logistics, and Jarrod Taylor designed a beautiful and inventive cover, whilst Brittany Morris and Bella Roberts managed marketing and publicity. They and the entire team at Amazon Publishing gave a gargantuan company human nuance and were a pleasure to work with.

Eric Smith, my book agent, read each chapter as it came and clapped in the margins with such sincerity that I believed him. Max Grossman and Geoff Morley at UTA, my manager Ashley Bernes, and my attorney Richard Thompson complete my representative team, and I owe them all more than commission. Megan Beatie and Olivia Haase were energetic publicists for the book.

Cavan Ash, Armand Richard David, Dave Rudden, and Richard Smith all read early drafts, and their feedback and encouragement provided a first-time prose novelist with the juice he needed to keep going.

Paul Redford first prompted me, over lunch nearly a decade ago, to take a fresh look at Raffles and Bunny. When I did, we decided it was time for them to make a reappearance. Our joint attempt, a television pilot, was mangled to death by the network development process, but it is evidence of Paul's graciousness and generosity that he blessed me running solo in this new direction.

Tarquin Pack suggested to me that Lord Greystoke was a far more interesting character in London than he is in Africa, and I hope he'll forgive me for not making the young rapscallion the hero.

That I had the time to write this book at all, in the same year as opening two new plays, is largely thanks to my producing partner at Mostly Harmless Productions, Tamar Climan, and to Scott Kay, my business partner at Prodigal. They took care of a thousand important things on two different continents so I didn't have to.

Allison Caviness listened to pitches and excerpts on many long car journeys, giving valuable insight and suggestions along the way, but more importantly, she continues to inspire, comfort, and challenge me as Maud does Bal, keeping my heart safe and my flame burning.

My father, G. A. David Dass, who abandoned a PhD in constitutional law at King's College London to return to help build the nation of Malaysia out of the British colony of Malaya, set a standard in real life which fiction can never meet. My mother, Professor Maya Khemlani David, born in India on July 12, 1947—a midnight's child forced to flee her home province of Sindh as it was torn apart by partition—went on to become one of the world's leading experts on Sindhi culture and language, a living reminder that the cruelty of empire can result in unexpected outcomes. I think, in this, I may have finally told a story they will both enjoy.

On the other end of the generational spectrum, my daughter, Odetta Elsie N'jie David, child of Gambia, England, Wales, Scotland Ireland, America, India, Malaysia, and Pakistan, descendant of both colonist and colonized, displays more bravery and provides more inspiration in every moment of her life than I could ever hope to do in a million pages of prose. This one's for you, Bug, as are they all.

Arvind Ethan David

Santa Ynez, California, December 2025

ABOUT THE AUTHOR

Photo © 2026 Valerie Caviness

Arvind has written seven graphic novels, including most recently his adaptation of Raymond Chandler's *Trouble Is My Business* (Pantheon, May 2025) and the Bram Stoker Award–nominated *Darkness Visible* with Mike Carey. Arvind has also written multiple hit audio originals, including the science fiction anthology series Earworms, *The Crimes of Dorian Gray*, and the nonfiction audiobook *Douglas Adams: The Ends of the Earth.*

In theatre, Arvind's plays include *The Hitchhiker's Guide to the Galaxy* and *Dirk Gently's Holistic Detective Agency*, both based on the novels by Douglas Adams, and he received an Olivier nomination for his family musical *The Boy With Wings*, based on Lenny Henry's children's book. He also contributed additional material for David Baddiel and Erran Baron Cohen's musical *The Infidel* and was a lead producer of the Grammy and Tony Award–winning Broadway musical *Jagged Little Pill*.

Arvind has written and produced extensively in television, including *Dirk Gently's Holistic Detective Agency* for Netflix, *Anansi Boys* for Amazon, and the Asian Academy Award winner *The Garden of Evening Mists* for HBO.

The Great Game is his debut prose novel.